Conn

of se

His hands slid under her blouse and over the flesh of her back. She trembled at the contrast between the roughened pads of his fingertips and the smoothness of her flesh. Sylvester shuddered as she ran her fingertips along the back of his neck and through his hair. It was an endless kiss, and Connie murmured softly into Sylvester's mouth.

"Don't tell me that wasn't meant to happen." She didn't want to plead with him, but if that was what it took...

"I think we both know it *is* meant to happen. It's going to happen." His hands moved down to her hips, holding her closer to him so she could feel him throbbing against her. "I don't want to hurt you, Connie."

She pressed tighter against him, fitting herself to him blatantly, showing him with her own body exactly what she wanted. "Maybe I want you to."

Jane Godman writes in a variety of romance genres, including paranormal, gothic and romantic suspense. Jane lives in England and loves to travel to European cities, which are steeped in history and romance—Venice, Dubrovnik and Vienna are among her favorites. Jane is married to a lovely man and is mom to two grown-up children.

Books by Jane Godman

Harlequin Nocturne

Otherworld Protector
Otherworld Renegade
Otherworld Challenger
Immortal Billionaire

Harlequin E Shivers

Legacy of Darkness
Echoes in the Darkness
Valley of Nightmares
Darkness Unchained

IMMORTAL BILLIONAIRE

JANE GODMAN

HARLEQUIN® NOCTURNE™

ISBN-13: 978-0-373-63987-8

Immortal Billionaire

This edition published by arrangement with Harlequin Books S.A.

For questions and comments about the quality of this book, please contact us at CustomerService@Harlequin.com.

HARLEQUIN®
www.Harlequin.com

Printed in U.S.A.

Dear Reader,

Immortal Billionaire represents a departure from my usual paranormal romances. For one thing, the setting is a luxury, privately owned Floridian island instead of a mystical otherworld inhabited by warring races of faeries, vampires and wolves!

In this book, the paranormal elements are implied rather than overt, with a strong theme of romantic suspense infusing the story.

On the island of Corazón, a curse from the past spills over to haunt the present. Dark secrets still linger from a time when the brave Calusa, the Shell Indians who inhabited Florida's golden shores, defied the invading conquistadores. It's a legacy that leaves the heroine, Connie Lacey, caught up in a web of intrigue and danger, not knowing whom she can trust.

In spite of the all-pervading sense of peril, the attraction between Connie and her billionaire host, Sylvester de León, is instant and overwhelming. But the clock is ticking and the curse of Corazón cannot be denied...

I'd love to hear from you. You can contact me at my website, www.janegodmanauthor.com, on Twitter, @JaneGodman, or on Facebook, Jane Godman Author.

Happy reading,

Jane

This book is dedicated to my new grandson, Luke, who arrived while I was writing it and gave me a whole new perspective on life!

Chapter 1

It is easy enough to list in advance, and with absolute certainty, those things for which we are prepared to die. Family, country, religion, the one we love, a valued way of life. Until we are faced with a situation that puts our convictions to the test, we can never know for sure which of these will hold true. There were many lessons to be learned during those strange weeks on the island of Corazón, but, for Connie Lacey, this would prove to be the most important.

Four years of running and hiding. Four years of looking over her shoulder. Of viewing every man she met with suspicion. Of waking every morning, wondering if today was the day he would finally catch up with her.

The relief of being offered somewhere to hide was so huge it drove every other thought out of her head. She had a brief mental image of herself as a disaster survivor and the man opposite as the rescue worker who had just draped an emergency blanket around her shoulders. She resisted the temptation to cling to him, garbling out incoherent thanks until he was forced to gently pry her hands away. They were the wild thoughts spinning through Connie Lacey's mind as she listened to the clipped tones of the attorney.

With hindsight, she probably should have paid more attention to the strangeness of the offer he was making and the diffident manner with which he made it. *Gratitude will do that to you*, she decided later. At the time her attention was taken up with grabbing this opportunity. *Nod, smile and sign on the dotted line. Don't ask questions that might make him withdraw this incredible invitation.* All she could focus on was the fact that—for thirty days, at least—she would not have to sleep with a knife under her pillow.

"You have one week." She realized Mr. Reynolds had finished outlining the details of the proposal. "My client will expect you to be in Florida in exactly seven days' time."

Connie swallowed hard. She might have known there would be a catch. The logistics of getting to Florida posed a massive problem. Mentally, she reviewed the contents of her wallet. She knew exactly how much cash was in there. It wouldn't get her across town let alone across the country. Before she could speak, Mr. Reynolds reached into the desk drawer and produced a hefty roll of banknotes. His expression softened slightly as he passed them across the desk.

"Expenses. For the journey and such sundry other items as may be necessary." He cleared his throat with a hint of something that might have been embarrassment. "My client is a very exacting man. His guests will, for example, be required to dress for dinner during their stay on Corazón."

Darn! And there I was thinking I had successfully managed to hide the fact that the sole is hanging off one of my sneakers and this sweater has forgotten what color it used to be.

Connie stuffed the wad of cash into her shoulder bag with a muttered word of thanks. If an encounter with Sylvester's attorney could reduce her to the status of a gibbering wreck, how on earth was she going to cope with the man himself?

As she got to her feet, Mr. Reynolds rose and came around the desk. He held out his hand. Surprised, Connie took it. Instead of the handshake she had expected, he clasped her hand between both of his. It was an oddly tactile gesture for such an aloof man.

"However this venture may turn out..." He paused and Connie sensed he was fighting an internal battle. As if the personal and professional were at war within him. The result felt like his version of a truce. "I wish you well, Miss Lacey."

It was only later, when she got back to her grim, one-room apartment and counted—then, in disbelief, recounted—the money, that she began to truly appreciate the gulf between her world and that of Corazón. What constituted "sundry other items" to Mr. Reynolds was almost a year's salary to Connie.

Laughing, she tossed the notes into the air and briefly contemplated just disappearing with them. To hell with "second cousin several convoluted times removed" Sylvester and his mysteriously worded proposition. This money could buy her the freedom from fear she had been dreaming of. Temporarily, it was true, but even that was so much more than she had wished for. No more moving from town to town and job to job? No more looking over her shoulder? *Yeah, I'll take that and deal with the future when it gets here.*

A pang of guilt tugged at her. Backing out wasn't an

option. She had just accepted Mr. Reynolds's wretched invitation and a promise was, after all, a promise. Besides—despite its reputation—she was intrigued enough by Corazón to want to see it and, even if she admitted it only to herself, she wanted to meet the legendary Sylvester.

The ease with which Arthur Reynolds, senior partner in the firm of Reynolds, Prudah and Taylor, had tracked her down was unsettling. Even if she hadn't been contemplating answering Sylvester's eccentric summons, it would have been time to move on. *Goodbye*—she experienced a minor moment of panic as she tried to remember where she was. It had to happen one day—*Farmington, Missouri. The last month has been okay, but it was never a long-term thing. We both knew it. No hard feelings.*

She had a week to prepare for the journey. With a shrug, she tucked the money away at the back of her closet and curled up on the bed with a book. Connie could have her belongings packed in an hour. She'd done it often enough.

Mr. Reynolds's emailed instructions were meticulous. The launch that was to take her to Corazón would meet her at the marina in Charlotte Harbor. He had even included a map showing the exact location.

Charlotte Harbor was a vacationer's paradise. The hotel where she'd spent the night, although modest, had been way beyond her usual budget. Eating shrimp and drinking beer at a beachside restaurant, she'd watched the sky fade through shades of bright blue and burnt orange to black. It had crossed her mind—how could it not?—that this was all some elaborate trick. That, at some point, *he* would appear before her and gloat over how easily she had fallen for this whole trick. Then he would pull out the knife... *Stop this. Every time you think of him, every time you remember, he wins.*

An internet search had revealed nothing irregular about Mr. Reynolds. His was a well-respected, international law firm, with offices all over the country, including one in St. Petersburg, Florida. The company dealt with wealthy clients and celebrities, even those as well known as Sylvester. And the de León family *were* some sort of relatives of her mother's, however distant. Connie had always known that. The last few years had taught her to be watchful. With good reason. But perhaps it was time to put caution aside? What did she have to lose by going to Corazón? Unless she was brave enough to seize this chance, she would never know. According to Mr. Reynolds, who had, after all, personally traveled all the way to Missouri to meet with her, she might even stand to gain a great deal.

Connie reached the quayside a few minutes before the time Mr. Reynolds had specified. It was busy without being bustling, mostly with fishing charters and tourists embarking on a day of island hopping. There was no reason for the horrible crawling feeling of nervousness that caused her to keep glancing over her shoulder. She wasn't being watched. *He* couldn't possibly know she was here. It was just habit kicking in. She had gotten used to sensing his presence everywhere. It was called self-preservation.

The email had said there would be other guests traveling to Corazón with her. Sylvester had no close family, but he had invited several distant relatives. None of them knew the reason for the invitation. That was something Sylvester probably intended to reveal once they were on the island. She couldn't see anyone who looked like they might be waiting for a launch to take them for an extended stay on a luxury island. The thought of enforced proximity to strangers made Connie shudder slightly. Compulsory enjoyment. Was Sylvester some sort of masochist? *Look on the bright side.* Wherever this adventure might lead, at least it was not into a temporary job in a poky office where she would be chained to yet another dreary desktop computer.

A slightly shrill voice interrupted her thoughts. "Hurry up, Guthrie! I told you we should have left the hotel earlier. And I still don't understand why we couldn't have flown first-class. No, don't put my cosmetics case there! Oh, for heaven's sake." The woman exuded restless, perfumed elegance. Connie decided her companion must be her husband. Who else would obey her staccato instructions so meekly? The hapless Guthrie followed in her wake, carrying a quite astonishing array of suitcases from the cab onto the quayside. Then, as his companion found the original arrangement unaccountably displeasing, he obligingly reorganized them.

"But that was how you told me to do it, Lucinda." His protest was made in tones of mild confusion.

Looking up, Connie encountered the gaze of a tall, fair-haired man who was wheeling a single suitcase as he approached her. There was something vaguely familiar about him, but she couldn't quite place what it was. From his frowning expression, he appeared to be thinking exactly the same thing as Connie. They both regarded Lucinda and Guthrie in dawning horror. *Oh, please, God, no. Surely life could not so be unkind?* A paradise island, even one with a sinister reputation like Corazón's, deserved pleasant—if not perfect—company. *Let my instincts be wrong. Just this once.*

"The email said nine-thirty and it's exactly that now.

Unpunctuality is abhorrent to me. Don't stand there, Guthrie. I can't see the harbor with you blocking my view."

The man with the suitcase drew level with Connie. She felt her cheeks burn as he gazed down at her. Four years after the attack that had left her scarred, she should be used to people staring at her, but it had never become any easier. Obviously realizing his silence was making her nervous, he made a visible effort to strive for normality.

"Are you waiting for the de León launch?" When she nodded, he held out his hand. "My name's Reynolds."

"Oh!" Connie was taken aback. That was the name of Sylvester's attorney, but this was not the same man she had met with in Missouri. He was younger, fairer, and there was less formality about him. She regarded him a little doubtfully. There was a definite resemblance, however.

"From your expression, I suspect I was right. I take it you are on your way to Corazón, having met with my father a week ago?"

Connie felt the frown clear from her brow. Her nervousness began to disappear like champagne bubbles rising to the top of the glass. "Oh, yes. I can see it now. You look a little like your father, you know."

"I hope to God that's not true. He acts like he's got a baseball bat rammed up his ass most of the time. Although I shouldn't complain. I'm a junior partner in the firm and, even though it leaves him short-staffed in the Florida office, he's given me as much time as I need to go on this little jaunt of Sylvester's." His voice was cheerful. "Allow me to put my powers of deduction to the test even further by using a process of elimination to decide which of Sylvester's relatives you might be." He tilted his head to one side and studied her face.

Connie had the distinct impression the gesture was for show and that he already knew who she was. How could he not? Her hand went to her throat in a protective gesture and she thought she saw a glimmer of something in his eyes. Probably sympathy. She hated that look. It was too depressingly familiar.

"I was going to guess that you must be Constance Lacey. But I'm not sure you're old enough."

"If you are on your way to Corazón as your father's representative, Mr. Reynolds, you will know I'm twenty-seven. Since I look every day of my age, I'm going to accuse you of being the most outrageous tease."

His eyes twinkled in response and she decided she liked him. He was easy to laugh with.

"Acquit me, Miss Lacey," he said, adopting the same mock-formal tone. "I was trying to flirt, not tease, and I'm never outrageous. You are wrong about one thing, however. I am on my way to Corazón, but not as my father's representative. Like yours, my mother was a distant relative of the de León family. I have been summoned as part of this curious proposition of Sylvester's."

"Oh." Connie fiddled nonchalantly with the top button on her shirt. "Have you met him?"

"Sylvester? Oh, yes. Many times."

Connie succumbed and allowed her curiosity to get the better of her. "What is he like?"

"Exactly as he appears in the press. Handsome. Charming. Witty. Unfathomable. Sylvester has never been anything less than pleasant to me, but, at the same time, I wouldn't want to cross him. I've never been allowed to get close enough to him to know how he'd react." Lifting one hand, he shielded his eyes against the brilliant sunlight. A sleek, white boat with a rampant lion emblazoned on its bow was approaching the quay. "Unless I'm very much mistaken, this, Miss Lacey, is our lift."

"My friends call me Connie." Even as she said it, Connie tried to remember the last time she'd trusted anyone enough to say those words. It was no good. Whenever it had been, it was far enough in the past for her to have forgotten it. Trust and friendship were words that had been missing from her vocabulary for a long time. It was too soon to say if the younger Mr. Reynolds would restore them but she experienced a tiny flare of hope that he might. She didn't feel anything other than friendship toward him, but even that was much more than she'd experienced for a long time.

"Mine call me lots of things, most of them unrepeatable. I hope you'll settle for Matt." It was said with an ironic smile that Connie couldn't help returning.

Of course Connie had known that Corazón was an island. And of course she'd known it was remote, part of a far-flung, jeweled string on Florida's westernmost edge. Through media coverage of his lifestyle and daring exploits, didn't the whole world know that Sylvester—one of the wealthiest and most well-known men on the planet—protected his privacy by disappearing off to his privately owned little heart-shaped paradise whenever it suited him? She just hadn't added the anxiety induced by a boat journey into this already stressful venture.

Connie had never been fond of boats and, after the fuss of ensuring Lucinda's luggage was safely stowed had died down, she stepped nervously onto the elegant launch. This was unlike any other boat she had ever been on. It was piloted by a man in an impeccable uniform—also bearing the de León logo—who introduced himself as Roberto. In his capable hands, the vessel skimmed the water with barely a sound from its powerful engines and only the faintest suggestion of movement. *You're in de León territory now. You sold out.* Connie could almost feel her mother's disapproving gaze. As always, the bright shard of pain triggered by the memory of her drove itself deep into her chest.

Once clear of the marina, the waters were as smooth as a sheet of shimmering blue silk spread before them. Overhead the sky was an unrelenting, uninterrupted shade of azure and they passed tiny green islands ringed with sea grasses and golden sands.

"You look like you're on a white-knuckle ride rather than a leisurely boat journey." Matt lounged against the rail at her side.

"I'm not great with boats." Connie adjusted her floppy straw hat so her face was shaded. It would be just her luck to turn up at her first encounter with Sylvester looking like an overheated beet.

"Bad experience?"

"No." It was true and yet… His question touched a chord, something deep and unexplored within her. Her thoughts were interrupted when Matt leaned excitedly over the side, making her panic that he might fall in.

"We've got company."

Connie forced herself to shift slightly to one side so she could follow the direction of his gaze. A group of playful dolphins had joined them and was swimming alongside the launch. In the pleasure of the moment, she forgot to be afraid. Laughing at their antics, the breeze on her face, the salty tang in the air, all of those things combined to lend poignancy to the atmosphere. She was reminded of childhood beach holidays spent playing among sand dunes. A brief pang of wistfulness for those days, for her big, laughing father and quiet, kindly mother, tried to tug at her, but she brushed it aside. Not now. This was not the time for sadness and nostalgia.

Sometime later Matt drew her attention to Corazón as it came into view. Although most of the island sat low in the sparkling waters, the northernmost edge reared high and craggy above green-tipped cliffs. Connie could just make out what appeared to be a tall building perched on the highest point of them all. By keeping her eyes focused on it, she gained a clearer image of the unusual outline as the launch drew closer.

"Is it a lighthouse?" She turned questioning eyes to Matt.

"It is. That is also the site of an original property, a fortress built by Sylvester's ancestors." He pointed to where the headland trailed long, rocky fingers into the water. "See those openings in the rocks, almost like windows?"

Connie shielded her eyes with her hand, following the direction of his finger. There were four crude, almost square shapes high up near the top of the cliff.

"When the de León family first made their home here and built that fortress, they had to fight hard to keep their island safe. Sylvester's ancestors were forced to take drastic measures. Those windows are part of the dungeons they built beneath the fortress. Any prisoners who managed to escape from their cells were likely to blunder around in the darkness and fall out of one of those openings."

Now they were closer to them, Connie studied the apertures. "Couldn't they climb up from there and reach the top of the cliff?" Even as she asked the question, she decided it seemed unlikely. Although the openings were close to the top of the cliffs, it would still entail a long climb up a sheer rock face with no rope or other safety equipment.

"I suppose if the climber possessed superhuman powers, they might. We'll have to ask Sylvester if anyone ever achieved it." He turned his head to look back at the lighthouse. "These cliffs have always been a danger to boats coming into this stretch of water, and several ships ran aground in close succession in the nineteenth century, with the loss of all lives on board. This tower was built in response, but it was never entirely successful in its job as a beacon for sailors. There is some debate about the motives of Emilio de León, the man who chose to build it."

"How on earth do you know so much about it?" Connie was fascinated by the story but couldn't help wondering at the source of his in-depth knowledge.

"The de León account is one of my father's most lucrative. As a junior partner, I took over part of the workload and started coming to Corazón regularly. I drank in the stories of its history, particularly because of my own family connection.

"Why were Emilio de León's motives questioned?" Matt was a born storyteller and Connie found her fear of the water relegated to second place in her fascination to hear the rest of the story.

"Wrecking," he replied bluntly. "It has been rumored that the de León fortune is founded on the lives of the hundreds of men who died when their boats were deliberately lured onto these rocks. In fact, some went further than that and called Emilio a murdering bastard." He must have seen the change in Connie's expression, because he switched to a lighter note. "The lighthouse was decommissioned not long after it was built. The island has always belonged to the family, and the de León home, site of the modern-day mansion, was built on the other side of the island."

The boat skipped over the waves and around the tip of the island. They were looking up now at the lighthouse. Or rather, it was looming over them. The distinction seemed important. Despite the bright sunlight, Connie shivered slightly. It would be foolish to suppose those lost souls lingered here still in some guise or another. Or that they wished for vengeance. Yet there was something about this lonely place that invited fanciful thoughts. Some of the stories she had heard about Corazón resurfaced in her memory. She had always dismissed them as just that. Stories. Fiction. Perhaps initiated by the de León family to make themselves appear even more interesting to the outside world. Although why that would be the case when they were known to have had more than their fair share of mystery, heartache and misery, she couldn't fathom.

All she knew was that the island's name always carried with it a sinister undercurrent. A darker side to its status as the paradise escape of a billionaire that it had never quite shaken off. As if a cloud passed over the sun each time the word *Corazón* was spoken. Connie almost laughed at the foolishness of her thoughts. A combination of her fear of boats and Matt's story was probably not the best way to start her visit to this island.

"I don't know what possessed Sylvester to invite such a crowd." Although Lucinda had determinedly kept her distance throughout the journey, her voice reached Connie now above the sounds of the seabirds and the waves buffeting against the side of the boat. "I thought this was going to be a select *family* party."

"It might be fun." Guthrie gave an apologetic grimace as he met Connie's eyes. "Like a school outing."

Lucinda looked at him as though he had just slapped her before turning away in stony silence.

Connie's attention was drawn back to the island. The scenery was changing now from the drama of the cliffs to lush, tropical splendor. This was an island with a split personality. Theater and danger were replaced by peace and serenity as the boat slowed on its approach to a private dock. The main house was before them in all its traditional grandeur. Even Lucinda descended from her sulks for long enough to look impressed.

Bordered by white sands and protected by palm trees and majestic pines, the stunning Spanish-style mansion was perfectly matched to its surroundings. A riot of flowers in shades from royal purple to palest mauve hung from every balcony and overflowed from giant terra-cotta pots onto the patios.

Even before the boat had docked, the scent of citrus, pine and blossom—the scent of Corazón—was fresh in Connie's nostrils. It was new and yet hauntingly familiar. At some point in the past, she must have smelled this delicious combination and stored it away in the recesses of her memory. Time and distance had caused her to forget when it was, but it tugged at her now like a nostalgic melody, making her think of sultry nights and lazy days, of drama, passion, laughter and warmth. For some reason, it held within it an enticing whiff of promise and welcome.

Her thoughts about the elusive scent were quickly relegated to second place, because there, descending the steps of the house, was the man himself. Even at a distance, he was unmistakable. The thought that Sylvester must have been looking out for them was ever so slightly breathtaking.

Get a grip, Connie. He probably greets all his guests in person. It's called courtesy. Or did you expect him to prove his conquistador heritage by charging across the beach, sword held aloft?

Dismissing her strange imaginings as relief at having arrived safely, Connie stepped onto the wooden boards of the dock. Soon she felt the sand crunch beneath her feet and her nerves stopped jangling for nautical reasons. Instead her tension found itself a whole new focus.

In person Sylvester was even more stunning than in the newspaper photographs and internet searches Connie had devoured over the years. There was something about him that harkened back to another era.

Sylvester de León's looks were wasted on the casual linen pants and lightweight sweater he wore. He was as tall as Matt but broader across the shoulders and slimmer through the hips. His light brown hair, which had a reddish gold tinge, was swept back from a heroically broad brow and his features were masterfully carved. A charming, easy smile curved his near-perfect lips. He looked relaxed and completely in tune with his surroundings as, wineglass in hand, he trod barefoot onto the sands.

Lucinda, with a burst of speed worthy of an Olympic sprinter, dashed ahead of the others. "Sylvester, how delightful." She lifted her face to his so he was obliged to kiss her cheek. "You remember my brother Guthrie, of course."

Obedient to her imperious summons, Guthrie bustled forward and thrust out his hand. Sylvester was forced to switch his wineglass to his left hand so he could shake Guthrie's with his right.

With a skill Connie suspected had been born out of years of dealing with similar situations, Sylvester sidestepped Lucinda. His smile of welcome encompassed the rest of the group. Up close, his eyes were the bluest Connie had ever seen.

"I hope you all had a pleasant journey? I am so sorry—" His gaze had been scanning the group, then, as it reached Connie's face, he broke off abruptly. She spared a second to wonder what Sylvester had felt the need to apologize for. Then her thoughts were distracted. His smile froze and then vanished. After he stared down at Connie in silence for a full minute, there was a loud crack as the glass in his hand shattered. Blood and alcohol mingled in a stream and dripped onto the sand.

Without another word, Sylvester turned on his heel and walked back into the house, leaving his visitors staring after him.

Chapter 2

Why? It was the wrong question. Yet it persisted, only to be followed by another, equally senseless and unrelenting, demand. *Why now?* These were the thoughts tormenting him as he made his way blindly into the house and up the stairs to his room. Once inside the sanctuary of his suite, Sylvester turned the faucet in his bathroom on full, wincing as he held his lacerated hand under the cold water. He bent his head, battling to get his breathing under control. *What the hell is going on?*

This couldn't be happening. Not now. Not when he had spent so long planning. Not when he was so close to seeing this scheme through to its conclusion.

Turning the water off, he went to the medicine closet and managed—with one-handed clumsiness—to tend his wounds, covering the deepest cuts with waterproof dressings. Conscious he had been guilty of monumental rudeness, he went through to his bedroom, picked up the house phone and dialed his housekeeper's number.

"Vega, I had a slight accident and had to leave my guests on the beach. Can you go down and escort them into the house?"

"Mr. Matthew has already brought them inside." There was a trace of disapproval in Vega's voice. That was the problem with servants who had worked for you for years. What you gained in loyalty, you lost in distance. "I organized drinks. They are waiting for you in the salon."

He couldn't do this now. He needed time—and plenty of it—to collect his thoughts before he could even think about being sociable. "Make my apologies. Explain that I have something urgent to attend to and I'll see them at dinner. When they've finished their drinks, show them to their rooms, please."

"I hope everything is well, sir?"

He hung up without replying, knowing she would be worried at his unaccustomed abruptness but not having the mental energy to deal with it. *I need to find the strength to cope with what's going on in my own head. The rest of the world will have to wait.* That decision seemed to restore some of his equilibrium. One thing at a time. Losing the bloodstained clothing seemed to be a good starting point.

Standing under fierce jets of water in the shower, he replayed that heart-stopping, brain-numbing moment on the beach. Could he have dealt with the shock any differently? Hidden his feelings? He choked back a laugh. Not a hope in hell. Living his life in the public eye, Sylvester had developed plenty of coping strategies. The easy, unruffled persona he showed the world had become second nature. Up until half an hour ago he thought he was prepared for any eventuality. But a pair of wide, golden-brown eyes peeping shyly at him from beneath the brim of a straw hat had just shaken him out of that certainty forever.

Impatient now to find out more about her, he turned

off the shower. Wrapping a towel around his waist, he returned to the bedroom. Opening a drawer in his dresser, he extracted the six identically bound files Arthur Reynolds had sent him. Each had a name written on the front in Arthur's meticulous, sloping handwriting. The carefully made-up blonde had introduced herself as Lucinda. He discarded her file. So she must be either Ellie Carter or Constance Lacey.

Arthur had set each file out in the same way. As soon as Sylvester opened Constance Lacey's file, a head-and-shoulders photograph—obviously taken some years earlier—gazed up at him from inside the buff cover. The same shock waves hit him immediately. Thankfully the sensation was muted, presumably because this was a picture and she wasn't here in person. Nevertheless, the impact of looking at her face zinged through to his nerve endings once more. *Good thing I'm not holding a glass this time.*

In the black-and-white picture, it looked as if the photographer had caught her unawares. Like she was in midsentence. Her hand was raised to brush her dark mane of hair back from her face. Her lips were parted, her eyes just crinkling into laughter. She wasn't beautiful in any conventional sense of the word. She was stunning in every unconventional sense.

Gazing at her for a protracted, aching moment, Sylvester was overcome with lust and longing. *Really? The man who can have any woman he wants...so they say. Getting hard and drooling over an old photograph. Nice image, Sylvester.* Even as he gave himself the mental lecture, another voice spoke up in his mind. *You know that's not what this is about.*

Who was she? He remembered thinking when Arthur had sent him the files that Constance Lacey's was thinner than any of the others. Of course, he hadn't actually opened any of them until now. He hadn't seen any reason to read about their backgrounds until they were actually here on Corazón. Would he come to regret that decision? What would he have done if he had seen this photograph before meeting her in the flesh? Changed his mind? Withdrawn his invitation? It was too late for those questions. She was here. He had to deal with the reality of her on his island.

Sitting in a chair close to the bed, he skimmed the brief paragraph on their family connection. Arthur, as always, had been meticulous in his research. Sylvester recalled their conversation two years ago. "You want me to find *anyone* who is remotely related to you?" The attorney had clearly been struggling to keep the incredulity out of his voice. "You do know we will be talking hundreds of people?"

"Theoretically, yes. With any other family, that might be the case, but you know how small my family is. You are then going to narrow it down those de León descendants who are between the ages of twenty-five and thirty. Who are of sound mind and body, have no criminal record, no dependents, no marital ties and who are available to come to Corazón on the specified date. Given some of them will think I'm a raving lunatic, I imagine we'll be talking a mere handful, don't you?"

Arthur, still regarding him with a measure of disbelief, had agreed. Despite his misgivings, the attorney had done an outstanding job and Sylvester had been proved right. The handful had, of course, included Arthur's own son. Hardly surprising, since the family connection was the reason Sylvester had entrusted the Reynolds family with his secrets for so many years.

Constance Lacey's grandmother, Sylvester read now, had been some sort of de León second cousin, back in the mists of time. Could that be considered related at all? *We aren't related.* The feeling brought a sense of profound relief, one that he instantly dismissed. The rest of the file contained frustratingly few biographical details. Her father, a Cuban immigrant, had died following a brief, violent illness when she was in her early teens. There was a newspaper cutting included in the file, and Sylvester glanced at. It told him Constance's mother had been murdered a few years ago.

Constance had studied graphic design at college. Following that, she seemed to have a promising career as a model. Then she had simply…disappeared. Or deliberately made herself invisible. Clearly something traumatic had happened to her. That much was obvious from her appearance. When Arthur had tracked her down and traveled in person to Missouri to interview her, she had been working as a temporary clerk for a back street insurance company. None of this mattered. She might be something of an enigma, but her private life was her own affair. The task ahead of him was too important for Sylvester to be diverted by any imaginary connection he might feel to Constance Lacey. She was here now, in his space, on his island. It was an unexpected complication, but he couldn't allow it to upset his meticulously laid plans. His lifestyle meant he'd had plenty of practice at keeping people at arm's length when he chose. Doing the same to Constance Lacey shouldn't be a problem. *Should it?*

Even as he asked himself the question, his fingertips strayed with a will of their own to one of the glossy photographs and traced the near-perfect oval outline of her face. But to find her now, after an eternity? He had always thought he was meant to suffer this alone. Determinedly, he put the picture aside. *I* am *meant to suffer this alone.*

They are a star-crossed family. With a name that brings bad luck to anyone who speaks it.

The words had been uttered with absolute finality by her usually unsuperstitious mother. Connie had been forced, therefore, to glean what she could about her famous relatives by scouring the gossip columns. Luckily, since Sylvester was a close friend of celebrities and princes, it had not been too difficult to follow his progress. Not a week went by without a photograph of him appearing in the press. Inevitably, he would have a drink in one hand and a woman on his arm. It was a different woman in each photograph, the common theme the adoring gaze up into his eyes. No matter who he was with, it was Sylvester on whom the paparazzi focused. He had that sort of charisma. His eyes indulged the world with a charming, if slightly cynical, smile. He was one of the elite, a member of that absurdly famous group of people known throughout the world only by their first names.

In addition to his wealth and celebrity lifestyle, Sylvester attracted attention for his determined daredevilry. He seemed to have an ongoing desire to kill himself in the most outrageous way imaginable. Now in his late twenties, he had climbed Everest, trekked to the North Pole, broken trans-Atlantic sailing records, flown around the world single-handed and had recently climbed one of the most perilous rock faces in the world. Those blue eyes scorned danger, their mesmerizing stare challenging death to try to take him if it dared.

Because of her mother's prohibition, Connie had been cut to the core that she couldn't boast to the other girls at college that she was related to Sylvester. *Yes,* that *Sylvester. I mean, what was the point of having a ridiculously famous relative when I was strictly forbidden to talk about him?*

When this strange invitation had come along, she couldn't help wondering what her mother would have made of her acceptance. Principles, Connie decided, were all very well. Surely even her mother would have put superstition aside and obeyed a summons from Sylvester if the alternative was more fear and running and hiding? But Sylvester's odd behavior when he greeted them on their arrival had brought her mother's words back to her all over again.

"Is this Sylvester's idea of a joke?" Lucinda's voice had broken the stunned silence that descended as they watched the rear view of their host when he stalked away from them into the house. "Because if it's not, he is quite insufferably rude."

Connie remained perfectly still, feeling the slow-burning color creep up from her neck to her cheeks. She gazed after Sylvester in the grip of the same sort of trance that had held him as he had looked down at her. What on earth had just happened?

"Are you okay, Connie?"

The concern in Matt's voice made it all so much worse. *Because it confirms that Sylvester's reaction was about me. And they all know it.* Pride made her tilt her chin a fraction higher. "I'm fine."

"Right..." Matt hesitated, glancing around. He was clearly striving for a more decisive tone. "Well, it's obvious it was the unfortunate accident with his glass that caused Sylvester to walk away the way he did. I expect he'll join us again as soon as he has tended to the injury to his hand. In the meantime, why don't we make our way inside?"

"Do you think we should?" Guthrie's expression was doubtful. "Perhaps we ought to wait until he comes back?"

"Nonsense." Lucinda had already started walking across the beach toward the house. "Even if he's severed an artery, Sylvester can't seriously expect us to stand here waiting for him."

Those blunt, and rather brutal, words had been the deciding factor. Since Matt was the only one among them who already knew his way around, he led the way up the beach and into the house.

Once there, they entered a staggeringly beautiful reception salon. Six floor-to-ceiling, arched windows lined each side of the tiled room. The furnishings were perfectly matched in shades of beige and gold and were opulently comfortable. Connie experienced an incongruous urge to kick off her shoes and curl up into a corner of one of the huge, squashy sofas. Marble columns, exquisite oil paintings, elegant rugs and ornamental chandeliers provided reminders that this was no ordinary family home and that such blatantly make-yourself-at-home conduct might be frowned upon.

She was experiencing a kaleidoscope of emotions. Could they all be attributed to the shock of Sylvester's conduct? She wasn't sure. So many conflicting thoughts were vying for her attention that she felt slightly dizzy. Her reaction to the house itself confused her. She had never in her life stepped foot inside a place so grand, yet it felt comforting and easy to be here. As if the house was wrapping her in a blanket of well-being and contentment. Yet lying in wait beneath that, there was darkness. Raw, greedy and merciless. Connie was used to fear, but this was more. Another layer of watchfulness had been added to her everyday dread. Resolutely she turned her thoughts away from soul-searching. *This is because of Sylvester. You are allowing his behavior to color how you feel about Corazón.*

Their arrival had attracted attention and a small, stout woman with a face like polished mahogany came to greet them. Her calf-length, black skirt and white blouse—while not precisely a uniform—together with the way she wore her blue-black hair in a neat bun effectively proclaimed her status as an employee. When she saw Matt, a grin almost split her broad face in two.

"Vega!" He held out his hands.

She turned from greeting him to speak more formally to the other guests. "I'm the housekeeper here at Corazón. Anything I can do to make your stay more comfortable, just let me know. For now, you sit down while I fetch a pitcher of my lemon iced tea."

"Given the circumstances surrounding our arrival, I'd have thought something a bit stronger was in order, wouldn't you?" Guthrie muttered as Vega departed.

"It's not even noon." There was something tired and automatic in the way Lucinda said the words, as though they were overused. Her eyes, bright and curious, turned to Connie. "I thought Sylvester was supposed to be known for his diplomacy. He did a very poor job of hiding his emotions on this occasion. Although you really should consider wearing a scarf. Your appearance can be quite alarming."

Connie rose from her seat and moved to one of the tall windows, gazing out at the breathtaking vista with unseeing eyes. One hand remained over her neck in a familiar, defensive gesture.

Matt came to join her. "Take no notice. She's wrong."

Connie shook her head. "What else could it be? His whole manner changed as soon as he saw me."

"I know Sylvester well enough to say this with complete confidence. Whatever it was about you that startled him—and I suppose it would be pointless to try and deny it *was* about you, Connie—it had nothing to do with your scars."

Connie's thoughts were diverted from the drama of their arrival by the view from the balcony outside her bedroom. The sensation that she was soaring out over the bay with nothing anchoring her to the land was breathtaking. Midday sunlight cast its rays over the scene, changing the water's hue as it became more distant from the westernmost edge of the island. Close by, a satiny trim of color turned the sea a bright turquoise. White-tipped waves of brilliant cobalt played and gurgled against the rocks farther from the house. Beyond them, a midnight-dark band signaled deeper waters. Overhead, the sky was a blaze of blue so bright it hurt. The scene was framed on either side by fronds and feathers of lush plants. It was a perfect noonday paradise, its soundtrack the song of cicadas. In spite of Sylvester's strange reaction to her, she felt a sense of peace washing over her, as if the island itself was welcoming her.

"It is beautiful." She turned to look over her shoulder at Vega.

"I have always thought so," the housekeeper replied in her serene way. "You will be careful, won't you? It is a sheer drop down onto the terrace from there."

She was referring to the waist-high, wrought-iron balcony rail on which Connie was leaning. The words made Connie feel suddenly nervous and she turned back into the room itself. It was dominated by a vast bed with a carved head, and legs as thick as tree trunks. A colorful, embroidered quilt in shades of gold and blue covered the mattress. The pictures on the walls and the rugs on the floor reflected the same scenes depicted in the embroidery.

"This is the Sea Shell Room," Vega explained. "The quilt is a copy of one that was in the de León family many centuries ago."

Connie ran a hand lightly over the intricately patterned needlework. A faint tremor, reminiscent of a slight static shock, tingled through her fingertips and she withdrew her hand with a frown. That sort of friction was something she associated with man-made fibers, not the cotton of this bedspread. Whatever it was, she really didn't want that sort of irritation associated with her bedding for the duration of her stay. *If I stay here at all.* She was still undecided about that. The comfortable atmosphere of the island might have swept over her, but the welcome party hadn't exactly been encouraging. And she hadn't forgotten that other, deeper, feeling she had experienced. It had faded now but, like a bad taste, the memory of it lingered. *You are so used to sensing evil, you've forgotten how to stop*, she told herself firmly.

The embroidery showed a series of scenes of people engaged in a variety of activities, all of them featuring beaches, boats, shells or water. "Who are they?"

"The Calusa. They were the original inhabitants of this chain of islands."

It somehow felt wrong to visit a new place and not

have taken the time to learn something about it. But life on the run didn't exactly allow for research, and Connie had only had seven days to get ready for this unexpected journey. Even so, she felt uncomfortable with the confession she was forced to make. "I know nothing about the Calusa."

"They were the Shell Indians, the people who lived along the sandy shores of this part of Florida." Vega, seeming untroubled by the static electricity that had affected Connie, traced the embroidered pictures with one fingertip. "These are scenes that show their daily lives. Fishing, boating, collecting shells. Although the Calusa tribe died out completely in the eighteenth century, they had already been driven out of many of these islands long before then. The arrival of the Spanish brought chaos to their lives."

The mention of the Spanish prompted Connie to ask another question. One her mother, because of her prohibition about the de León family, had been unable to answer. "Is it true Sylvester is descended from the conquistadors? Or is that just a fairy tale?"

"Ah, the master tells the history of his family so much better than I ever could." *The master?* It was like stepping into a black-and-white movie. Or someone else's privileged lifestyle. One in which Connie didn't belong. "I'll leave you to unpack. Dinner is at eight."

When Vega had gone, Connie returned to the balcony. Her thoughts were in turmoil and even the idyllic view couldn't soothe them. Could she remain here on Corazón and face Sylvester again after that devastating first encounter? Surely the right thing—the only thing—to do would be to leave? Just turn around now, steel her boat-induced nerves, and ask Roberto to take her back to Charlotte Harbor on the launch? If she did, she would have to return the money Mr. Reynolds had given her, including the amount she had already spent on clothes. She had no savings on which to draw.

No money. No job. Nowhere to go. It wasn't exactly a new situation. In fact, it pretty much summed up the last four years of her life. But Mr. Reynolds—or, through him, Sylvester—had given her a little glimmer of hope, a brief respite from loneliness and running. Just for once she had the chance to break out of her discarded, unwanted and unloved life. He had offered her safety and he would never know—how could he?—what that had meant to Connie. Then, with one glance and one shattered wineglass, Sylvester had cruelly dragged that vision of security away again.

What if I stay anyway? We have an agreement. It doesn't say Sylvester has to like, or even tolerate, me.

The thought made her straighten her shoulders. Could she spend the next few weeks on his beautiful island and enjoy the luxury of this house without having to spend time with her host? Accept this sanctuary as a much-needed breathing space from which to plan her next steps? If she could hang on to that remaining money, it might just get her a plane ticket to Europe. A new life could be within her grasp. All she needed to do was to be Sylvester's invisible guest for the next month. It seemed like a plan. As far as she could see, there was only one problem with her idea…

Dinner was at eight.

Chapter 3

Mindful of Mr. Reynolds's comments, Connie had dutifully purchased some new clothes. She had been reluctant, however, to spend too much of the cash he had given her on expensive outfits. Those crisp notes were her insurance policy, the cushion between her and the harsh reality of a job scrubbing floors. She wasn't going to part with a single one of those dollar bills for frivolous reasons unless she absolutely had to. So the week between her meeting with Mr. Reynolds and her journey to Corazón had been spent visiting vintage clothing stores and dressmaking outlets.

Connie's mother had been a talented seamstress, with an eye for color and style. After her husband's death, she had supplemented her income by doing alterations and making clothes for friends, including one who had won a luxury cruise holiday. Once the excitement about the prize had died down, a panic about purchasing expensive cocktail dresses on a limited budget had followed.

"What you need—" Connie could hear her mother's calm voice as if it was yesterday "—is a few simple, neutral gowns. Then you change the trimmings on them so people are fooled into thinking you're wearing a new dress each time."

She had demonstrated by swiftly pinning a length of cream silk around her friend. One minute it was decorated with a spray of tiny crystal flowers curling lovingly over one shoulder; the next, two rows of diamanté decorated the scooped neckline. "Two different dresses. You see?"

For that first dinner Connie chose a white gown of Grecian simplicity, in a draped style that left one shoulder bare. When it came to hair and makeup, she knew she wouldn't be able to compete with Lucinda's expensive sophistication. Shrugging, she decided she would have to rely on the novelty of simplicity instead. Arranging the glossy length of her hair in a single thick plait over her exposed shoulder, she finished the look with a touch of coral lip gloss.

Simplicity seemed to work. When she appeared in the doorway of the salon, every eye turned her way. Guthrie actually did her the honor of choking slightly on his drink. Lucinda looked thunderous but, for once, had nothing to say. Instead she rearranged the folds of her designer gown and patted her immaculately styled hair before whispering behind her hand to the woman who sat beside her.

"You look stunning," Matt said, coming forward to greet Connie.

"Stunning in a good way?" She winced at how needy the words sounded. Four years ago she had made a vow never to cover up the scars on her neck. They were proof that she was a survivor. But on a night like tonight—wearing a dress that attracted rather than deflected attention—she needed all the reassurance she could get.

"Definitely in a good way." He guided her into the

room. "Let me introduce you to Ellie and Jonathan Carter, who must, like else everyone in the room, be some sort of distant cousins of ours."

Ellie, Connie was relieved to note, was considerably less threatening to look at than Lucinda. Connie judged her to be a couple years older than herself and she had a chatty manner and bright eyes that missed nothing. Ellie explained she was a New Yorker, born and bred. She was also unmarried.

Jonathan was her older brother. Tall and handsome, with dark hair and penetrating green eyes, he was quiet to the point of taciturnity. Ellie informed Connie that he worked for a firm of accountants, but he was also an aspiring author. Jonathan, who seemed annoyed his sister had shared this personal information with a complete stranger, moved away to look at the view out the window.

"The news of the moment is that Sylvester will be joining us anytime now." Ellie clearly had no idea of the heart-dropping effect those words had on Connie.

A light step outside was the signal they had all been listening for. A laughing, masculine voice responded to something Vega was saying and then Sylvester stepped into the room. He paused on the doorstep, those brilliant eyes scanning the company.

Connie willed herself to remain outwardly calm, despite the fact her heartbeat was thundering in her ears. Thinking fast, she placed her glass on a nearby side table so no one would notice and comment on the sudden trembling of her hands.

Sylvester's eyes seemed to linger on each face. Except hers. He didn't even glance in Connie's direction. Yet she knew, just knew with a certainty that branded itself into her heart, that he was as intensely aware of her as she was of him. *You can't possibly know that.* She tried to force her rational self to take over, to stop this nonsense now. *You are trying to make this into something it's not.* It was no good. Whatever this force was that existed between her and Sylvester, the very air between them shimmered with the ferocity of it.

"What sort of dreadful host arrives after his guests have assembled? I do hope you'll forgive me." Sylvester's easy charm was legendary. Up close, it was devastating. In an instant the whole room was his to command. Connie was immediately aware of the strangeness of the phrase. *Why would he want the sort of power that allows him to command us?* It was a long time since she'd drunk alcohol and a few sips of Guthrie's potent rum punch were clearly sending her imagination into overdrive. *Water for you from now on, my girl.* If only she could do something about the equally forceful impact of Sylvester's presence. "Vega tells me dinner is ready."

He led them into a long, hacienda-style dining room. The arched, full-length windows were open onto the terrace, allowing them views over the beach. A light breeze wafted the mingled scents of mimosa flowers, citrus and the tang of the sea into the room. Connie couldn't help contrasting this elegant scene with years of eating takeaway meals, or sometimes nothing at all, alone in a meager room, while planning her next one-step-ahead-of-the-madman journey. Would she take luxury and tension over poverty and terror? She almost laughed aloud at the stupidity of her own question.

Sylvester took his place at the head of the table and immediately started a conversation about sailing with Ellie, who was on his right. Lucinda was quick to claim the seat on his left. Connie moved to a chair as far away from Sylvester as possible. She was glad to look up and receive an encouraging smile from Matt as he slid into the seat opposite her.

Guthrie was next to Connie, and she was surprised to learn he and Lucinda were twins. She wondered why on earth he allowed himself to be bullied by her and supposed it must be a habit that had started in the womb.

Vega's food was delicious. Made with fresh ingredients, each dish was well cooked and plentiful. For Connie, who had spent plenty of time wondering where her next meal was coming from, it was heavenly. As she ate, Connie found her ears tuning out Guthrie's comments and listening, almost with a will of their own, to the conversation going on beyond him at the head of the table.

"Whatever have you done to your hand?" Ellie asked as Sylvester struggled to cut his food.

"Didn't you hear?" Lucinda cut in before Sylvester could speak. "Cousin Sylvester was so shocked by the appearance of some of our little group that he crushed his wineglass in his hand."

Connie risked a glance at Sylvester's face. It was impassive, but there was a flash of something in those blue eyes that might have been anger. He turned to Ellie. "Lucinda is joking, of course. I have nothing to blame for my injury other than my own clumsiness." His voice was dismissive and Connie got the distinct impression he was making an effort not to look in her direction as he spoke. Perhaps he was able to convince himself that what he said was true. She knew better, and so did everyone else who had been present at the time.

Determinedly, Connie turned back to Guthrie. She had made a pact with herself to keep her distance from Sylvester. She should probably include eavesdropping on his conversation as part of the deal. Not an easy task in a group as small as this one.

Once he was free of Lucinda's tight rein, Guthrie proved to be surprisingly good company. He kept Connie entertained with a steady stream of anecdotes about his job as a junior manager in a convenience store chain.

His life appeared to lurch from one comical episode to another. Although he was at pains to let Connie know how invaluable he was to his company, reading between the lines she speculated about how competent he actually was. An alarming number of unfortunate incidents seemed to occur in his working life. She decided Guthrie was one of those people for whom it was always somebody else's problem or somebody else's fault. He consumed a remarkable amount of alcohol during the course of the meal and Connie couldn't help wondering how much of a contribution drink made to the mishaps that befell him.

It was during the main course of Spanish-style chicken and rice that Connie's attention, along with that of everyone else at the table, was drawn back to Sylvester as Lucinda began to question him about the history of the island.

"The word *Corazón* means *heart* in Spanish, of course." Lucinda's penetrating voice carried around the room. "And the island is well known for its heart-shaped coastline. So I assume that is where the name came from?"

"You assume wrong." Although Sylvester's tone was softer, his words were equally compelling. Other conversations stopped as they all turned to look at him. "The island's full name is Corazón de Malicia. It means 'malevolent heart' or 'heart of malice.'"

"But that's nowhere near as pretty." Lucinda pouted. "In fact, it makes it sound quite nasty."

"That's because the story of how the island came by its name *is* nasty." Sylvester paused, taking a sip from his glass.

As though drawn by a force beyond his will, he looked directly at Connie for the first time since he had entered the room. And nothing else mattered. The people around them faded into insignificance. Time stilled. In that instant she could sense his feelings as clearly as she knew her own. There was no doubt in her mind. She knew his reaction on the beach had not been about the scars on her neck. This was something deeper and darker, and it was inside them both. Neither of them wanted it, yet at the same time it was unavoidable. They could be silent and reserved, avoid each other's gaze and pretend, but when their eyes did meet—as they met now—there was no hiding place for either of them. Connie didn't try to understand what was going on; all she knew was that when she gazed into Sylvester's eyes her heart leaped with a combination of joy, fear and something older and unfathomable. And she never wanted to look anywhere else.

"Well, you can't say that and then not explain!" Lucinda's indignant exclamation had the effect of rousing Sylvester from his trance.

Connie caught a brief flash of regret in his eyes as he withdrew them from hers. Then a slightly mischievous smile touched his lips as he turned to Lucinda. "Very well, but it's a strange tale and an old one. I can't vouch for its truthfulness. It concerns an ancestor of mine, one Máximo Silvestre de León y Soledad."

"Are you named after him?" Ellie asked.

The smile deepened. "Of course. The name was

handed down through the generations...and Americanized in the process, of course. Máximo was the founder of our great family."

"And is it true? Are you descended from Ponce de León himself?"

"There are no formal records, but it's a link that has repeatedly been made. Not necessarily within my own family."

"How amazing!" Lucinda's eyes sparkled. "To think you can trace your family tree back to the man who discovered Florida."

Sylvester's smile had vanished now and his voice held a harsh note that was unlike his usual charming tone. "I prefer to think Florida was here all along and needed no discovery by the Spanish. But, back to the story of Máximo...

"Juan Ponce de León's intention when he arrived here in 1521 was to set up a Spanish colony in La Florida, or the place of flowers, as he had named it on his earlier visit. When he arrived, he encountered a hostile reception from the native Calusa Indians. In a skirmish, Ponce de León was shot in the thigh with a poisoned arrow and, although he managed to escape to Cuba, he died of the wound. Máximo fared rather better. His life was spared by the Calusa. It was an unusual move. They were not known for their merciful nature. On the contrary, they were known to be quite savage to their enemies."

"Is it known why they changed their habits for Máximo?" It was Matt who spoke up this time. Although he lounged back in his seat, he, like everyone else around the table, appeared to have picked up on the tense atmosphere generated by the story.

"There has been much speculation. Perhaps it was

Máximo's personal charm—according to records kept at the time, he was accounted a very charismatic man—although the ability to enchant an entire warlike tribe must have been quite an achievement."

Watching his face as he spoke, listening to that, soft, lyrical voice, Connie could believe the Máximo of all those years ago had possessed that sort of magnetism. His descendant certainly did.

"The most popular theory is a high-ranking Calusa maiden, possibly the daughter of a chief, appealed for mercy on his behalf."

"So Máximo was a bit of a ladies' man?" Guthrie gave a smirk around the table.

"What makes you say that?"

Somehow, although she couldn't say how, Connie sensed an undercurrent of anger in Sylvester's question.

"Well, you know…"

"On the contrary. We don't know. So let's stick to the facts, shall we?"

Guthrie, muttering under his breath in the manner of a sulky schoolboy, subsided into his seat.

"Although we can only speculate about the reasons, Máximo lived among the Calusa for some months. It's not clear how he parted company with them, or how he came to claim this island. One thing we do know is a curse was placed upon our family by the mother of the Calusa king. It was that curse which gives this island its name." When Sylvester paused, the only sound was of the waves caressing the sands.

"What was the curse?" Overcoming her nerves, Connie spoke directly to Sylvester for the first time. For some reason she really needed to know the answer to that question. Her mother's words came back to her. *They are a star-crossed family.* Yes, there was that. But her yearning for more went deeper. Like the pull she felt to Sylvester himself, there was something drawing her into this story.

Sylvester's eyes returned to hers and, although she drew in a sharp breath as that electrical current of energy surged through her once more, she managed to maintain the contact. "It was in the dead language of the Calusa, but the translation was that Máximo's descendants must forever remain pure of heart. If they do not, any drop of impurity contained within them will, from then on, be magnified a thousandfold, damning the house of de León forever. Word of the curse spread and that was how the name Corazón de Malicia came about."

"It seems a strange curse. Why not simply condemn him to die a horrible death? Surely that would be a more effective way of dealing with him?" Matt's finely tuned legal mind honed in on the detail.

"Revenge is a sweeter wine when sipped slowly. It seems to me the whole point of curses and hexes is to strike a fear into the soul of the receiver that lasts long after the point of contact with the person delivering it. This one certainly did that.

"Instead of Máximo's life, the old Calusa woman took from him all he cherished. His proud name, his heritage, his status. For generations she has defiled the de León family name, sapped our strength and eroded our pride. I am branded with an island home named Heart of Malice. Each of you, just like anyone who has heard of us, will be aware of the rumors about this place." He encompassed his house with a sweep of one hand. "It's the same old story. I've lost count of the number of newspaper and magazine articles that have been written about the family who have everything. Except good fortune. You know what the press say. Don't marry a de León...unless you want to die young."

Connie winced. A quick glance around the table told her everyone was thinking the same thing. They were all remembering the shocking reports of car, plane and boat accidents, terminal illness, murder and suicide. How many ways could the members of one family die too soon? Fate seemed to grow ever more creative where the family was concerned. No wonder the world believed Corazón was doomed. And now Sylvester himself seemed to be providing irrefutable confirmation. This island's beauty was a thin veneer beneath which black poison oozed.

"So the curse became a self-fulfilling prophecy that has lasted almost five hundred years?" Matt's skeptical voice broke the mood.

"Yes. Far more effective, wouldn't you say, than simply striking Máximo down on the spot?" Sylvester waited while the words sank in. "And now I suppose you must all be eager to discover why I have invited you—who are all de Leóns, however distant—to spend the next month here on my cursed island?"

Chapter 4

Throughout the remainder of the meal, Sylvester did his best to avoid looking in Connie's direction. It wasn't good for his heart rate or his self-control. Whenever he did lose the battle with his willpower and glance her way, she immediately made sure she was looking elsewhere. Once or twice she wasn't fast enough and he caught those glorious dark eyes staring at him with a mixture of curiosity and something more. Something primeval and longing. *She feels it, too!* The realization sent a surge of triumph through him, like a wildfire singeing his nerve endings. Unlike him, she didn't know what "it" was. *How could she?* That thought instantly quenched the fire.

His eyes were drawn to the way her hand repeatedly touched the slender column of her neck, attempting to hide the disfigurement but drawing attention to it instead. The action touched him because it lacked guile yet it told a story. She wasn't seeking attention. She was avoiding it.

The white scars stood out in stark relief against the olive smoothness of her skin. No accident could have caused those linear marks. One scar went almost all the way across her throat from left to right. Then there were a series of other, smaller marks running parallel above and below it. Someone had taken a knife to Connie's smooth flesh and dug it in deep. Someone, not something. His hand clenched hard on his thigh. He thought he was ready to face any challenge, but nothing could have prepared him for this. The thought came again, stronger and more despairing. *Why now?*

Anger flared within him. It was two-pronged, directed at the person who had wielded that weapon, but also at a fate cruel enough to twist another knife. One that was cold steel tearing at his gut because, just as everything was in place, along had come Connie Lacey to turn his orderly plans upside down.

Sylvester knew better than to let his feelings of rage spiral out of control. The de León family could never be cold-blooded. Their emotions ran deep and strong. It would be easy to blame the curse, to pass responsibility for their actions on to the story of the old Calusa woman. In the past, that was what many de Leóns had done. Because he knew what was to come, Sylvester had never allowed himself that luxury. If anything, the curse had made him keep a tighter rein on his emotions.

His awareness that the darker side of his de León personality could easily become magnified had forced him into a heightened awareness of his own faults. Quick to anger, he had learned early how to keep his temper in check. A perfectionist, he had trained himself to relax and let the details go. Impatient of idle chitchat, he had cultivated a manner that hid his intolerance under a guise of genuine interest. No one, Sylvester had determined, would ever be able to say the master of Corazón had a "heart of malice."

Now he tightened his grip on the anger that wanted to become a frenzy. He wanted to fire questions at Connie about what had happened to cause those scars and that haunted, hunted look he saw in her eyes every now and then when she thought no one was looking at her. He also wanted to storm and rage at a set of circumstances that had brought him this dilemma.

All the pathways in his well-ordered life had been leading him here. Everything he had ever done since that first conscious memory had brought him to this point and now he was confronted with…what? *Not a change of plan. That can never happen.* So Sylvester kept his anger to himself, finished his meal and maintained his role as the perfect host.

Sylvester was aware his guests were all speculating on his story about the curse of Corazón. Oh, they were too polite to do so openly. The conversation over dessert was all about the weather, the Floridian cuisine, this island chain known as Corona de Perlas and the activities and sightseeing they hoped to engage in during their stay. But the undercurrent was tangible. The atmosphere had changed the moment Sylvester mentioned his reason for inviting them. Behind the polite chat, each one of them was wondering why they were here and what they could gain from their visit.

The temptation to keep them guessing a while longer was almost irresistible, but Sylvester hadn't brought them here to toy with them. No matter how grasping the light in Lucinda's eyes or speculative the expression in Ellie's, they were here for a reason. He might as well get this over with.

"We'll take coffee on the terrace, Vega," he said when everyone had finished dessert.

The marble-tiled terrace overlooked the beach. Comfortable furnishings reflected the golds and blues of the seascape and climbing plants trailed colorful fingers over the wrought-iron balustrade. Waves washing onto the shore and the light breeze rustling in the trees provided a backdrop of sound, breaking the silence that fell over the group as they realized the time for the truth had arrived.

Sylvester noticed Connie hung back until she saw where he was sitting before deliberately taking the seat furthest from his. He felt a pang of annoyance at such obvious reticence and then dismissed it. It suited him not to have her close by. Her nearness disrupted his equilibrium, something he needed for the task he was about to undertake.

Vega took her time serving coffee and liqueurs and then, after checking she would not be needed again, left them alone.

"It must have seemed strange that I chose to invite you, a group of complete strangers, to join me in my home." Looking around him at their faces, Sylvester could see each of them was hanging on his every word.

"We are not all strangers," Lucinda pointed out with something approaching a pout. "Guthrie and I have met you once before, remember?"

Ignoring her comment, Sylvester continued. "I asked Arthur Reynolds, Matt's father, who has been my trusted attorney for many years, to trace as many of my relatives as he could who were between the ages of twenty-five and thirty. They had to be of sound mind and body, have no criminal record, no dependents and no marital ties." Sylvester smiled as he looked around. "You are the people he found who fitted those criteria and who were able to come to Corazón on the dates I had specified."

"It did seem a little—" Ellie appeared to search for the right word "—*unusual.* But I thought it was a charming idea."

You are a liar. Sylvester refrained from saying the words aloud. He wondered what her reason for being here was. Probably money. That's what it usually came down to.

"And so to my reason for inviting you. I have decided the time has come to make my will." There was a faint ripple of interest. *Yes, I thought that might grab your attention.* "I have no heir, no one to inherit Corazón or the fortune that goes with it. My reason for asking all of you here is simple. I intend to leave my estate divided between as many of you as I consider worthy of it."

There was a brief, stunned silence, broken only by the high-pitched chipping sound of a distant osprey.

"Well!" It was Lucinda who spoke first, her voice cutting through the silence like a razor-edged knife. "I would have thought it was fairly obvious who Corazón should be left to, without any need for this drama. Guthrie and I are your nearest relatives, after all."

"Yes, but you will note I said I wished to leave my estate to the person, or people, I consider the worthiest." Sylvester ignored her outraged expression. "Most of you can be said to have some claim of birth, however remote." He allowed his eyes to skim quickly over Connie. Her link was so tenuous it was almost nonexistent, but there was no need for the others to know that. "Matt is here to oversee the legalities. Being a relative himself, he is also included in my proposition."

"I'm an employee. There is no need to include me in this," Matt protested in embarrassment.

"There is every need, if I choose to do so." Sylvester's voice was smooth. "There is just one condition. It is simple and not negotiable." Everyone went very still. Sylvester was reminded of those old black-and-white movies. This was like the scene where the detective gathers everyone together and unmasks the murderer. Cue dramatic music.

Everyone was waiting for him to continue speaking. "In order to be included in this proposal, you must remain here at Corazón, as my guests, until my thirtieth birthday in thirty days' time. Those of you who are still here to raise a glass on that day will be named in my will as my heirs and will inherit an equal share in my fortune. As for the island itself, I will leave that to the individual I decide is worthiest of it."

"Seems a decent arrangement," Guthrie said. "I, for one, am quite happy to live in the lap of luxury at your expense for the next few weeks, Sylvester."

"I thought you might be." Sylvester kept his voice perfectly even, although his eyes dropped briefly to the empty liqueur glass in Guthrie's hand.

"But you've said people tell such strange stories about Corazón." Lucinda cast a theatrical glance over her shoulder at the dark beach. "How do we know we will be safe here?"

"If you have the slightest fear about staying under my roof, you have only to say the word and Roberto will have the launch at your disposal within the next half an hour." Sylvester's words cast a hush over the terrace. His meaning was clear. *Stay and risk the hidden dangers that are rumored to lurk within these heart-shaped shores. Go and forfeit your share of a fortune.*

The atmosphere changed in that instant. It had become a competition.

After dropping his bombshell, Sylvester went away, leaving his guests on the terrace. His departure provoked a storm of conversation, one from which Connie remained detached. She didn't feel part of this strange arrangement, so she didn't feel she had any right to comment. Or maybe her inclination and willpower weren't strong enough to insert herself into the storm.

"It's ridiculous," Lucinda was saying sulkily. "And probably illegal."

"If my father is advising Sylvester, it's certainly not illegal," Matt commented. For some reason, his words didn't seem to reassure Lucinda.

"We've all sustained a shock. I think a drink is in order," Guthrie said. "I'll go and fetch us something." Eagerly, he hurried away.

"What is Sylvester worth, do you think?" Ellie glanced around each of them in turn.

"Billions." Jonathan's voice was calmer than the others. "The exact amount would be speculation."

Ellie's eyes sparkled. "So all we have to do is sit tight, and we each get a share of that. And one of us will inherit this island, as well."

"When Sylvester dies," Matt pointed out. "He's a young man."

"But as his heirs, we would be entitled to some sort of privileges during his lifetime, surely?" she insisted.

"That would be entirely up to Sylvester."

"This is ridiculous!" Lucinda had been pacing the length of the terrace but she paused now, her face suffused with fury. "This should be done properly. Mr. Reynolds should have been given the task of finding Sylvester's closest relatives. That would be Guthrie and me. We should be his heirs. We could challenge this—"

Matt's calm tones cut across her heated ones. "I hope you won't. You'd look very foolish. It is up to Sylvester to decide who he leaves his money to."

Before Lucinda could reply, Guthrie returned with a tray laden with drinks and proceeded to dispense these. The interruption lightened some of the tension. "It's like an old-fashioned horror story," Guthrie commented cheerfully.

"Don't be absurd." Lucinda frowned at him.

"No, I mean it." He lowered his voice dramatically. "Who will be the first to succumb to the curse of Corazón? The first one to go is usually the quietest. My money's on you, Jonathan."

"Thank you." Jonathan raised his glass in a mock salute.

"Connie won't be first," Guthrie continued. "The prettiest girl always lasts until close to the end."

"It's interesting that no one wants to leave," Matt said. "Which means none of us are taking the story seriously."

"Do you think Sylvester believes so strongly in the curse he is convinced *he* will die young? Is that why he has never married?" Ellie turned to Matt for answers.

Matt shrugged. "I'm not in his confidence. Sylvester doesn't strike me as an overimaginative person, however."

"If we chose to stay and don't remain pure of heart, surely we risk becoming victims of the second part of the curse?" After remaining quiet for so long, Jonathan seemed to have found his voice. It was laden with doom.

"You mean there's a chance we could die young? Within the next few weeks?" Ellie's voice became more high-pitched with each word. "I hadn't thought of it that way."

"We'll just have to think pure thoughts and do pure deeds for the next three weeks," Guthrie said as he drained his glass. "Who's for another?"

Since Jonathan's words had cast a gloom over everyone's spirits, no one took him up on his offer and Guthrie was left alone among the bottles as the others wandered away.

Matt caught up with Connie as she strolled along the edge of the beach. "You were very quiet back there. Everything okay?"

She turned her head to smile up at him. "I'm not sure what to make of it all. Do you believe the curse story?"

"No, but I think those sorts of things can have a powerful influence. Once they take hold of an individual's imagination, they can do some damage. If anyone back there actually believed their darker traits might be enhanced by this island—that they will develop a heart of malice while they are here—then the power of suggestion could be strong enough to make it happen."

There was enough light cast by the moon and from the house itself for her to see his expression. A mischievous smile lit up his features. "So we might see Lucinda change from the dear, sweet girl she is now into someone altogether more unpleasant."

Connie couldn't help laughing. "When you put it like that, it does sound foolish to think a place can change someone's personality." She looked at the house. It was so beautiful; how could it possibly be bad?

"Do you believe the past can influence the present?" His voice was suddenly different. Some of the humor had gone, to be replaced by a sudden urgency.

Connie shivered slightly. Wasn't she living proof it did? Every day? "It depends. Are you talking about living memory or the distant past?" She'd spent so long worrying about what the next ten minutes might bring, tonight was the first time she'd thought about the past in a true historical sense—beyond the pages of a book—in a very long time.

Matt ran a hand through his hair. "To be honest, I don't know what I'm talking about, or where the hell that question came from. I'm going to blame Guthrie for mixing an overly powerful drink and go in search of a strong coffee. I'll leave you to your stroll."

Slipping off her shoes, Connie stepped up to the water's edge, feeling the grains of sand crunch and slide between her toes. She wondered if she was the only person who felt safer here, despite the curse. Or did the other five all have equally powerful reasons for staying? *I have faced the prospect of dying young every second of every day for the last four years. What does another few weeks matter?*

Sylvester's proposition meant nothing to her, except as a means of escape from fear. If she was still here in three weeks' time—and she'd become used to thinking of her future in much shorter time scales—she'd deal with the implications then. Perhaps Mr. Reynolds could help her? If she survived and emerged as one of Sylvester's heirs, surely she'd have more options. She smiled. One of Sylvester de León's heirs. The thought was too ridiculous for words.

The thought that she was here at all, thinking about Sylvester, imagining that there was something in his eyes when he looked at her, was all too far-fetched to be true. Perhaps that was another reason why this talk of curses hadn't affected her as much as it had the others. Her heart rate had still not recovered from the intensity of that magnetic blue gaze. Unlike everyone else, her biggest challenge would not be to withstand the effects of the curse; it would be to resist the lure of the island's owner.

As she turned and walked back, the view of the house, golden and welcoming in the darkness, was stunning. It beckoned to her as nowhere in her life had ever done, stirring emotions she didn't understand. Sweet wistfulness twined its way around her heart, slowing her limbs and softening her gaze. Decorative arches were lit by lamps and light shone from each of the windows. The walkways through the gardens were also now lit and Connie caught glimpses of pretty fountains shimmering with reflected color. As she walked toward them, she experienced the oddest feeling of déjà vu. The thought amused her. *Because my life has been all about spending time in the garden of a billionaire's island mansion.* Moving closer still, the feelings persisted. It was much more than a brief sensation of having been here before. It was an emotional pull accompanied by a strange, proprietorial pride.

There were four identical Spanish-style fountains, each hexagonal in shape with mosaic tiles in green, white and blue decorating their bases. The walkway between them was lined with fragrant blue sage flowers and a stone bench had been set at the end, affording a perfect view over the whole area. Connie surveyed the scene with her head to one side.

Perfect. Just like the old house at Valladolid.

The strange thought, quick and fleeting, was gone as soon as it had entered her mind. Connie shook her head. What did she know of old houses in Valladolid? This strange night was getting to her in more ways than one.

As she drew closer to the fountains, she could hear two men talking. They were walking toward her. Recognizing Sylvester's voice, she pulled back into the shadows. She wasn't ready for a conversation with him yet. She might never be ready for that.

The other man was Matt. Clearly he had been sidetracked from his coffee, and he was the one speaking as they drew level with Connie.

"Sylvester, this plan of yours is ridiculous. You'll marry and have children of your own. There is no need for this—" Connie could hear the frustration in Matt's tone as he ground out the words, then paused to seek the right one to come next. "Theater."

"No, you couldn't be more wrong. I will never marry. No child of mine will inherit Corazón."

"I don't wish to pry, but are you ill, Sylvester? Is that what this is all about?" Matt sounded concerned. "Because we can get you the very best doctor money can buy."

As the two men continued on their way, Connie heard Sylvester's laughter. It was a bitter, mirthless sound, carried to her clearly on a warm island breeze together with his words. "I wish it was that simple, Matt. Really, I do."

Chapter 5

Connie slept well in her shell-themed room, although her slumber was plagued by odd snippets of dreams. These were fanciful glimpses into another time when there were shells to be gathered and fish to be speared. She had never before had a dream in which the sense of heat was so real. Connie could taste it in the sand-blasted, flower-scented air. It shimmered around her as she walked, clinging to her bare legs and plastering the strange garment she wore against her body. It seemed to be a short dress made of tanned deerskin decorated with interwoven grasses, moss and shells.

Waking the next day, she felt the oddest sense of loss, as though her dreaming self wanted to cling to something that never was. The feeling persisted as she showered and dressed.

These strange imaginings must have been prompted by Sylvester and his talk of the deeds of long-dead de León ancestors. After all the talk of history and curses, it was probably only natural her subconscious mind should have taken her on a journey away from this beautiful house that gazed out onto calm seas. Behind the luxurious façade, there was drama and legend enough to sweep her back through the centuries to the point in time when Spanish conquistador and fierce Calusa had collided.

She was relieved to find she was the only person at breakfast. Vega informed her that Sylvester, always an early riser, had already eaten and gone for his customary morning run. No one else had emerged from their rooms. Vega imparted the news with a vague air of condemnation.

"Are there any books about the Calusa in the house?" Connie asked when Vega brought her coffee and eggs. "I'd love to learn more about them."

"You should ask the master. He knows more than anyone alive about the 'fierce people,'" Vega told her with a trace of pride. "But I think he does have some books in the den."

The day stretched ahead of Connie, the first one she could remember in which she had no plans. It was a strange feeling. No work. No furtive, over-the-shoulder glances. No raised heart rate. It was too soon to say there was no fear. She had been conditioned to feel fear. Her hand went to her throat. *He has brainwashed me to be afraid. The way a master trains his dog.* The thought roused a flicker of anger deep within her and she welcomed it as a sign she wasn't completely under his control.

When she had finished eating, she took a second cup of coffee into the den. As with every room at Corazón, it was both luxurious and comfortable.

Connie found the Spanish style that pervaded the house soothing to her nerves, and that feeling was more apparent in this room than any other. The huge fireplace dominating the room was decorated with a brass plate.

When she stepped closer, Connie saw it depicted scenes of the conquistadors' battles. The den had a high, arched ceiling of light oak paneling with the wood continuing halfway down the walls. This had also been used to build the bookcases that lined one wall.

Vega was right, and Connie discovered several books about the Calusa on the shelves. Taking these down, she placed them on a side table and, kicking off her shoes, curled into one of the huge, cushioned chairs at the side of the fireplace. What heaven! A chance to read without having an eye on the clock and the other on the door. Within minutes she was completely lost in the world of the Shell Indians. Her ears, accustomed to listen for changes, picked up on movements within the house without allowing them to disrupt her concentration. She tuned out Lucinda's complaints about the noise of the cicadas, Ellie's inquiry about whether the coffee was decaf and Guthrie's good-natured banter with Vega about the size of the breakfast and his fears for his waistline.

It was some time later that the door clicked open and she finally glanced up from her book, reluctantly leaving behind a world when shells counted as currency and the word of the king and his high priests were the laws that mattered. The smile faded from her lips as she encountered the blistering blue of Sylvester's gaze.

"Oh." Connie snapped the book closed. He looked annoyed. Shouldn't she be here? Perhaps he didn't like people helping themselves to his books without asking first. She felt the blush burn her cheeks and her hand stole to her throat. "I'm sorry. I wanted to find out more about the Calusa. I should have asked..." Her voice trailed off and she rose to her feet, gathering up the other books and turning to the shelves, preparing to replace them.

"No." Sylvester strode into the room, stopping when he was a few inches away from her. His eyes raked her face hungrily and Connie held her breath. Was he going to say something about whatever it was that existed between them? This nameless, aching longing that gripped them both? Was he going to acknowledge it so they could talk about it, even do something about it? Because those inches separating them were alive with a crackling intensity that made her want to reach out a hand just to see what would happen. Would blue sparks leap between them? Would they both be engulfed in flames?

Sylvester looked like a man whose very soul was in torment. He drew in a breath and tore his eyes from hers. "It's fine—help yourself to any books you want. I'm sorry I interrupted you."

Turning abruptly away, he walked out of the room, leaving Connie staring after him with her hand half-raised.

Connie arrived late for lunch, having lost track of time. Murmuring an apology in Sylvester's general direction, she slid into a seat. It seemed there was a determined effort taking place to get this strange house party fully under way. Connie's introverted soul withdrew further at the idea. Ellie seemed to have appointed herself group leader and Guthrie was happily assisting her in planning a number of entertainments. Matt caught Connie's eye a few times, his droll expression causing her to hide a smile.

"We must do all the things Sylvester's other house guests do," Ellie decided. The subtext was clear. *We must behave the way celebrities do when they visit*

Corazón. "The weather is perfect, so there is no excuse for staying indoors." She directed a frown in Connie's direction. It was clearly a condemnation of the person who had remained buried in her book most of the morning while the others socialized on the terrace. "There are any number of activities to occupy us." She began to list them on her fingers. "Swimming, sailing, walking, fishing, water sports—"

"Are you trying to wear us all out?" Lucinda asked. "I'm more in favor of lounging by the pool."

"I think we'll quickly end up at each other's throats if anyone feels obliged to do anything he or she has no inclination for." It was a lengthy speech from the generally quiet Jonathan.

"What do your guests usually do?" Ellie appealed to Sylvester for help.

"Whatever they choose. My home is at your disposal." He cast a glance around the table. "You should remember that, apart from the brothers and sisters in the group, none of you know each other. In the unusual circumstances that brought you together, enforced exposure to strangers might be difficult. I think you should take care to respect each other's privacy."

Did Connie imagine it or did he cast a brief, sympathetic glance in her direction?

"Following that wise advice, I'm going for a swim. Anyone care to join me?" Guthrie rose from the table.

Ellie jumped up enthusiastically. "Swimming is my passion. I do it every day. I'm a competitive long-distance swimmer..." Her voice faded as she left the room and Connie felt a sense of relief at the prospect of being spared any more planned amusement.

Matt caught up with her as she left the house. "Any plans for the afternoon?"

"I want to explore the island."

"Care for some company?"

She agreed readily, although her conscience troubled her slightly as they followed a path that led them inland. Was she consenting to his company because she liked Matt or because of his closeness to Sylvester? She hoped it was the former.

She didn't think of herself as a manipulative person, but that raised its own set of problems. She felt safe in Matt's company and he was the first man close to her own age about whom she had been able to say that in a long time. He alleviated some of her fears over this strange holiday and took away some of her nervousness around the others in the group. But she'd seen the admiration in his eyes when they'd rested on her. That was something she didn't want to encourage. The idea of a new friend was an unlooked-for pleasure. Anything more, even without the complication of her feelings for Sylvester, was out of the question.

Matt glanced down at her once or twice, but remained silent until they reached the top of a small hill. Looking back, they could see the house and the beach, ahead of them another tiny bay and a cluster of small buildings.

"It looks like a miniature village," Connie said.

"I suppose it is, in a way," Matt agreed. "Looking after an island like Corazón takes some work. This is the staff quarters. It was where the landscapers, house maintenance staff, boat keepers, fishermen, dive experts lived. The list used to be a long one."

"Used to be?"

"As technology has advanced, the number of staff has reduced. Many services are brought in. Now there are just four permanent, live-in staff. Vega and Roberto, whom you've met, and two others who do more general roles," Matt said. "I know so much about it because my father's firm oversees a lot of Sylvester's contracts."

"And the curse doesn't bother the staff who live here?"

"The curse was aimed at the family, remember? Also, Sylvester pays well, which takes some of the sting out of the old legends."

They continued on the downward path, reaching the bottom of the hill and finding themselves among a group of small, thatched huts and a larger, wooden building that was open to show kayaks stored inside. Two men at the water's edge were working on a traditional-looking canoe and, as Matt approached, they greeted him with pleasure.

"Stranger," one of them said in a teasing voice. He was younger than the other man, but the likeness between them meant they could only be father and son. "We thought you'd lost your directions for how to get here."

"Connie, this is Juan and his son Nicolás. They are responsible for all things water-sport-related on this island. If you want to try water-skiing or kayaking, you know where to come." Seeming unaware of her look of horror, he looked over the craft they were working on. "What model is this?"

"Mark four." Juan eyed the canoe with pleasure. "We think this is the one."

"You said that about the last three."

"Care to put your money where your mouth is?" Nicolás challenged.

"No, because when you sink between here and Cuba, how will I collect my winnings?"

Connie looked from one to the other. "You are going to Cuba in this?" Her surprise cut across their banter.

"That's the plan." Nicolás laughed at her expression. "How long has it been your ambition to do this, Dad? Thirty years?"

"At least. And it has been done before. We are trying to replicate the voyages undertaken by the Calusa in their hollowed-out cypress logs. There is plenty of evidence to show that they reached Cuba and even possibly Mexico in vessels such as this one."

"Dad likes to think he's a Calusa at heart." Nicolás quirked an affectionate brow at his father.

"Were they your ancestors?" Connie remembered the book she'd been reading that morning and the fascinating stories it contained. Could these two men with their weathered, brown skin be descended from that ancient tribe?

"No." The voice came from behind them and they swung around. None of them had heard Sylvester's approach. Not even Connie, who prided herself on having a sixth sense for people approaching her from behind. "There are no living descendants of the Calusa."

"We're from Cuba," Juan explained. "Where some people like to claim they have Calusa blood. They think it makes them sound fierce and interesting. What do you think, boss?" He pointed to the boat.

"I think you're going to die."

Juan certainly did look fierce as he turned away with a scowl, Connie decided. That was about the only thought she had to spare, since Sylvester's presence instantly took up every part of her awareness, her senses, her very being. She remembered a solar eclipse when she was young, and her father telling her solemnly that she mustn't look directly at the sun because it would burn her eyes. *I can't look directly at Sylvester. He burns my heart.* Just as they had done with that long-ago eclipse, her eyes refused to listen to the instruction. They kept finding their way back to the source of the danger.

Sylvester had taken Juan aside and was talking to him about sporting equipment. No doubt warning him there were some very persistent guests who might not necessarily put their own safety first. Matt was still teasing Nicolás about their bet.

Connie wandered a few feet away along the edge of the water. The shells were plentiful here and she stooped to pick a few up, examining them, marveling there was once a society built upon their fragile beauty. *There are no living descendants.* Sylvester's words saddened her way beyond anything she should feel for a people to whom she had no connection beyond one book she'd browsed a few hours earlier. It made her feel unbearably sorry to think such a proud people no longer existed. The closest feeling to which she could compare it was one of mourning.

She was turning back when Sylvester fell in step beside her. *Okay, I can do this. I can ignore the pounding of my heart and make polite conversation. He is just being a considerate host.* She reminded herself Sylvester had no idea of the impact he had on her. Or perhaps he did? Perhaps he knew women became fluttery and tongue-tied whenever he approached them? "It's sad to think of a whole complex civilization being wiped out. How did it happen?"

"They were mighty warriors, and they fought the Spanish bravely. But they were not equipped to fight the diseases the Europeans brought with them. When the Spanish arrived in South Florida in the 1500s, it is estimated there were twenty thousand Calusa here. By the time the English gained control in 1763, their number had been decimated and only a few hundred of the Shell People remained. It is believed those survivors left Florida for good, following the Spanish to Cuba. So, perhaps Juan is right and there may be a few descendants in his country…your country, too. Wasn't your father Cuban?"

She blinked slowly at the sudden question. How did he know about her father? "Yes, although he had lived in this country most of his life." She gave a self-conscious laugh. "He used to call me Constanza, while my mother insisted on Constance. In the end, they compromised and I became Connie. I always felt it lacked the romance of his version and the dependability of hers.

"My father certainly never believed he was descended from the Calusa. Or, if he did, he never mentioned it." She turned the subject back to her original question. "Was it disease that wiped out the Calusa who lived on this island?"

"The story on Corazón is a different one…because of Máximo de León's wife." He paused, turning to face her. His eyes were bright, almost demanding, as they examined her face. It was as if he was gauging her reaction as he said the next words, expecting something from her. "She *was* a Calusa."

Sylvester saw Connie's eyes widen at the mention of Máximo's wife and the shells she held slipped from her fingertips back into the water. Nothing more. *What did you expect? And what the hell are you trying to do here?*

"Theirs must be quite a story." Her eyes were fixed on the horizon.

"It's an epic saga that would sound like a work of

fiction if it wasn't well documented. Máximo and his Calusa maiden had to travel across two continents and face some formidable opposition to be together." He kept his eyes on her profile. What was she thinking and feeling?

"But they did it."

"Was that why they were cursed? Because they came from different worlds?"

Before Sylvester could answer, Matt approached. "This looks like a deep conversation."

"We were talking about the Calusa."

Matt grimaced. "Don't get Sylvester started on his favorite subject, Connie. He turns into a bore."

She withdrew her gaze from the water with what appeared to be an effort, a smile dawning in the depths of those amazing eyes. Shyly, she turned to Sylvester and his heart somersaulted. "I find it fascinating. I'd love to know more."

This was too dangerous. Her nearness was intoxicating. If only he could tell her. Explain why he couldn't allow himself the luxury of getting closer to her. If only he didn't have to brutally snuff out that half hopeful, half scared light in her eyes.

Getting a grip on his emotions with difficulty, he injected a note of steel into his response. "Matt's right. If I'm not careful, I can turn my hobby into something resembling a lecture. Now, if you'll excuse me, I have things to do." He turned away, but not before he saw the flash of pain in her eyes or the surprise in Matt's.

You bastard. His lips compressed into a thin line as he marched back to the house. If she had to be here at all, why did Connie have to be so vulnerable, so easy to hurt? Why couldn't it be brittle Lucinda or robust Ellie? Why shy Connie, who was already so damaged? *Some-*

one took a knife to her throat not so long ago, and now you are doing the same thing to her heart.

Because she'd fallen in love with him at first sight. Of course she had. Just as he had with her. It was inevitable when you'd shared all they had before they'd even exchanged that first glance.

Sylvester wanted to turn back, to draw her tenderly into his arms and kiss away the hurt before explaining it all to her. But he didn't want to see her expression change to one of horror. He didn't want the ensuing speculation about his mental health, the stares, and the whispered comments behind hands. He didn't want anyone to try to stop him seeing this final task through to its inevitable conclusion.

Ignoring the sounds of revelry from the pool area, he made his way up to his room. Going to the drawer in his dresser where he kept the files on each of his guests, he reached beneath those and withdrew the portrait of Máximo de León y Soledad. The face that stared back at him was proud and noble. A perfect, precise, mirror image of his own.

"This had better be worth it." Five hundred years ago, Máximo had set off on a journey into the unknown. Now it was time for modern-day Sylvester to do the same.

He didn't know how long he sat in his room, gazing at that picture, but it was some considerable time later when he was roused from his thoughts by the sounds of shouting, running footsteps in the hall below and a woman screaming. Frowning, he replaced the portrait and made his way down the stairs. When he reached the foot of the staircase, there was already a crowd in the marble-tiled hall.

"What's going on?"

The group around an unconscious figure on the floor parted in recognition of Sylvester's authority. Guthrie, clad in swim shorts, and still wet from the pool, was lying on his back, a puddle of blood forming behind his head. A smashed glass lay beside him and a strong smell of liquor pervaded the scene.

"Somebody find Roberto. He's a trained paramedic."

Sylvester knelt beside Guthrie, checking his pulse. It was regular. Clad only in a bikini, Lucinda was still screaming. Sylvester glanced over his shoulder. "Can someone get something to cover her up? Keep her warm. Vega, maybe a cup of tea..." The message behind the words was clear. *Get her out of here.* Making soothing, clucking noises, Vega led Lucinda away.

"Shall I help you lift him onto one of the sofas?" Jonathan offered.

"Let's wait for Roberto."

Roberto arrived a minute later, carrying his medical bag. Sylvester rose so Roberto could get better access.

Turning Guthrie's head, Roberto discovered a nasty wound on the back of his skull. The movement caused Guthrie to groan and open his eyes.

"What the hell hit me?"

"You fell." Jonathan told him. "You left the pool to come and fix yourself another drink. When you didn't come back, Lucinda came looking for you and found you here. You must have knocked your head on the floor when you fell."

"No, that's not right." Guthrie winced as Roberto began to clean the wound. "I'd got my drink and was on my way back to the pool. As I was passing the stairs, something hit me on the back of the head and I went down. That's what happened. Not the other way around."

"But that can't be how it was. Who would hit you?" Jonathan insisted. "It's much more likely you fell and banged your head. Your feet were wet and—" he gave Guthrie an apologetic glance "—you had been drinking."

"I know what happened, damn it!"

Sylvester met Roberto's eye over Guthrie's head and Roberto shook his head with a frown. "This needs stitches, boss. I can do it, but he should probably get it checked by a doctor, as well." He beckoned Sylvester to take a look. The cut on Guthrie's scalp was circular and deep. "He's right. It looks like he's been bashed hard with a heavy object. No way was this caused by hitting his head on the floor."

Chapter 6

The dream is so vivid it feels like reality. More than reality. Even the sounds and scents of the beach come to life. Connie can hear the shouts of the Calusa braves as they drag the Spanish prisoners ashore. She can smell the sweat, fear and blood mingling with the everyday aromas of sea, salt and pine. If she reaches out her hand, surely she will be able to trail her fingers in the azure waters and rub the golden sands between them? Instead she watches, along with the whole village. Everyone has come out to see the light-skinned devils who have, it is said, traveled across oceans, to murder the Calusa and rob them of their islands.

But we fought. And we won.

In the midst of the mayhem around him, one man catches her attention. She doesn't know what she expects a devil to look like, but this is not it. The Calusa braves around him are tall but, even slumped in pain, this man is taller than his captors. The red-gold tint to his hair shines through the dirt and blood. They kick his legs from beneath him and he stumbles to his knees on the shell-encrusted sand. Does he know he is about to die? If he does, his gaze remains proud and defiant.

"We must help him," Connie says to the old woman at her side, in a language she doesn't know.

Her grandmother stares back at her in horror and tugs on her arm to draw her away, but Connie resists her.

His eyes are blue. As endlessly, perfectly blue as the sky above their heads. Connie has never seen such eyes. They fascinate her. She takes a step closer and he looks up at her.

"I will help you."

He doesn't know her language, but those beautiful blue eyes tell her that he understands.

Connie woke abruptly at that point, feeling restless and unfulfilled. That was the problem with falling asleep in the afternoon. Not that she would usually know. It was a luxury she generally couldn't afford.

On returning from her walk with Matt, the house had seemed oddly quiet. She had expected to find a group around the pool and dreaded the prospect of an invitation to join them; instead she'd caught a glimpse of Jonathan and no one else. Glad of a chance to escape any company and to reflect on her humiliating encounter with Sylvester, she had made her way up to her room. Within minutes of lying on her bed, she had fallen into a deep sleep.

It was one of those rare dreams in which, upon waking, she could remember every detail. One that made perfect sense and to which she wanted to return so she could find out the ending. Did the handsome Spanish prisoner—*who, let's face it, Connie, looks a hell of a lot like your host. I wonder what his starring role as the hero of your dream tells you about your feelings toward him?*—die? Did Connie, as the heroine of the dream, save him the same way legend suggests a Calusa maiden did with Máximo? Or did the story degenerate as dreams tended to? Something bizarre happening to derail the whole story?

Glancing at the clock on her bedside table, she decided it was time to dress for dinner. Just the phrase made her feel like she was in some strange parallel universe. Never in a million years would she have imagined herself at any point in her life "dressing for dinner." As she stepped into the bathroom and turned on the shower, she gave her reflection a grim smile. *Never in a million years did I imagine that, this afternoon, I would be snubbed by one of the richest men in the world.* She stepped into the shower, allowing the powerful jets of water to wash away the last remnants of sleep.

Sylvester had hurt her with his abrupt words down at the beach, and she couldn't shake the feeling he'd done it deliberately. Shyly, she'd extended a tentative offer of...what, exactly? Friendship? She almost snorted with laughter. As if Sylvester was in need of new friends. A way of getting to know each other? Of exploring these wild emotions between them? It didn't matter. He'd curtly let her know he wasn't interested.

Yet she sensed he had known how hard it was for her to open up to him. She even got the feeling he hadn't wanted to reject her.

She shook her head. If that was the case, why did he do it? He was as aware as she was of the atmosphere between them. He wanted her as fiercely as she did him. What they felt for each other transcended anything either of them had ever felt before. She knew that was the case for him as strongly as she did for herself. She didn't have to question it. It just *was.* It wasn't physical; although the attraction was fairly spectacular, it went deeper than that. It was love, and much more than love. *You love me, Sylvester, but you don't want to love me. I get it. I don't understand it, but I get it. I'm scared, too, but I was prepared to give it a chance. I wanted to explore it.* She'd gotten the message today. Sylvester didn't want to go there. It had cost Connie a lot to make that first move. She would never do it again.

Emerging from the shower wrapped in a huge, fluffy towel, she surveyed her dresses and selected a plain black gown with a high neckline and a low-cut back. Once her hair was dry, she piled it on top of her head in a loose updo.

When she reached the salon, Guthrie was entertaining everyone with the story of how he had come by an injury to his head. He was wasted in retail, Connie decided. Guthrie really should consider a career in stand-up comedy. It was strange the way his extroverted tendencies and skill at storytelling seemed to have developed in the short time he had been on the island.

Connie was shocked to learn she had slept through so much drama, particularly since everyone else seemed to have been roused from the four corners of the house by the noise. The fact that it must have happened very soon after she'd returned from her walk made it even more surprising she had heard nothing. Yet Connie had fallen into that instant and uncharacteristically deep slumber, as soon as she'd reached her room.

The conversation at dinner continued to be mostly about Guthrie's injury. Guthrie remained adamant he had been hit over the head by an unknown assailant. Although there were some skeptical remarks, notably from Jonathan, Sylvester surprised everyone by supporting Guthrie.

"Roberto informs me the most likely cause of Guthrie's head wound *was* a blow to the back of the head with a hard, heavy object. Something like the poker from the fireplace in the den."

Guthrie muttered an expletive under his breath. "If someone hit me with that, they could have killed me."

"Has anyone checked to see if the poker is still there and, if so, if there is any blood on it?" Matt, as always, went straight for the practical aspect of the matter.

"Good God." Ellie lifted a hand to cover her mouth. "We are not in a 1930s detective novel."

"The poker is in its usual place and there is no blood on it." Sylvester ignored her interruption.

"So either something else was used, or whoever hit Guthrie cleaned the poker after they hit him and then replaced it."

"Oh, I see. We *are* in a 1930s detective novel." Ellie took a long slug of her drink.

Connie took a deep breath. "Can I ask what may sound like a silly question?" Sylvester nodded, those endless eyes probing her face, tilting the world off its usual axis. "Why would anyone want to hit Guthrie over the head?"

Lucinda, who had been uncharacteristically silent throughout the meal, gave a bitter, little laugh. "Don't you see? It's the curse of Corazón."

"What do you mean?" Ellie turned on her sharply. "Surely you can't be implying one of us attacked Guthrie?"

Sylvester answered for her. "I think what Lucinda means is exactly that." He waited for a moment until Lucinda nodded. "If that's the case, someone either intended to genuinely harm Guthrie or to force him into being the first to leave Corazón. Whether that was because he was injured or too frightened to stay…well, I don't suppose it matters. The end result would have been the same."

Guthrie raised a tentative hand to the back of his head. "I'm a tougher nut to crack than that."

Jonathan offered an alternative suggestion. "Or there was an intruder on the prowl and Guthrie disturbed him."

Sylvester's expression was not quite a smile. Connie thought the weight of experience of the Corazón curse—real or legend—glittered in the blue of his eyes. "We can tell ourselves that. By all means."

"But none of us would have done such a dreadful thing." Ellie shivered slightly as she looked around the table.

And now we are all covertly studying each other and wondering who did it. Connie glanced down at the half-eaten meal on her plate. Paradise had suddenly turned nasty. "This is the point in the book where the detective would question us about where we were and who we were with." Ellie laughed at her own feeble attempt at a joke. It was a hollow sound.

"I'll go first. I was lying on the floor with a hole in my head," Guthrie said brightly.

"No one could suspect me. I'm Guthrie's sister."

"But where were you at the time?" Jonathan's eyes probed Lucinda's face. "You weren't out at the pool. You went into the house a minute or two after Guthrie did."

Lucinda flushed. "I went to the bathroom."

"What about you, Ellie?" Jonathan turned to his sister. "You'd left the pool about five minutes before Guthrie."

"I went to my room to get a book."

Jonathan held his hands palm upward in a helpless gesture. "I was still out by the pool. So any of the three of us could be guilty. We were all alone at the time and we can't provide each other with an alibi." He turned to Matt and Connie. "What about you two?"

Matt shook his head. "We walked down to the beach and met Sylvester. After he left us, Connie headed back here and I kept walking. We can't vouch for each other, either."

"I came back and went to my room." Since the provision of an alibi seemed to be expected, Connie felt obliged to offer her own at this point.

"I was also alone in my room. So it seems any one of us had the opportunity to attack Guthrie." Sylvester's calm tone lowered the mood even further.

"And all of us, with the exception of Sylvester, have a damn good motive." Matt sounded almost cheerful as he took a sip of his wine. "Maybe we should make sure we stay together in groups or pairs in future?"

"My God." Ellie lifted a hand to her throat. "Do you seriously think someone at this table is capable of harming the rest of us? To get us to leave the island so he or she inherits a greater share of Sylvester's fortune?"

"I'll show you the stitches in my head if you have any doubts," Guthrie offered.

"This seems like a good opportunity to remind you the launch is at your disposal, should any of you decide you wish to leave," Sylvester said.

Six pairs of eyes turned to regard him. Then silence reigned as everyone, with the exception of Connie, continued with their meal.

"How strange there are no animals here. I'd have expected a house like Corazón to have a few cats and dogs around." Connie thought back to her childhood. They'd had a big, friendly dog that had been her father's favorite, while her mother's elegant cat had ruled the household. A morning walk after breakfast had become her routine. A dog would have been good company and a distraction from her thoughts.

"Sylvester doesn't like animals," Lucinda had informed her. She'd seemed to feel she had somehow triumphed over Connie with this little piece of information. As if, by knowing something about Sylvester that Connie did not, she had gained a sort of superiority over her. Connie had wanted to tell her she needn't have worried. There was no danger of Connie finding out any information about him. She had been on his island for almost a week and, since that day at the beach, he had been carefully avoiding her.

Connie walked farther inland this time, along a rough path through pine woods she hadn't taken before. The trail was easy and she walked much farther toward the center of the island than she had planned. Her other explorations had taken her into the tiny beaches and rocky bays around the perimeter.

After walking for what she judged to be about half a mile, the route became steeper and she heard the sound of running water. Before long, its source became clear. The trees opened and Connie caught a glimpse of a lake into which a stream, tumbling over rocks, splashed. As she drew closer, she saw that, where the path ended, the only way forward was to cross a wooden bridge to the other side of the lake. On the opposite bank, there was a wooden building. Too small to be a house, too large to be a summerhouse.

Connie hesitated, looking around at her surroundings. It felt like she was intruding on someone's private property, yet there was no fence, no warning signs. And didn't the whole island belong to Sylvester, anyway? There was a surreal feeling about this place. Because of the way the trees grew around the lake, sunlight shone down in almost a perfect circle, as though an artistic film director had carefully planned the lighting for a dramatic scene. The background music should be tranquil, Connie decided, with just a hint of unease.

What is this place? And why is it here? And why do I really, really, want to cross that bridge and go through the door of that miniature house?

A house built for one.

She supposed she should turn back. Ask someone about it. Get Sylvester's permission to explore another day. But like the girl in the horror film or the child in the fairy tale, her head refused to listen to the warnings. Her foot felt the wooden slats of the bridge beneath the sole of her sneaker before she even knew what she was doing.

It wasn't so much an electric shock. More a subdued feeling of static tingling through her nerve endings as soon as she placed her hand on the rail of the bridge. The wood was old. Centuries' worth of other hands had imprinted themselves upon its grain, and something in that knowledge shimmied through Connie as she gazed over to the other bank. She cast a quick look back over her shoulder.

There can be no turning back. I must go to him.

Although she didn't understand it, the thought spurred her on and, with a renewed determination in her stride, she crossed the bridge. The building was a curiosity. It looked like someone had built it from oddments of wood scavenged from the surrounding forest. As though it shouldn't have lasted. But there were signs it had been carefully preserved. Recent repairs had been carried out on the roof and the exterior had been freshly varnished. This funny little house meant a lot to someone.

The door was open—*just as it always was*—and Connie stepped inside. Her heart was beating wildly but she couldn't name the emotions that caused the wild hammering. The only item of furniture inside the room was a narrow bed, long since stripped of any bedding. The bed itself looked to have been made from pieces of wood bound tightly together with narrow strips of hide. Closing the door behind her, Connie breathed in the stale, pine-scented air. Some compulsion took her to that bed.

She ran a hand over the planks of wood. Wood that should have rotted centuries ago. As her hand connected with the grain, sorrow so profound it felt a lot like fear swept over her in a sudden swoop. Connie gave in to the utter hopelessness of the emotion. Lying on the uneven slats, she pressed her face to the rough wood. Without knowing why, she began to cry as though her heart would break.

The feelings that racked her body were a tidal wave of grief so intense she doubled up in pain. She was consumed by a restless, burning longing—almost a memory—for something beyond her reach. She couldn't name it but, like a winter storm brewing below the horizon, it rumbled and raged just beyond her vision. It was a void, a desperate aching need inside her that, now she was aware of it, seemed to have always been there. Weighing her down with its intensity, it took all her emotions and drew them out until she couldn't think; all she could do was hurt and feel.

Connie didn't know how long she lay there with her

tears soaking into the ancient wood. Eventually she managed to get a grip on her emotions and sat up, propping her back against the wall and drawing her knees up to her chin. She'd read about places where past events leached into the present atmosphere. Battlefields where flowers didn't grow. Murder houses that, no matter how beautifully renovated or reasonably priced they might be, no one would buy. Tragic, haunted places where birds didn't sing.

What had happened in this tiny space, no more than eight feet across, that it could have such a profound effect on her?

Or was it her surroundings, at all? Was it simply that, having finally stopped running, the horror of the last four years had caught up with her now that she had relaxed? No, she shook her head. Connie knew for sure this wasn't about anything other than where she was right now. Her feelings ran the whole range from deep sorrow to wild elation. A tremor of excitement ran through her as she touched the wooden bedpost. Excitement and more. For the first time since before she had been attacked, she felt the first stirrings of arousal. She almost laughed aloud at the bizarre thought. *Am I remembering a sexual encounter in another narrow bed? I think maybe the last time I felt like this might have been when I was a student, so, yes, that would have been in a tiny room and a cramped bed. Oh, dear God, do I have a* fetish*?*

With humor replacing her sadness, she wiped away the last traces of tears.

Determinedly, she stopped trying to dismiss or to make light of the intensity of what she was feeling. *Just let it happen.* She closed her eyes. When she unwound, the sensations rushing through her grew stronger. It was all about this place. This bed. And it was about Connie. That was as far as she got before she heard the unmistakable sound of a footstep.

When she opened her eyes, Sylvester was glaring at her from the open doorway.

Restlessness surged through him and there was only one place he could feel at peace. The place where it all began. His guests were planning a tennis tournament for the afternoon and seemed content to spend the morning pursuing their own activities. Slipping out of the house—the good thing about having a reputation for being solitary and enigmatic was that people assumed you wanted to be alone and didn't offer you their company—Sylvester made his way toward the cottage in the wood.

As always, just the sight of the wooden bridge and the tiny dwelling soothed him. It was incredible how this place had the ability to take the sting out of any situation.

Crossing the bridge with quick strides, he entered the place he had come to think of as his personal haven and stopped short in shock to find Connie sitting on the bed.

"What the hell are you doing here?" The words had left his lips before he'd known what he was going to say.

She visibly gulped. "I'm sorry. I didn't know it was private."

Seeing her there, on *that* bed, aroused a storm of emotions so violent Sylvester was helpless to withstand them. For the first time in his life, he acted without thinking. Going over to the bed, he sat on its edge and gazed down at Connie's face. He took in her look of shock, the signs of her recent tears, but his eyes lingered most on the soft invitation of her parted lips. Taking her face between his hands and smoothing a few stray strands of hair away from her cheeks with his thumbs, Sylvester bent his head and succumbed to the impulse that had been tempting him since he'd first seen her.

The initial pressure of his lips on hers scorched him, burning its way from the mild connection of their mouths into his bloodstream and sizzling through to his groin. One touch and he was iron hard. It was exactly the effect he knew she would have on him.

Powerless to resist, he deepened the urgency, snaking his tongue between her parted lips. Connie's response was instant, her hand coming up to clasp the back of his neck, drawing him closer. The heat that had existed between them since the first moment they'd met grew and intensified so they were caught up in their own shimmering maelstrom. Minutes flew by in an exchange of crushed lips and exploring tongues.

Triumph surged through him. *This*. How long had his body been waiting to feel like this again? This tumultuous half pleasure, half pain sensation? It felt like his very soul was burning up in the violent flames of the passion that melded them together. The ache and sorrow that had been pent-up inside him for so long, the same feelings he had seen reflected in Connie's eyes just now, were ashes in the scorching desire that screamed at him for release.

Consumed by his need for more, Sylvester reached for the buttons at the front of her blouse, his fingers uncharacteristically clumsy. Tugging aside the lacy cup of her bra, he covered her breast with his hand. Her flesh was so soft, so incredibly sweet to touch, like cushioned silk. As he rubbed his thumb over her nipple, Connie moaned into his mouth. The soft, insistent sound brought him back to reality with something resembling a thud. What the hell was he thinking?

Breaking the kiss, he sat straighter, trying to ignore the look of hurt in her eyes.

"That wasn't meant to happen..."

Before he could say anything more, she jumped up from the bed, clutched her blouse closed with one hand and raced out of the cottage.

Muttering a curse, Sylvester ran after her. She was moving fast, but he caught up with her on the other side of the bridge.

"Let me explain."

Connie kept her eyes downcast as she buttoned her blouse. He had a feeling this wasn't going to be easy, particularly as he couldn't tell her the truth.

"I can't get involved with anyone right now."

"Okay." The word came out stiffly. Still not looking at him, she started to walk away.

Sylvester caught hold of her upper arm, turning her to face him. It was a mistake. Touching her was always going to be a mistake. As soon as his fingers connected with her flesh, that electricity was there, urging him to do more, to move his hand, to stroke the soft flesh of her inner arm with his thumb...

He released her and gazed down into those sherry-brown eyes. "You don't understand."

"I think I do. You believe I'm here for a share of your money. That makes me a gold digger, right? But what better way to ensure I get the biggest prize of all than to exploit this attraction between us? Or are you going to deny there is an attraction between us?"

He could tell how hard it was for her to make this little speech. Confrontation was not her style. She waited, and he shook his head in response to her questions.

"You think I'm out to snare *you*, instead of waiting it out to get my portion of the inheritance. You couldn't be more wrong about me, Sylvester. I don't want your money. Unlike the others, your proposition is not the reason I chose to stay on Corazón."

"You don't need to explain yourself to me." The pain in her eyes tugged at his heart.

"You're right, I don't. Which is why I'm not playing this game of yours anymore."

Her lip trembled and he wanted to reach out and smooth his thumb over its plump cushion, feel its soft warmth responding to his touch, see the hurt in her eyes disappear. "What do you mean?"

"You can ask Roberto to get the launch ready. The first of your guests is leaving Corazón."

Chapter 7

Connie felt curiously calm as she packed her clothes away. Having made the decision to go, she now felt only a sense of relief. It was what she should have done as soon as Sylvester walked away from her at that first meeting. Nothing was worth this sort of humiliation. She paused, touching a finger to her lips. She could still feel the imprint of his kiss. There was a strong chance she always would. Her breasts still ached to feel his touch once more. Angrily, she shook her head. No, even another kiss as magical as that one wasn't worth waiting around for. Sylvester had made his feelings clear. He wasn't going to change his mind, and Connie had too much pride to try to persuade him. It was no use dwelling on something that wasn't to be. She had more important things to think about. Like where the hell she was going next.

Sylvester had let her go when she had announced her intention of leaving the island. He hadn't tried to stop her. Of course he hadn't. What else could he do? He was hardly going to persuade her to stay here when it must be a profound relief to him to see the back of her. Now he could get on with this Machiavellian scheme for the rest of the group without any fear this intense attraction between the two of them might interrupt his plans.

A knock on the door made her start in surprise. Despite her lecture to herself, her mind instantly leaped with the hope it might be Sylvester. With her heart pounding wildly, she went to open it.

Matt was standing outside, his expression shocked. “Roberto said you’re leaving. Tell me it’s not true.”

“It’s true.” She stepped back into the room, allowing him to follow her.

“But why? I don’t understand. Is it because of what happened to Guthrie? I have a theory about that. I reckon Lucinda brained him with the poker to stop him drinking the island dry.”

Connie smiled but shook her head. Throwing the last few items into her suitcase, she closed and locked it. “I’m just not happy here.”

“Because of Sylvester?”

She glanced up in surprise. “What makes you say that?”

“Oh, come on, Connie. You come into a room, he goes out. He spends all his time watching you but pretending not to. He goes out of his way to include everyone in the conversation, but he can’t string two words together to speak to you. If I hadn’t seen it with my own eyes, I wouldn’t believe the legendary Sylvester de León could behave so awkwardly.”

Connie felt something suspiciously like tears sting the backs of her eyelids. She didn’t have time to indulge in an in-depth discussion about Sylvester, no matter how much she might want to. “It doesn’t matter. We’ll both be happier if I go.”

“Well, I won’t.” Matt sounded like a sulky schoolboy.

"My God, look what you're condemning me to. Do you want me to end up a gibbering wreck after another few weeks with no one normal to talk to?"

"I'm very flattered to be thought of as normal," Connie assured him with an attempt at a smile. "I must go. I don't want to keep Roberto waiting."

Matt made a final attempt. "You don't like boats."

"It's hardly an excuse for staying. I have to leave here sometime and the only way to do that will be on a boat. I can't stay marooned here forever."

He stared down at her, but she had the strangest feeling he wasn't really seeing her. "No, I suppose not." It seemed to take an effort for him to rouse himself from his thoughts.

Matt carried her suitcase down the stairs for her.

Sylvester was waiting on the beach as they walked out of the house. Matt handed Connie's suitcase to him and then turned away, leaving them alone.

"I can carry it to the boat." Connie held out her hand for the case.

"Don't go." Sylvester's voice was hoarse.

She shook her head, unable to look at him. "I have to. This isn't doing either of us any good."

"Please. I've behaved like an idiot. Stay and let me make it up to you."

Connie managed to lift her eyes to his face. If she'd been undecided then, the blaze of emotion in those blue eyes was all she needed to convince her. Her throat hurt so much she wasn't sure she'd be able to speak. When she tried, the words came out stiffly. "Do you know what it is, why it's happening? This thing between us?"

"Yes, I do."

"But you can't tell me?"

"No. Maybe if we knew each other better I could…

but it sounds so crazy you wouldn't believe me." He sighed, running a hand through his hair. "We don't have enough time."

"If I stay, will you promise me something?"

Sylvester smiled properly at her for the first time. It was an irresistible expression and it took every ounce of Connie's self-control to remain serious and not return it. "If I can."

"This is the first vacation I've had since I was a child. Will you stop being such a pain in the ass and make sure I get to enjoy it?"

Clearly he had been expecting her to ask him for something deeper and more intense. Shock made him pause. Then he started to laugh. "You have yourself a deal." Taking her hand, he tucked it into the crook of his arm. Leading her toward the house, he called back over his shoulder, "Roberto, we won't be needing the launch today, after all."

The decision to ask Connie to stay had come from his heart not his head. Now it was made, Sylvester somehow felt lighter and freer. Was it the right thing? Reason told him it wasn't. As he watched her while she ate her lunch, he decided reason could go to hell. *I have a few weeks left. Just this once, let me put duty aside and have some pleasure.*

That other, insidious voice at the back of his mind tried to start up again. *What about her? What about after?*

For the first time ever, he silenced it. *This is about now, not about forever.*

After lunch he approached Connie. "After your request this morning, I'm at your command. What would you like to do this afternoon?"

She bit her lip. "I didn't mean you had to devote yourself exclusively to me."

Sylvester took a step closer to her. He couldn't help himself. "I want to."

Her eyes sparkled. "I would like to see the lighthouse."

"Very well. There are two ways of getting there. We can walk, but it's faster by boat."

The sparkle vanished instantly and something shifted in Connie's eyes. A shadow, haunted and fearful, lurked in their dark depths. "I don't like boats."

Sylvester's impulse was to sweep her into his arms and kiss away that look. Instead, with a superhuman effort, he forced himself to keep his distance. "Then we'll walk." He glanced down at her sneakers. "It's a good thing you're wearing some sturdy shoes."

They set off across the island.

At first, Sylvester confined his conversation to information about the landscape, pointing out different plants and telling Connie stories about his childhood exploits.

"What's the little cottage we were at earlier?" He sensed she had been building up the courage to ask him the question.

"After Máximo was captured by the Calusa, he lived among them for some time. That was the house he built himself. It has been preserved for posterity." He smiled. "*Preserved* is probably the wrong word. I'm guessing very little of the original actually remains. Nevertheless, I suppose it's a sort of shrine. The place where the de León dynasty was founded."

"And I crashed in there and sat on the bed." Connie groaned. "No wonder you were angry. I'm so sorry."

He caught hold of her arm, the action halting her and swinging her around to face him at the same time.

"Did you think it was anger I was feeling when I kissed you, Connie?"

Although she swallowed hard, she tilted her chin bravely. "I know it wasn't. I was there, remember?"

The pulse that beat wildly in her throat fascinated him and he reached out to touch it. Connie flinched away from him and he immediately knew why. Cursing his own clumsiness, he moved his hand, tracing the white lines on her throat tenderly. "Who gave you these scars?"

Her eyelids fluttered down, hiding the expression in her eyes. "I don't know his name." A single tear slid down her cheek and her body slumped against his.

Leading her to a large pine, Sylvester sat in its shade with his back against the tree and gestured for Connie to join him. After a moment's hesitation, she sat, drawing her knees up and wrapping her arms around them in a defensive gesture.

"Can you talk about it?"

"I don't know." Her voice was shaky. "I've never tried."

"Not even to the police?" Sylvester did his best to keep his voice even. He sensed if he followed his instincts and drew her into his arms, she would run from him like a frightened animal.

"Yes, at first, but…" She lifted a hand in that unconscious gesture he'd noticed so often and covered her neck. "I'll start at the beginning…

"I studied design at college and it got me noticed by a few photographers. I signed with an agency and started doing some modeling. I was actually quite successful at it and my career looked set to take off. The police think that's possibly how he first noticed me. But it wasn't a classic case of stalking. There was no build up to it."

"So he didn't feel he had a relationship with you?"

Connie nodded, apparently pleased he understood. "That's it exactly. The attack came out of the blue. I lived with my mother. We'd been out for dinner and a movie. When we got home, he was in the house. Waiting in the dark for us..." Her voice became choked.

Sylvester risked placing an arm about her shoulders. Connie didn't resist. "You don't have to continue if it's too painful."

"No, it feels good to finally talk about it. He wore a mask and he didn't speak. Not once throughout the whole thing. Not even when he killed my mother." She turned her face into his shoulder and sobbed.

Sylvester held her close and murmured words of comfort into the silken mass of her hair. *Words of comfort?* What could he possibly offer to take away the pain of what she had just described?

After a few minutes Connie sat straighter and rummaged in the pocket of her shorts for a Kleenex. She dried her eyes and blew her nose.

"The police couldn't understand why he didn't kill me, as well. They said he stopped just short of it. Almost as if he knew just how far to go to leave me badly scarred but still alive." Her fingertips skimmed the scars. "He was branding me, leaving me with a permanent reminder of him on my body I would have to live with every day."

"Was he interrupted?"

"That was the police theory, but I know it isn't true." Her eyes were huge and haunted. "I didn't lose consciousness. He wasn't interrupted. He just stopped. Walked away and left me in a pool of blood next to my mother's body."

Sylvester's hands clenched into fists on his knees.

"And in all this time, they've never found a single clue about his identity or his motive?"

"No. But that was four years ago and he has been taunting me ever since."

"Didn't the police do anything to protect you?"

Connie gave a soft laugh. "I had a panic button and they monitored my calls, but he just found new ways around it. He would break into my apartment and leave notes to remind me about the night he attacked me, or tell me what I'd done that day, describe what I'd eaten in a restaurant, so I knew he'd been watching me. In the end, I gave up going to the police and started moving on each time he found me. He always found me."

Sylvester slid an arm around her shoulders and she didn't resist. No wonder she had wanted this respite, this haven Corazón offered. And he had almost driven her away because of his own selfishness. As her head came to rest on his shoulder, he made a promise that, in the time he had left, he would do his best to protect her from any further hurt. And that would include protecting her from him.

They sat under the pine tree in silence for some time. Telling Sylvester about the attack had left Connie emotionally wrung out, yet with a curious feeling of comfort. It was as though her muscles had been energized after being tightly wound for so long she couldn't remember what relaxation felt like. Now, when she stood, her body felt ready to face new challenges.

As they continued walking across the island, the scenery gradually changed. Instead of lush vegetation, their feet encountered uneven rocks. Although Sylvester reached out a hand to assist Connie over the worst of these, there were some points when they had to scramble over deep fissures. In the distance, she could make out the shape of the lighthouse perched on the very tip of the island.

She paused to catch her breath. "Matt told me the lighthouse might have been used for a disreputable purpose. He said the man who built it was a murdering bastard."

"Is that what he said?" Sylvester's expression was unreadable. "It's true people believed Emilio de León was evil. Hundreds of people lost their lives on these rocks after this lighthouse was built. He, meanwhile, amassed a fortune from the goods he collected from the wrecks of their ships. Don't let anyone tell you the de Leóns are nice guys."

She looked up into his face. "Are you trying to convince me you are a bad guy?"

He grinned. "I'm not perfect, but at least I decided against going into the family business of wrecking ships."

Since he'd persuaded her to stay, Connie felt some of the barriers between them had come down. *Some.* That was the important word. Sylvester still put up invisible boundaries. She didn't know what they were or where she would find them until she encountered one. She was discovering one now. It was as if she had gotten a bit too close and he was gently pushing her away.

Frustrated, she turned to look at the lighthouse again. "Let's go."

Sylvester caught her arm. "Not that way."

Confused, Connie pointed. "But it's right there." Surely they just needed to walk in a straight line?

"We can't go directly across those rocks. There is a chasm too wide to be crossed."

That sounds like a metaphor for us, Connie thought,

following Sylvester as he took a route that appeared to lead them away from the lighthouse. *A chasm too wide to be crossed. Whatever your secret is, Sylvester, it must be pretty wide if you can't tell me and then let me decide whether I want to cross it to reach you.*

After walking for a little while, they approached the lighthouse from a different angle. The closer they drew, the more imposing the structure became. The ruined walls of the old fortress ran along the cliff edge on one side, meeting the lighthouse at the tip of the island. Built from a stone so light it appeared white, the lighthouse had withstood the demands of time and weather, although the ironwork on the viewing platform around the light itself appeared rusted. Sunlight glinted on the glass dome and on something else. Something set into the fortress walls that was pointing out to sea.

Connie turned wide eyes to Sylvester. "Is that a cannon?"

"Didn't I tell you the de Leóns were not always nice? The wreckers would use the light to warn ships of the rocks, then confuse them by extinguishing it. Once they were close enough in the darkness, they made sure they were wrecked on the Corazón rocks by firing a couple of cannonballs into them." He led her to the fortress walls. "Any survivors—and there weren't many—were brought ashore and imprisoned here." He pointed to a metal ring in the rock. "These still lead to the fortress dungeons."

Connie shivered and decided she didn't want to see the cells. She remembered Matt's story about the prisoners blundering around in the darkness before falling to their death from the openings in the cliff face.

Turning away, she looked up at the lighthouse itself.

"Didn't the authorities do anything to stop the wrecking?"

Sylvester started walking again and, although the atmosphere of the whole place was brooding, Connie was relieved to leave the dungeons behind. "Emilio de León *was* the authorities. This was his island. He was a wealthy and well-respected man, a friend of the governor. But he decommissioned the lighthouse and it fell into disuse."

They had reached the base of the lighthouse itself now and Connie looked down onto the rocks below. The waves churned wildly, just as they must have done in the darkness all those centuries ago. She could picture the scene. Sense the confusion and fear. Hear the shouts and cries. Smell the saltwater tang and the acrid gunpowder. Feel death and defeat. All because one man wanted more gold to add to his already bulging purse. What sort of man must Emilio de León have been? The thought made her shudder.

"Are you still with me?" Sylvester's voice jerked her out of her trance.

"There's something about this island, isn't there? It holds on to its memories, locks them into its fabric, and refuses to let them go."

"Sometimes it releases them. When the time is right." The sadness in Sylvester's voice made her turn her head to look at his face. Quickly he changed his expression to a smile. "Shall we go inside? It's not locked."

The interior of the round tower was cool in comparison to the heat of the day. A dusty tang in the air conveyed the message no one had been there for a long time.

"Is it safe?" Connie placed a hand on the spiral staircase.

"Perfectly, although it does creak a bit."

Sylvester followed her as she made her way up the narrow, winding, iron steps. He was right about the creaking. With each step the staircase groaned and complained as though it was trying to pull itself away from the wall. Although the tower narrowed as it got higher, the top of the staircase opened into a circular room, the center of which housed the huge light. The space around the light was limited to a narrow strip.

"Do you want to go outside? You need a head for heights." Sylvester paused with his hand on the door leading to the platform that ran all the way around the outside.

"I'll risk it." The last four years had taught Connie it was no good having unnecessary fears. When you were running for your life, you tended to focus on the important things. Spiders, flying, heights…they faded into the background. The only thing she hadn't quite been able to consign to the back of her mind was her fear of boats. Although irrational and completely without foundation, that one refused to go away.

There was a breeze up there that hadn't been apparent on the ground. It ruffled the fine cotton of Connie's blouse and blew her hair across her face. The view across the vast expanse of water was breathtaking, giving a sense of the remoteness of Corazón in relation to the nearest land. The sheer height of the lighthouse on its perch high above the rocks made Connie feel as if she was soaring out over the clear blue sea. When she did look down, the effect made her feel slightly giddy.

Turning inland, Sylvester pointed back the way they had come. "That's why we couldn't walk in a straight line across the rocks."

From their superior vantage point Connie could see a cleft in the rocks, splitting it neatly into two cliffs. The waves pounded into the gap in a near frenzy. "I can see why that might have been difficult."

"It's known as the Salto de Fe. The Leap of Faith," Sylvester said. "Over time it has also become the Corazón equivalent of a lover's leap."

"Does that mean lovers have to leap across it as a test of their devotion?" Connie asked dubiously. The gap was wide enough to make her question whether such a feat could be achieved. "Because if a man asked me to do that, I might have to seriously rethink the relationship."

"No, it serves a very different purpose. Those who leap into the Salto de Fe don't die, they find their way to a new life. Blighted lovers over the centuries have leaped hand in hand to their deaths into the Salto de Fe. If those who cannot find happiness in this life leap into it, they will find the lasting contentment they seek in another life. Or so Corazón legend would have us believe."

"Corazón seems to have a lot of legends, most of them unpleasant." Connie stared down into the furious foam churning between the rocks. "You'd have to be desperately unhappy to resort to such a desperate step."

"Desperately unhappy…or very much in love."

"If you are very much in love, surely there are no obstacles so great they cannot be overcome?" Connie risked a glance at his face and was shocked at the desolation she saw there.

"There are some things even love can't put right."

He lifted his hand, as though fascinated, and moved a strand of her hair away from her cheek. As soon as his fingers touched her skin, they were both lost. Connie turned her head so her lips brushed his hand and Sylvester gave a growl of surrender. Enchantment, lust—Connie didn't know what it was and she didn't care as it pounded through them both, sending waves of energy pulsing between them. She didn't know who moved first—maybe they moved together—but she was in his arms and the soaring sensation no longer had anything to do with the height of the tower.

Sylvester kissed her as if he knew her body, understood what she needed. His lips brushed hers. Ever so gently. Teasing her slightly, knowing how much she wanted more.

Connie rose on the tips of her toes, fitting her body to his, something in the back of her mind telling her this was too familiar.

Sylvester murmured appreciatively, threading his fingers into her hair, tilting her head back as he deepened the kiss. It was warm and sweet. A tender exploration of tongues stroking, lips caressing and nerve endings tingling.

Connie was instantly lost in a whirlpool of sensation. His hands slid under her blouse and over the flesh of her back. She trembled at the contrast between the roughened pads of his fingertips and the smoothness of her flesh. Sylvester shuddered as she ran her fingertips along the back of his neck and through his hair. It was an endless kiss, and Connie murmured softly into Sylvester's mouth. Rocking her pelvis against him, she felt his hard erection press insistently into the sensitive flesh of her stomach. Gently, he broke the kiss, resting his forehead against hers.

"Don't tell me that wasn't meant to happen." She didn't want to plead with him, but if that was what it took…

"I think we both know it *is* meant to happen. It's going to happen." His hands moved down to her hips, holding her closer to him so she could feel him throbbing against her. "I don't want to hurt you, Connie."

She pressed tighter against him, fitting herself to him blatantly, showing him with her body exactly what she wanted. "Maybe I want you to."

Chapter 8

When they got back to the house, Connie felt the warmth of its welcome wrap around her. It would be easy to fall in love with this place, and she had to remind herself her stay here was temporary. Did her fondness for the house have a lot to do with its owner? It didn't matter. In both cases, she had to avoid getting too attached. A few weeks might seem like a long time to someone with her transient lifestyle, but in reality she would soon be gone from here and this interlude would be no more than a pleasant dream, fading into obscurity over time.

She shivered when she remembered that kiss at the lighthouse and the conversation that had followed it. It was only a matter of time before she and Sylvester made love.

A matter of time.

Was she really starting to believe the unthinkable? She shook her head. Corazón certainly knew how to make her think some strange thoughts. She stood on her little balcony and looked out across the bay, trying to come to terms with the extraordinary idea that had taken hold of her mind.

Strange or not, her thoughts were interrupted by a commotion within the house. Raised voices and scurrying footsteps were signals something was wrong and she decided to go and investigate. Aware she was gaining a reputation among her fellow guests for being "the aloof one," she knew she should make more of an effort to mingle. *I'm just not the mingling sort*, she thought. Even before the attack that had left her scarred, she had experienced a sense of separateness. As a child, her mother had labeled her shy, and perhaps that was it. To Connie it had always felt like more. It was a sense of being different without really knowing what her differences were. Of not belonging. As she walked down the stairs at Corazón, a sudden revelation occurred to her, blinding in its intensity. *Here. This is where I belong.*

"She said she was going swimming in the sea." Jonathan was standing in the hall with most of the others gathered around him. A swift look showed Connie only Ellie and Guthrie were missing.

"How long ago was this?" Sylvester asked.

"She went just after lunch." Jonathan appeared genuinely worried as he checked his watch. "That's almost three hours. I've walked right along the water's edge as far as I could and there's no sign of Ellie anywhere."

"I'll get the staff together and we'll all start looking. I'm sure she'll turn up." Sylvester went away to get organized.

"Where's Guthrie?" Matt turned to Lucinda.

"I don't know." Her voice was tearful. "I thought he was in his room, but when I knocked just now to see if he knew where Ellie was, there was no answer."

"So perhaps Ellie went for a swim, met up with

Guthrie and they've gone for a walk somewhere?" Matt spoke reassuringly to Jonathan.

"I suppose anything is possible." Jonathan's expression was always serious, now it was somber in the extreme. "I just want to be sure she's okay."

"While Sylvester's getting his search party organized, why don't we go out and see if we can find her ourselves?" Matt suggested. "You and Lucinda go in one direction and Connie and I will go the other way."

They split up as Matt had suggested. Connie walked slowly along the water's edge at Matt's side, alternately looking out to sea and then inland. The water was calm, with only the slightest swell of waves lapping the golden sand. It didn't look like the sort of day when a swimmer would get into difficulties.

Connie recalled Ellie's words. "She said she swims every day, and she's a long-distance swimmer. That must mean Ellie is able to look after herself."

"It depends how far out she went." Matt's eyes scanned the horizon. "It's okay here close to the shore, but the currents farther out at sea can be dangerous."

Connie lifted a hand to her throat. "You don't think…?"

"God, no. At least, I hope not." He gave a slightly nervous laugh. "Corazón is weaving its dark spell on our imaginations. She's probably wandered off somewhere and she'll laugh at us when she sees us at dinner and knows we were all worried about her."

No one was laughing several hours later when dinner was delayed because there was still no sign of Ellie. Jonathan was almost frantic with worry and even Sylvester seemed ruffled out of his usual calm.

Guthrie, wandering down the large staircase, blinked in surprise to see he was the only one who had dressed for dinner. "I hate to say it, but standards seem to be slipping around here."

"Ellie is missing." Sylvester summed the situation up. "And where the hell have you been?"

"In my room." Guthrie jerked his thumb upward. "I was reading for a few hours, then I must have fallen asleep."

"But I knocked on your door over and over and got no answer," Lucinda protested. "And how on earth could you sleep through all the commotion of everyone looking for Ellie?"

Guthrie's shrugged. "I sleep soundly. So, have the police been called?"

"Jonathan is going to check her room first to see if anything is missing. It's hard to see how Ellie could have left the island without Roberto knowing about it, but it's not impossible. There are other boats coming to and from Corazón now and then with deliveries. She could have hitched a ride with one of them."

"But Ellie didn't want to leave Corazón," Jonathan burst out. "She was the most determined of all of us to stay."

"Nevertheless, it will be the first thing the police will ask. And you should check to see if her phone is in her room."

"Has anyone tried calling it?" Matt asked.

"Several times. It goes straight to voice mail." Jonathan's face showed his frustration. "Connie, will you come with me while I check?"

Although Connie was surprised to be asked, she agreed. Of all Sylvester's house guests, Jonathan was the one with whom she had had the least interaction. He was the other introvert, the other person who seemed to find the proximity of strangers difficult. She supposed it must be painful for him to be confronted with his sister's belongings when he was so worried about what might have happened to her. Possibly he was also thinking of all the comments that had been made about old detective stories and alibis. Maybe he wanted someone with him so he couldn't be accused later of tampering with Ellie's stuff.

Or am I starting to overdramatize things, as well? She decided the tense atmosphere was getting to them all. Overthinking wasn't going to help anyone, least of all Ellie.

They made their way up to Ellie's room in silence. Connie tried to find something reassuring to say, but the words wouldn't come. It occurred to her this was exactly the reason Jonathan had asked her to accompany him. Bland, overused clichés were not going to be welcome to Jonathan on any occasion, especially not this one.

When they entered Ellie's room, Jonathan flicked on the light switch, illuminating the scene. The room was immaculately neat.

"That's strange." Jonathan's brow wrinkled into a frown. "Ellie is usually the untidiest person I know."

He went to the wardrobe, flinging the doors wide. It was empty. Connie checked the dresser, opening each of the drawers in turn. None of them contained any items of clothing. There were no personal possessions in this room, belonging to Ellie or anyone else. It was as impersonal as an empty hotel room.

Jonathan surveyed the room with an expression of shock. "It's as if she had never been here."

The water slaps the rocks with the same soft, unrelenting rhythm it has used for thousands of years. The connection penetrates deeper than her dreaming self, connecting her to a reality she has been striving for since she arrived at Corazón. If she could only see beyond that final, invisible veil. She is walking, feeling the grains of sand sliding wet and warm between her toes. Dreaming, Connie half closes her eyes against the brilliant rays bouncing off the sea. Humming softly to herself, she stoops to gather shells, examining each one carefully before either discarding it or placing it in the bottom of her basket made of woven palm leaves. In the distance, she can hear the sounds of the village children laughing and splashing at the water's edge.

Ahead of her, the men are fishing. Tall and straight, they stand waist-deep, like statues in the water. Their hair is tied back from the finely sculpted features of their faces. One man stands out as the sunlight glints a giveaway and reveals the reddish tinge to his brown hair. As always, Connie's eyes are drawn away from the Calusa braves and straight to the Spaniard.

His skin is bronzed from long days of working in the sun. The bulging muscles in his arms are defined as his spear is poised, ready to strike, the concentration on his face clear. Even across the distance between them, she sees the bright blue gleam of his half-closed eyes as he brings his hand down. The strike is swift and true. When he holds the spear aloft, the wriggling fish is large, its scales iridescent in the sun's rays. There is a murmur of approval from the other fishermen. The harvest has been good recently. Since the Spaniard came among them, the gods have been kind.

Connie walks on, passing the fishermen. She can feel the intensity of that blue gaze following her now, knows his eyes are on the sway of her hips, the dark waterfall of her hair and the long, slender length of her legs. She likes his eyes on her body, craves it. At night, when she lies alone in her narrow bed, she listens to the sounds of the ocean and imagines what it would be like to have his hands touch the places his eyes caress. A warm, sweet ache thrums between her legs.

Casting a sidelong glance under her lashes in the direction of the Spaniard, she sees he is leaving the water and coming toward her. Her heart gives a wild thud. This wasn't meant to happen! What if her grandmother should see him approach her? Or if someone else should see and take their tales to her father, the chief? She walks fast, heading away from the beach, toward the trees.

With his long stride, he catches up to her easily, falling into step beside her and not even noticing she is hurrying. He says a few words she doesn't understand and, keeping her eyes lowered, she shakes her head. They have reached the cover of the trees now; at least here the prying eyes from the beach cannot see them. Gently the Spaniard catches her arm, bringing her to a halt. He seems to be telling her not to be afraid of him. It is clearly very important to him. Oh, those eyes are so blue...

He taps his chest. "Máximo."

She laughs. It is the most ridiculous name she has ever heard. She tries to repeat it and her attempt makes him laugh. In return, she tells him her name and he frowns. Clearly he isn't even going to try to say it.

He places both hands over his heart, then points to her. "Cariña."

She shrugs her lack of comprehension. What is he saying? He repeats the gesture, saying the word again.

This time he steps closer. She backs up so she is leaning against a tree trunk, looking up at him.

"Cariña." His voice is husky. Very gently, he takes her chin in his hand, tilting her face up to his. Then his lips softly brush hers.

Connie lay awake thinking about her dream. *Cariña.* The Spanish endearment meaning "my love" or "my darling." Yet the word meant more than that. She knew, without knowing *how* she knew, that those three syllables were the key to the mystery of Corazón. She lay still, not forcing her thoughts, trying to capture why that single word should matter so much. Stubbornly, it refused to come. Connie sighed, turning her thoughts back to the substance of the dream. It didn't take much to analyze what the latest one was all about. In her dreams Máximo and Sylvester were the same person.

You don't say? I wonder why that is? Could it be you want to get into Sylvester's pants so desperately that fantasizing about him as his half-naked ancestor has become the next best thing?

A flush burned her cheeks. Since reality wasn't going to allow them to have a happy ending, her subconscious mind seemed determined to invent a love story for her and Sylvester. It was harmless enough and—my God!—the kiss in her dream had been steamy. She squirmed slightly at the memory. *I had no idea my imagination was so good!*

The light through the blinds and the silence of the house told her it was still early. Lying propped on her pillows, Connie allowed her thoughts to wander to their strange house party. With Ellie's departure, it had gotten slightly stranger. Those character traits that already seemed to be developing disproportionately in each individual were now more marked than ever. Guthrie was becoming louder. He had to take center stage and, of course, he had to have a drink in his hand. Lucinda was more demanding, her own craving for attention just as strong as her brother's but less jovial. Jonathan was more withdrawn and taciturn. It was increasingly apparent how much he hated this enforced proximity to other people.

Turning the spotlight on herself, Connie could see her own faults highlighted. Fear still had her in a strong grip, to the point where she occasionally wondered, even here on Sylvester's paradise island, if she could feel *his* presence. Every now and then she would sense him—the stalker who, in Connie's opinion, wasn't a stalker because he didn't seem to have any connection to her other than a desire to harm her—watching her, planning his next move, gloating at the control he had over her life, enjoying his power over her…

He's not here!

Even now, comfortable and safe in her shell-themed room, she had to remind herself. That was how deep inside her head he had managed to get. So Connie couldn't claim immunity from the curse of Corazón. Her paranoia was heightened along with her shyness.

We make a great combination at the dinner table.

There was only Sylvester to keep the conversation flowing normally. And Matt, of course. Of all the guests, he alone didn't seem to be affected by his surroundings.

After thinking about him, it seemed strange Matt was the first person Connie encountered when she emerged from her room. Or not strange at all. Perhaps it was one of those strange quirks this island seemed to conjure up so easily. Instead of going for breakfast, they took a walk along the beach first, pausing to sit on the rocks and look out at the tranquil ocean.

It soon became clear Matt had been having similar thoughts to Connie's. Coincidence or Corazón? "It can't really be a curse, can it? We must be going a bit crazy because we're all cooped up together on an island with not much to do."

"I was just thinking you are the only one who doesn't seem to be bothered by it all." Connie was surprised to see a slightly haunted look in his gray eyes.

"Were you thinking about me, Connie?" The look changed, became almost hungry for a brief instant as he gazed at her.

"Matt, I..."

He laughed, a touch of embarrassment in the sound. "Take no notice of me. I know you have eyes for no one but Sylvester." He turned back to the view and she studied his profile, gleaning nothing from it. "It seems to be inside my head, this curse thing, making me imagine things."

"What sorts of things?"

He shook his head. "It's hard to explain. It feels like the past is encroaching on the present. Like the barriers between then and now are being broken down."

It was an echo of what Connie had dared to allow herself to believe the previous night. The thought she didn't dare voice in case it was the first step on the road to madness. A friend at college had believed passionately in reincarnation, putting forward lengthy arguments in favor of the concept. Connie wished she'd listened more closely. Could a past life connection explain what she felt in this life for Sylvester? That feeling of recognition? The love at first sight? The certainty that he loved her in return? *Or is Corazón working its strangeness on me yet again?*

"Maybe it feels like that because there is so much history to this island?" She tried to apply reason to what Matt was saying as well as to her own thoughts.

"But it's not *my* history, so why should I feel connected to it?" He picked up a pebble and skimmed it across the water. "Do you think who you were in a past life can affect who you are in this life?"

"It's not something I've ever thought about until now. If I believed in it, then I suppose I would have to also believe it could."

When he turned back to face her, the look on his face made Connie draw in a sharp breath. "That's the scariest thing anyone has ever said to me."

Sylvester found Connie finishing breakfast. She seemed distracted, but the faraway look on her face cleared when she saw him and she smiled. It was an expression that tilted his world off balance. Made him think the unthinkable. Believe the impossible. Made him want to consider the future differently. As if he had a future to consider.

"I came to see if you wanted to accompany me to Mound Key? It is an artificial island built from shells by the Calusa. It became their ceremonial and military stronghold." He saw the hesitation on her face and immediately interpreted its source correctly. "Yes, it means a boat journey. Trust me?"

Her smile dawned again, chasing away the worried look. "I'd love to go."

"I'll get Vega to pack us some lunch."

Living on an island, Sylvester had grown up around boats, some of them far less reliable than his nifty little speedboat. Connie's genuine terror as she climbed into the vessel saddened him. "You really have no idea where this fear came from?"

"No." As he started the engine, she held on so tight her knuckles gleamed white. "I have never had anything much to do with boats. I've certainly never had a bad experience."

Something stirred in the recesses of his memory and he tried to capture it. Annoyingly, it eluded him. All his life it had been the same. He had flashbacks to another time, another place. *Another me.* Corazón was the catalyst. When he was away from his island home for any length of time, the feelings were muted, as though there was interference on a long-distance signal. When he was there, he gained no respite from them. He had never been allowed to escape from the certainty of his destiny. No matter where he was, that had always been with him.

"This group of islands were once all under the rule of one Calusa chief," he explained as they left Corazón behind.

None of the islands in the chain known as Corona de Perlas were geographically close to one another. On an aerial map they looked like a crown of pearls with Corazón, the largest and most westerly, as the jewel at the top of the crown. Most, like Corazón, were now privately owned. Celebrity hideaways and billionaire's mansions were tucked away on their emerald and gold shores, while luxury yachts were the most common craft in these waters.

"His home was on Corazón. Although this was the westernmost edge of the kingdom, like all the chiefs, he was required to pay homage to the all-powerful Calusa king, who lived on Mound Key."

"I read in the books you have that theirs was a complex society."

"Complex and hierarchical, with clear laws and religion."

Connie's expression was dreamy as she responded. "The Calusa believe each person has three souls. One is our shadow, the second is our reflection and the third is in the pupils of our eyes."

"I don't remember reading that in any of those books," Sylvester said.

Connie started as though rousing herself from a trance. "Nor do I." She gave a self-conscious laugh. "But it must have been there or else how would I know?"

Sylvester watched her. Sometimes he thought she had made the connection, that she knew the truth. Other times, like now, she seemed as far from knowing the reality of what was happening to them as ever. He waited, but Connie lapsed into silence and, once they were out into the open water, some of her former nervousness seemed to return.

To distract her, he continued with his story.

"There were always stories about the islands, which were given the name Corona de Perlas by the Spaniards. There were many mysteries and legends surrounding the Calusa. The fact they were able to withstand the Spanish for so long, the way they defeated Ponce de León, their fierce warrior attitude...all of these things added to the fascination they held for the conquistadors.

"But there was more to it with this particular group of islands. There was a darker side to de Perlas, a compelling, mystical pull even the Calusa felt. In their own ceremonies, the Calusa high priests reserved a special sacred chant for these islands to ward off ancient spirits. Yet from the very earliest days, the Spanish were casting covetous eyes in this direction."

"Why was that?" He was pleased to see Connie appeared so engrossed in the story she had relaxed slightly.

"There were rumors of Calusa treasure here. Stories that early explorer ships, even before Ponce de León's arrival, had run aground bearing Spanish gold, and the Calusa, captivated by its glitter but unaware of its value, had hidden it on these shores along with their own secret cache of the finest pearls."

"Was it true?"

He grinned. "No one knows. The Calusa treasure has yet to be found."

She laughed. "It's a good story and, if it was any other set of islands, I'm sure someone would cash in on its value by producing treasure maps and guide books. Since the de Perlas are rich people's hideaways, they are thankfully safe from hordes of day trippers with picks and shovels."

"Yes, or divers crowding the waters around them, all searching for sunken chests of gold coins. Helicopters are not unknown as a means of transport on some of the islands. I'm surprised no one has tried an aerial reconnoiter in search of buried treasure. It may only be a matter of time."

They were silent for some time as Sylvester steered the boat into open water. Although he'd played up the lighter side of the legends, he couldn't help dwelling on the other side. He knew too much of the islands to dismiss the stories of the ancient spirits lightly. He could only hope Corazón was not working its own dark magic once more.

"You look very serious. Are you thinking about

Ellie?" Connie's voice interrupted his thoughts. "I'm sure she'll be fine."

Sylvester wished he could share her confidence. In any other circumstances, a grown woman disappearing with all her belongings might be considered strange but not necessarily sinister. That had been the conclusion they had all reached the previous evening. Jonathan had decided he would keep trying to contact his sister by phone. No, he would not report her missing. He didn't want to make himself look foolish in front of the local police. He said Ellie had a tendency to make impulsive decisions and, although it seemed strange because she had been so determined to stay and claim her share of Sylvester's legacy, she had obviously succumbed to a sudden whim.

Sylvester had remained silent during the conversation. Unlike him, his companions had not grown up with the legend that was Corazón. It wasn't just the curse that made a de León fear the worst. It was their history.

Throughout the years, anything that could go wrong on this island paradise had gone wrong. It gave him a sixth sense. A supercharged pessimism. Sylvester had felt it more strongly than ever last night. He had asked Roberto to make discreet inquiries about Ellie's departure from the island. Roberto would check on the boats that made deliveries to Corazón yesterday and find out which of them she'd hitched a ride with. *If* she'd hitched a ride with any of them.

"Although, I was surprised at Jonathan's change of approach," Connie continued.

While Sylvester didn't particularly want to pursue this topic of conversation, he was pleased to see it was taking her mind off the boat journey.

"He was really worried about her at first, but then

he seemed to accept she was gone without any further concern."

"The Corazón effect," Sylvester said. Could he explain this without sounding like he'd lost possession of his wits? "It's as if the island has a soothing effect on the nerves, taking away violent emotions and replacing them with a less damaging feeling." That was a watered-down version of the truth. Sylvester had witnessed it many times. Corazón had a way of erasing strong reactions. Last night was a typical example. It was almost as if Jonathan had *forgotten* to be concerned about Ellie. By the time dinner was over, Sylvester was fairly sure all thoughts of his sister had faded to the back of his mind.

Connie wrinkled her nose. "It is an idyllic place."

He sensed she wasn't quite convinced, and was glad. He didn't want to lull her into a false sense of security. If someone had harmed Ellie, he wanted Connie to be on her guard. He had no proof Ellie had been harmed, of course. No proof, just a strong intuition…and a lifetime of experience.

Chapter 9

The island was at sea level, but there were seven raised mounds across its surface. As they waded ashore, Connie felt the strangest tingling. Like pins and needles starting in her hands and feet but rapidly spreading residual heat across her whole body. She felt lifted out of herself, as if she was looking back and remembering living this moment over again. Imprinting repetition in her mind. Her brow furrowed. *But how can that be?* She was living this now. *I have never been here before.*

"We must go to the highest mound first, so we can pay homage to King Yargua." She barely recognized her own voice.

Sylvester regarded her face intently. "Do you know what you just said?"

She nodded, shivering slightly. "But I don't understand why I said it. I've never been here before. How could I know where the king lived?" There it was again. A memory of a past she didn't know.

They followed a trail and, although there were informational displays, Connie walked purposefully, ignoring these. The island was built entirely of shells, piled up by generation after generation of Calusa Indians. Whelk, oyster and conch shells, together with fish bones, were scattered haphazardly beneath their feet.

"It was the sheer quantity of seafood available in the estuary that meant the Calusa could become such a complex society." Sylvester's voice penetrated Connie's trance. "Instead of tending crops, they could spend time devising elaborate ceremonies, creating lavish pieces of art and engineering canals. The Calusa from far-flung islands could travel here to bring their tributes to their ruler. In the 1500s, when Europeans first arrived, the Calusa king ruled an empire that stretched from the Atlantic Ocean to the Gulf, and from Lake Okeechobee to the Florida Keys."

Connie paused at the top of the mound, looking back the way they had come. She hadn't needed Sylvester's words to tell her all of that. She knew. More than that, she could see it. Feel it. As if she had been here before and been part of it. She could see the procession wending its way up the path they had just taken, hear the sweet singing of the Calusa maidens, the hoarse warrior cries of the braves, the king on his throne, that speculative look in his eyes as he gazed at her…

From this vantage point they could look right out across Estero Bay. It was exactly as the king had planned it when he'd built this mound. There were three canals, the means by which the Calusa could bring their canoes right up to their homes. Connie could clearly see the central canal, a long strip, where dark-leafed black mangroves crisscrossed the red mangroves. Tall papaya trees sprouted above the shrubs and prickly pears, and her taste buds tingled. How could she recall those sweet, succulent flavors when she knew she had never eaten either?

Tiny bugs inhabited the cactus plants. Connie pointed them out to Sylvester. "Cochineal bugs. The Calusa would carve wooden sculptures using bone and shell. Then they would paint then with the crushed juice from the bugs. I must have read it in one of your books."

His eyes were bright on hers. "I remember."

She nodded, tangling her fingers with his. His touch provided the reassurance she needed. Pausing, she stooped to pick a butterfly orchid, nestling the delicate pink-and-white blossom behind her ear. Sylvester drew in a harsh breath.

"What is it?"

"You remind me of someone."

Connie laughed. "Someone who wore a flower like this one in her hair?"

"Yes." There was something in his eyes that sent a shiver of raw desire down her spine. It was as if he couldn't get enough of her, as if he was spellbound by her.

Being here brought all that Connie had read and heard about the Calusa to life. But there was more to it. It brought something within her to life. Strummed a chord deep inside her so her senses were awakened by this place. It was tranquil and quiet, slumbering in the blistering Florida sunlight. She could see and hear, taste and smell all the things the Calusa had experienced all those years ago. Her senses were uniquely in tune with everything they had known back then.

But there was another side to her feelings. Standing at the highest point of the mound, she felt horribly afraid. A shadow inside her darkened the brightness of the day. There were undercurrents here, pulling her away from where she wanted to be, compelling her against her will toward something powerful and unknown. Without knowing why, she wanted to launch herself into Sylvester's arms and beg him to take her away from here forever.

Don't let them part us, my love.

"You look worried."

"Some places can do that to you, can't they? Find an echo of the past and send a shiver down your spine." She shook her head. "I've felt it on Corazón, but it seems to be just as strong here."

"Yet you don't know what 'it' is?" He seemed to be willing her on, wanting her to go further, to make that final connection.

She raised her eyes to his face, knowing it was there, just within her grasp. "Sylvester, who was Cariña?"

He relaxed, drawing her close and pressing his lips to her forehead. "I've been waiting for you to ask me about her."

Connie coped well with the boat, although it was obvious she was still nervous. Sylvester, who loved nothing more than the excitement of skimming at speed across the water, maintained a sedate pace as he maneuvered the little craft across to Lovers Key.

"There is a picnic area here," he explained as he helped Connie step out of the boat. "We can eat in peace and talk at the same time."

They found a pine table and bench under the shade of overhanging branches and Sylvester set out the small banquet Vega had prepared.

"How many people did she think were coming on this trip?" Connie asked with a smile.

"In Vega's opinion, you will need fattening up," Sylvester said. "It's nothing personal. She sees it as her mission in life."

They ate in silence for a while, sitting on opposite sides of the table and enjoying the stillness and the view of white sands and blue water. Sylvester watched Connie's face from time to time. Although her expression was serene, he sensed her thoughts were troubled. Her hands were tightly clasped on the table in front of her, betraying her tension.

"You wanted to know about Cariña?" She turned her head and he was caught in the golden-brown beam of those incredible eyes. "Before I begin, will you tell me where you have heard the name?"

A smile trembled on her lips. "This is going to sound silly, but I haven't heard it. I dreamed about her." She shook her head slightly. "Dreamed I *was* her."

"Cariña was the Calusa maiden who saved Máximo from death when he was captured. Her father was the chief on the island now known as Corazón. She begged him to spare Máximo's life and he did. It was because of her intervention that Máximo went on to live among the Calusa for several months before he..." Sylvester paused, searching for the right word. There wasn't one, so he came up with the only ones that would make sense. "Returned to Spain."

Connie exhaled abruptly, her body slumping over her clasped hands as she shuddered slightly. It was clear Sylvester's words had a profound effect on her. When she raised her head, her eyes had darkened. "I couldn't have known any of this, yet, ever since I arrived on Corazón, I have been dreaming about details of their life together. Intimate things that happened between them."

Sylvester decided it was time for her to hear it all. "Cariña was the name Máximo gave her because he couldn't pronounce her Calusa name. Because she was the daughter of the chief, any love affair between her and Máximo, who was still a prisoner, even if his life had been spared, was most definitely forbidden. Yet they did fall in love. Deeply, passionately and irrevocably. By doing so, they incurred the anger of the Calusa king."

Connie lifted a hand to her throat. "Because the king wanted Cariña for himself."

Sylvester's heart gave a thud. "How did you know that?"

She looked dazed. So adorably confused that he wanted to draw her into his arms and kiss away her bewilderment. But he also wanted her to get to the point where she knew the whole of the story. Their story. So she knew why it mattered so much. "I felt it, back there at Mound Key."

"Yes, Cariña had been promised to the king. Sadly, the Calusa language died out with its people, so his name has been lost in the mists of time. The best I can do is to give him a modern-day equivalent, which is Yargua. That's the name you called him, back there on Mound Key, although your pronunciation is slightly better than mine. Before the ceremony of marriage could take place, Yargua discovered Cariña had committed the greatest crime of all. She had already given her body to another man."

As he spoke the words, that magical sensation thrummed between them. It was uniquely theirs. He didn't need to explain it or to analyze it. Connie knew what it was now. Her lips were parted and she ran her tongue over them. He could see her nipples pebbling against the thin cloth of her dress. Her arousal was achingly obvious. Just as his was. Sylvester's erection jerked hard and insistent at the restraining cloth of his jeans. Forcing himself to ignore the wonderful, maddening sensation, he continued with the story.

"There could be only one punishment for both of them. The king gave the order for Máximo and Cariña to be put to death." Her eyes widened in distress and he placed his hands over hers. That wild, electrical charge of desire shimmered through him as soon as he touched her. Continuing with his story became more difficult than ever. "Máximo organized their escape. Sadly, on the night they were supposed to depart, word came to him that her grandmother, unable to live with her disgrace, had taken Cariña to the Salto de Fe and thrown her into its depths. The old woman had also killed herself. Devastated, Máximo left Corazón alone and returned to Spain."

Tears sparkled on the ends of Connie's lashes. "But that can't be the end." Her voice was husky. "Máximo must have returned to Corazón. And you told me his wife was a Calusa."

"That's where the story strays into the realms of the fantastic. Months after Máximo left Corazón and made a new home for himself in Valladolid, a young woman turned up in the town square. She was heavily pregnant, barefoot and dressed in rags. All she would say was Máximo's name. It was Cariña. She had followed Máximo across the world, suffering terrible hardship—including being shipwrecked—along the way."

"Shipwrecked?" Connie pressed a hand to her chest, the color draining from her cheeks.

Sylvester smiled tenderly, his grip on her hands tightening. "Yes. That would be enough to give anyone a fear of boats, wouldn't it?"

Her lips formed into a perfect O of realization. "She didn't die in the Salto de Fe?"

"Somehow she survived. It became a tale of Calusa legend, adding to the mystical qualities of the Salto de Fe. Although they were married in Valladolid and their first child was born in Spain, they both always knew they would return to Florida and make their home there. The details are hazy, but when they came back, Máximo purchased the island now known as Corazón."

"And the curse?"

"That was placed upon them by the mother of King Yargua. The king himself had died by the time they returned. He had been challenged by one of the island chiefs and was overthrown. The new king was happy to receive Máximo's Spanish gold in exchange for the island. Yargua's mother, however, saw things differently and refused to forgive or forget."

"Her name was Sinapa. She was an evil old woman, who always hated me." Connie's eyes narrowed slightly. "I remember her well."

Sylvester raised one hand to his lips. She knew. Finally, Connie knew. Not all of it, but her part in it. "Do you, Cariña?"

As they made their way back to where the boat was tied, a young dog ran up to them and jumped excitedly around their legs. Connie recalled Lucinda's comment that Sylvester didn't like dogs. He certainly gave no sign of dislike as, laughing, he patted the animal on its head and threw the stick it brought to him.

"Why are there no dogs on Corazón?" Connie asked as he started the boat.

He looked out at the water. "I have never had a pet. I can't allow myself to become too close to another living thing," he said softly. When he looked back at her, the light in his eyes was regretful. She couldn't help wondering if he was thinking about pets or people.

Their conversation at the picnic table had left her emotionally exhausted yet it had confirmed everything she knew. It was the final piece in the puzzle. This was the truth she had been searching for since she had arrived on Corazón. It excited and terrified her at the same time to know she had been Cariña in a past life. That the feelings she had for Sylvester were the remnants of their shared past. That the pull Corazón had for her was real.

When she told Sylvester she remembered Sinapa, the old woman who'd cursed Corazón, the memory in that instant had been real. But Connie found she could not summon up other memories of Cariña's story at will. Even now that she knew about it, she couldn't seamlessly recall her past life. The more she tried to force it, the more elusive it became. Like her dreams, the certainty of Cariña danced inside her while the details continued to elude her.

Connie knew Sylvester was giving her time to absorb the enormity of what he had told her, and she was grateful for his silence on the return journey. It never occurred to her to question the truth of his story. The realization of her past life as Cariña had struck a chord that resonated so surely with her, she knew it had to be real.

The intensity of what she was feeling went beyond shock, touching something deep within her, explaining everything, yet leaving her raw and shaken. It told her what she needed to know about herself, about Sylvester, about why, for her whole life, she had felt different.

Finally, she understood the all-pervading love she felt toward this man, even though they had only just met.

A love that had such quality, depth, beauty and power it scared her. The truth was perfect beyond words, yet utterly devastating. It left her shattered and hovering on the brink of tears. Were they tears of joy or sadness? Unsure, she forced them aside.

She watched Sylvester as he steered the boat. He had known her as soon as he'd seen her. She tried to put herself in his shoes at their first meeting, and her heart ached with sympathy. Imagine coming face-to-face with the love of your life after five hundred years! Recognizing her, yet knowing there was nothing you could do about it. No wonder he had broken that glass. And now? She knew beyond a doubt that whatever was going to happen on his thirtieth birthday was linked to the story of Máximo and Cariña. Some ancient duty was calling him to fulfill his destiny. *So why can't he tell me all of it? It's my story, too.*

Her heart cried out for her to get closer to Sylvester. What he'd said about the dog made her realize how lonely he was, despite the celebrity status he enjoyed. Connie knew what that felt like. She'd endured four years of having no one with whom to share life's littlest pleasures, of walking her own silent, solitary path, of being an observer, of keeping that hurt locked deep inside. Four years of believing her existence was insignificant, that she was meaningless to anyone and anything. That was the tragedy of loneliness. It was heartbreak and hardship neatly packaged together and wrapped in hurt. Four years? Sylvester had been feeling those things all his life.

Connie made a decision there and then. *Whatever momentous thing Sylvester has to do on his thirtieth birthday, we have until then. I'm going to make sure that, for these next few weeks, neither of us has to be lonely.*

Ignoring the sway of the boat, Connie closed the small distance between them, bringing her body up hard against the warmth of his. The arm that had been draped casually across the seat behind her immediately dropped lower, as if Sylvester had been anticipating her action. She shivered as his hand closed possessively around her shoulder. Slowly, Connie began to unbutton his shirt.

"Connie—" her name was a tormented groan on his lips "—I need to concentrate on steering this boat."

There was a plea in his voice and, although it was for her to stop, when her hand brushed his groin, she felt the rock-hard bulge that strained upward, urging her to continue. Connie decided to listen to his body and ignore his voice. Pressing a trail of kisses onto his chest, she slid his shirt open.

"You focus on the boat. Let me concentrate on you."

The heat that had been burning between them sizzled into a frenzy as Connie moved lower, reaching his belt. Sylvester's hips jerked convulsively as she loosened the buckle and lowered his zipper. The boat slowed almost to a standstill. Reaching inside, Connie freed his erection from the confines of his jeans and boxer briefs, her eyes widening as she looked at him. It was a very long time since she'd touched a man intimately, and never a man as big as Sylvester. She had certainly never behaved so boldly, yet, as she lowered her head, she felt no sense of shyness or hesitation. She knew without asking exactly what he liked.

She felt Sylvester's groan reverberate through his body and into her mouth as she slid her lips over the head of his cock. Taking a moment to accommodate to his size, she relaxed her jaw before easing him more fully into the wet warmth of her mouth. Guessing he wouldn't last long, and wanting to prolong his enjoyment, she pulled back, licking along the length of his shaft before returning to run her tongue lightly around the rim.

Sylvester tangled one hand into her hair, holding her head in his lap, and the gesture was hauntingly familiar. *God, I love this man so much.* Her whole body ached with longing. Her nipples were diamond-hard as they rubbed against his thighs, her sex burned with the need for his touch. What she felt went way beyond any physical connection. Her heart had been freed from the chains that had held it captive for the last four years. Swooping and soaring joyously, it was beating to a new rhythm. One that was wildly excited by this erotic experience but also deeply moved by their renewed bond.

When she took him back into her mouth, Connie could already feel Sylvester's climax building. Taking him as deep as she could, she moved her head up and down, reaching lower to cup his sac, feeling him bump the back of her throat. His body went rigid and she heard his hoarse cry, his warmth filling her mouth. Everything about it was so right. So perfect. *We have done this a hundred times before.*

When they reached Corazón a few minutes later, Sylvester had fastened his clothing. He was calm and in control as he helped her step out of the boat.

His eyes glittered bluer than the sky over his head as he gazed at her. Her whole body tightened and tingled with anticipation. She knew that look. It was loaded with erotic promise. "My room. Now."

Sylvester's room was actually a suite occupying the entire top floor of the house. There was a balcony overlooking the bay. Unlike the one in Connie's room, his had a waist-high, brick balustrade running along its length. Sylvester had poured two glasses of wine and taken them onto the balcony. Connie sipped hers as she looked out over the bay. It was tranquil and beautiful. Corazón at its best. They hadn't yet spoken about what had happened between them on the boat. Connie searched for the words to explain to Sylvester about her decision that, for the time they had left, they needed to be together. She hoped he wasn't going to try to put up more barriers. She didn't want to waste what precious time they had together arguing with him.

Before she could turn to speak to him, Sylvester's hands came down on the balustrade on either side of her, trapping her between his lean, muscular arms. Connie's world narrowed in a heartbeat. The view in front of her was forgotten as she focused on the body pressed up against her. It was strong, hard and undeniably aroused.

"It's a long way down." She nodded, reluctant to try her voice because her heart seemed to be trying to force its way out through her mouth. Then she gasped as Sylvester leaned even closer, lifting the length of her hair and moving it forward over her shoulder. His breath tickled the fine hairs at the back of her neck. "Are you scared?"

"No." That single monosyllable was all she could summon as she tried to fight down the fluttering, melting sensation turning her limbs to liquid.

"Nor am I. Not anymore." He moved his hips forward so Connie couldn't possibly mistake the iron harness of his erection. Unable to help herself, she arched her back a little, pressing her buttocks more firmly against that delicious length. Sylvester's next words came out on a slight groan. "Shall I tell you why?"

Connie managed to stammer out two words this time. "Y-yes, please." She felt extraordinarily proud of her achievement in speaking at all, since it was hard to concentrate on anything other than Sylvester's nearness and the exhilarating heat between her legs.

"I'm not scared because I'm with you, Connie." His charming baritone voice had become gruff with emotion. As he spoke, he removed his hands from the balcony rail and slid them up from her waist, cupping her breasts over the thin material of her dress. Connie gasped as his fingers found and teased her already pebbled nipples. "And because, ever since I met you, I've been thinking about doing this."

She leaned her head back against his chest, cupping her hands over his in encouragement. "I've been thinking the same thing."

Sylvester hissed through clenched teeth, pulling away for a second and then pressing forward with a groan, pinning her hard to the balustrade with his body. He ground his hips into her and she shivered violently, unable to focus beyond the wetness between her legs, the wobble in her knees and the mad thrill in her stomach. His lips brushed the ridge of her ear. "And right now, I can't think of anything except how much I need to be inside you."

His fingers left her breasts, but only to move lower so he could lift the hem of her dress. Hooking his thumbs into the waistband of her underwear, he pulled them down over her thighs and calves until she could step out of them. Nudging her legs apart with his knees, he moved closer, kissing the back of her neck. Connie was aware of him fumbling with his clothing and, with relief, she heard him tear open a condom wrapper. Thank goodness one of them was thinking straight. Then his muscled thighs were between her legs, spreading her wider.

She could feel his sheathed erection pressing hard against her. Standing behind her, supporting her against the balustrade, he positioned himself at her entrance and pushed all the way inside in one thick, hot rush. Rougher, faster and more completely perfect than anything she'd imagined. Connie wasn't sure she could bear it. The sweet heaven of him inside her, his hands firm on her hips, holding her steady while she grew accustomed to his girth. Then he started to drive in and out, and her whole body convulsed with pleasure at the rhythmic pounding that sent her thoughts scattering into a thousand tiny pieces. Pleasure built outward from her nerve endings, traveling through her bloodstream to the point where her body met Sylvester's.

Reaching a hand between them, he stroked her clitoris in time with his thrusts and Connie's internal muscles clenched tightly around him.

Sylvester groaned appreciatively, leaning closer so he could kiss the shell of her ear. "Feels so good when you squeeze me like that. Always has."

The words were too much for Connie. Obedient to the thrumming demands of the man inside her and his skillful, relentless fingers, she gave herself up to orgasm. Rapture crested, sucking her under so she was drowning in wave upon wave of delight. As if he had been holding back, waiting for her, Sylvester's thrusts accelerated. He gave an inarticulate cry before his body jerked out its release deep inside her.

Connie's body was still humming with pleasure as Sylvester withdrew and turned her to face him. Brushing the hair back from her face, he smoothed it gently behind her ear. Softly, his tongue traced the outline of her lips and she relaxed into his kiss, opening her mouth to allow his tongue to slip inside. They kissed hungrily, breathlessly, their tongues dancing together, his fingers tangling in her already tousled hair.

"I knew this time would be raw and out of control," he said when they finally broke apart.

She shook her head, trying to get to grips with what he was saying. "When were you planning on letting me into that little secret?"

"Around the same time you decided to let me into your body."

The eroticism of the words sent a renewed blaze of passion storming through her. She gazed up at him. "What will the next time be like?"

"Let me show you." He swung her up into his arms and carried her through the open glass doors and into his bedroom.

Chapter 10

Cariña sits on a rock and watches him as he works. The muscles in his back and shoulders bulge and relax as he hammers the wood in place, and her throat tightens painfully. Whenever she is close to Máximo, her body is gripped by a series of powerful emotions.

Sota has warned her to stay away from him, told her she was playing with fire. But what does her grandmother know? What harm can there be in coming to watch him build this funny little house in the pinewoods? In listening to his deep, melodic voice talking in that strange language from far across the seas? In gazing into those endless blue eyes? In imagining those big, powerful hands caressing her body...

Máximo is talking to her, trying out a few words of her language, and Cariña rouses herself from her daydream. She has placed a pink-and-white butterfly orchid behind her ear and he smiles, indicating the bloom.

"Pretty."

She blushes, unsure if the word is meant for her or the flower.

Máximo holds the door of the cottage open and, with

a flourishing bow, invites her inside. As soon as Cariña steps over the threshold, she knows what will happen. Sota was right to warn her. There is danger here, but it doesn't come from him. It comes from within herself.

Máximo has made himself a wooden bed and covered it with leaves and mosses. Filling most of the space in the cottage, it is a silent invitation. The very air between them thrums with the passion they have felt since the first day he arrived on Corazón. How can they possibly resist this?

He remains still. She knows he is waiting for her to move first. If she doesn't, he will keep his distance. With a sound midway between a laugh and a sob, she sways toward him and he catches hold of her waist in those strong hands. Rising on the tips of her toes, Cariña fits her body to his.

With a groan of surrender, Máximo slides an arm around her, moving his lips down her neck to the hollow of her throat. With one fingertip, he traces her lips, then her neck, pausing to follow the line of her dress where the deerskin covers the swell of her breasts. His lips find the sweet spot where her neck and shoulder meet and his fingers busy themselves undoing the ties of her garment. Spreading the deerskin apart, he slides it down over one shoulder, caressing her exposed flesh with his lips and tongue.

Máximo shivers at the sensation of his erection pressing into her stomach. She knows exactly what this evidence of his desire for her means and she wants more from him. Demands it. Together they push her dress down over her breasts, past her waist and stomach, until she is able to step out of it and kick it aside. She is naked except for the butterfly orchid in her hair.

Máximo's indrawn breath at the sight of her naked-

ness sends a shudder of renewed desire surging through her. He reaches out a hand and cups her breast while rubbing her nipple gently with the pad of his thumb.

Cariña tumbles headlong into a spiral of pleasure as his touch sends a shiver of delight shooting from her breast directly to that secret place between her legs. The place she has been achingly aware of ever since she set eyes on him.

She gasps as his hand moves lower, smoothing along her hip and across her stomach. She bites her lip as it dips between her thighs. How can he know exactly where she needs to feel his touch? Lightly, he skims the soft cluster of curls between her legs.

Pressing his knee between hers, he widens her stance. Using the tips of his fingers, he strokes the sensitive skin of her inner thighs. Moving his hand higher, his fingers part the soft curls and slide between her swollen folds. Her entire frame jerks wildly in response.

Máximo slowly draws his middle finger along her moist cleft, up and back down, probing her wetness. He finds and rubs the tiny bundle of thrumming nerves. When his movements quicken, Cariña whimpers. Her body, pulled taut and aching for release, gives way to an unexpected wave that crashes through her entire being. It is like nothing she has ever experienced. She tries to call out his name but no sound leaves her lips. The wave pounds through her again and again, and all she can do is cling to his shoulders with both hands, digging her nails into his flesh, until the tremors that shake her cease.

Máximo slides a hand down her back, over the curve of her buttocks and up her spine, calming her.

Cariña raises her eyes to his. What has just happened only makes her want him more. She takes his hand and leads him to the bed. When she sits on the edge, her eyes are level with his groin. He wears the traditional breechcloth of the Calusa brave and his bulging erection is evident beneath the brief garment.

She reaches out a hand and, sliding it beneath the deerskin, strokes his heated flesh. His whole body jerks in response.

Touching is not enough; she needs to look at him. Raising her eyes to his face, Cariña undoes the ties at his hips. His eyes gleam bluer than ever in the gloom.

The sight of him takes her breath away. So powerful and potent. So proudly masculine. She reaches out and grasps him, sliding her hand down his length. His groan and the way he grows even harder beneath her touch tells her the action is enjoyable, so she repeats it.

He closes his hand over hers, showing her exactly what to do, and together they stroke his shaft. Cariña keeps her eyes on his face, loving the faraway, dreamy look in his eyes. She wants more than this. She wants all of him. Releasing him, she lies back on the bed, parting her legs, offering herself to him. His eyes are hungry as he stares at her. She loves the sensation of him gazing at the intimate parts of her body.

"We can't." He says the words in her language, miming there may be a child if they make love.

Heat suffuses her face. She remembers what she has heard, the stories the women tell. There are ways to avoid it. She performs her own mime, blushing more at the smile in his eyes.

With a groan, he comes to lie next to her, drawing her close, kissing her, pressing his lips to the base of her neck and sighing unknown words of love against her skin. Lowering his lips, he trails a line of fluttering kisses down her body, lingering on a breast, on the tip of a nipple, along her collarbone. If there was only ever this one time, it would be enough magic for a hundred lifetimes.

He slides his middle finger into the wetness between her warm folds. Stroking her still-sensitized nub, he circles it with his thumb and flicks over it before sliding the same finger inside her. Seeking the sensitive flesh inside, he watches her face as she quivers at his touch. Slowly, he removes his finger and positions himself between her legs.

She murmurs his name and, needing no further encouragement, he enters her in one swift motion, stopping when he feels a barrier. Pausing, he pulls out of her slightly, watching her face intently.

Cariña lifts her hips, showing him she wants him to continue, to complete their love.

Biting his lip, he plunges into her as far as he can, halting again when he hears her sudden gasp.

Cariña squeezes her eyes shut as he penetrates her completely. The sense of him filling her is overpowering. The brief moment of pain is gone now, and Máximo begins to move. She surges up to meet him, wrapping her legs around his waist so he is buried even deeper in her. She needs him in as far as he can go.

Then he is pulling out and thrusting into her, over and over in a rhythm she matches with her pelvis pounding against his. There is a pulse beating deep inside her, the same sensations as before are building again. This time they are intensified by Máximo's hardness stretching and filling her. It is so perfect Cariña feels as if her heart might burst at the same time her body convulses with pleasure. She wants to keep his fullness deep inside her, igniting every nerve ending. At the same time, every grinding, undulating movement is driving them toward the soul-shattering climax they seek.

When Cariña's release rushes through her, it is a tidal wave of enormous pleasure that leaves her trembling on the brink of infinity. She cries out in unabashed abandon, the words unclear but the message unmistakable—she belongs to him, in that moment and forever.

She feels Máximo tense, and he withdraws from her as his orgasm rips through him. He grips his shaft, pumping it twice as it spasms. His body jerks and she feels his warm, wet release on her thighs. He buries his face in her hair; the Spanish words he utters are a muffled groan.

When Connie woke the next morning she was alone in Sylvester's huge bed. She glanced at the clock on the bedside table and did a double take. How did that happen? She had never slept so late in her life.

With complete wakefulness came the images of the previous night and she lay back, reveling in the warmth of her memories. Five hundred years ago Máximo and Cariña had been violently, passionately, in love. Theirs had been an intensely physical relationship. Her dream just now about the first time they had made love had been scorching. If it even approached the reality, then it was no wonder she had been wandering around this island in an erotic haze ever since she'd first seen Sylvester.

Face it, they couldn't keep their hands off each other. She set the dream aside—how did she know that for sure? A secret smile touched Connie's lips. *Because Sylvester and I recreated it last night. We had a lot of catching up to do on their behalf.*

Although there was still some residual shock there

when she thought of herself as Cariña and Sylvester as Máximo, the violence of her initial emotions was fading. Drama had given way to acceptance. Perhaps it was the strength of her connection to Sylvester that allowed her to acknowledge their past lives with so little hesitation. In spite of everything, this new knowledge brought with it a strange contentment.

Sighing, she slid from the bed and set about discovering the whereabouts of her clothing. Blushing, she retrieved her underwear from the balcony. When she was dressed, she made her way back to her own room, pleased not to encounter anyone as she left Sylvester's suite. It wasn't anyone else's business where she spent the night, she told herself firmly, but she didn't want to deal with explanations. Having showered and changed into shorts and a tank top in her own room, she made her way downstairs and onto the patio. The house seemed unnaturally quiet.

"Where is everyone?" she asked Vega.

"There's a problem with the mobile phone signal." Vega pulled a face as she poured coffee. "You know what men are like about these things. Suddenly they have all become technological experts."

"And Lucinda?" Somehow, Connie couldn't picture her getting involved with the intricacies of any technology problems.

"I haven't seen her this morning." Vega's tone, together with her brief shrug, told Connie everything she needed to know. The little housekeeper clearly did not approve of Lucinda.

Vega left her alone to eat her breakfast. Connie viewed the house differently now. *I was here when it was built.* This house was not the original, but some features remained. Those fountains in the gardens she loved so much were one example. *I built them.* They had been Cariña's tribute to the old house in the square at Valladolid.

"What are you smiling about?" Matt's voice penetrated her thoughts. Was it her imagination or was there an edge to his tone? A sharp note she hadn't heard before? Was it possible he had picked up on her newfound happiness and sensed something had happened between her and Sylvester? Connie wasn't sure how to react to Matt's feelings for her. They couldn't be very deep, surely? She'd known him such a short time and she had never given him any encouragement. If she acknowledged she knew how he felt, would he be angry? Hurt? She decided it was best to continue with her ongoing response and pretend she didn't know.

"Just enjoying the day," she said, as he took the seat next to her. "Aren't you tempted to get involved in the phone signal problem?"

He stretched his long legs in front of him. "God, no. There are enough conflicting voices offering advice on that issue already. I left them to it. Sylvester's expression was getting increasingly thunderous." He cast a sidelong glance at Connie. "Where did you get to yesterday?"

"Sylvester took me to Mound Key to see the ancient Calusa site. What about you?"

"I joined Guthrie, Lucinda and Jonathan in the launch. We went to Charlotte Harbor." He grimaced. "On balance, I think I'd rather have joined you and looked at an island made out of shells. I managed to escape for an hour and wander around on my own. Did you discover anything riveting at Mound Key?"

Deciding she could hardly answer that question truthfully, Connie opted for a noncommittal approach. "It was very informative."

Matt faked a yawn. "Sounds like a school outing. I told you Sylvester got boring about the whole Calusa thing. The only time I went to Mound Key, I couldn't get away fast enough."

Connie shifted position so she was facing him. "Why?"

It hadn't occurred to her until now, but Matt's whole personality changed whenever the Calusa were mentioned. He was instantly transformed from a charming companion to a sulky schoolboy. He became petulant and dismissive, doing everything he could to change the subject. It seemed a strange reaction to a very specific topic.

He lifted one shoulder in a sullen gesture. "I thought it was an eerie place. Gave me the creeps." He laughed self-consciously, becoming embarrassed. "History isn't for everyone. I'll leave that to you and Sylvester. I'm off for a swim. Coming?"

"I might join you later." Connie indicated her still half-full coffee cup.

Matt strolled away and Connie returned to her musings. Although Matt puzzled her, he couldn't hold her attention for long. Not when such momentous things were happening in her own life. It was so hard to reconcile the happiness she felt now with the knowledge it was all due to come crashing to an end in a few weeks. If only she could induce Sylvester to confide in her. Between them, they must be able to find a way around this. Whatever "this" might be. No problem was insurmountable. *We love each other. There has to be a way we can stay together.*

Restlessly, Connie rose from her seat and made her way onto the sand. Slipping off her sandals, she walked to the water's edge, allowing the gentle waves to cool her feet. A clear, bright image of Cariña in the demure clothes of a Spanish noblewoman, with her velvet skirts hitched up around her waist as she paddled in these very waters, came to her, and Connie laughed aloud. Máximo's unconventional choice of bride must have surprised his dignified Spanish acquaintances.

Although there had been too much else going on for her to dwell on it, she had been troubled by Sylvester's story about Cariña's grandmother, Sota. In her dreams, the old woman was a kindly figure who doted on her. Connie couldn't reconcile the benign person she saw in her nocturnal wanderings with the murderess Sylvester had described. It was strange how much, she mused as she walked, Cariña's life had been dominated by two older women. There had been the warm, watchful presence of the grandmother who'd brought her up and the contrasting malignant shadow of Sinapa, the woman whose curse blighted future generations of Cariña's family.

A flash of gold caught Connie's eye and she stooped to examine it. It was a half-buried object and she dug the fine grains of sand away from it. Her heart gave a thud of dismay as she recognized what she was looking at. Picking it up, she turned it over in her hand. It was a cell phone with an embossed gold cover. The initials E.C. were engraved across it. *Ellie Carter.*

Connie gazed at it in consternation. No wonder Ellie wasn't returning Jonathan's calls. How could she when her phone was still here on Corazón?

Sylvester ran a hand through his hair. Even though he was a de León, and genetically conditioned to think the worst, this was bad and looking worse with every new piece of information. "What the hell is going on here?"

Roberto held his hands palms upward in a helpless gesture. His face told its own story of complete bewilderment. "Someone is deliberately jamming the phone signals. It's easy enough to do—you can pick up a device cheaply enough."

"And it's someone on the island?"

"Has to be." Roberto nodded. "We are too far away from any other land mass for someone to be doing it remotely. I suppose it could have been done from offshore in a boat, but given all the other things that have happened, I'd say it has to be someone here."

"Talk me through the other things that have happened." Sylvester knew his voice sounded slightly stunned.

"We've lost our internet. As you know, we built a tower on the highest point on the island so we had a satellite WiFi connection." Sylvester nodded. "The dish has been smashed to pieces. Looks like someone climbed the tower and took a hammer to it."

"When did this happen?"

"It's hard to say, because I don't check on it very often. When I found out about the problem with the phones, I got my laptop out. I was going to contact the mainland to ask for advice. That's when I discovered there was no internet. I checked the tower and saw the damage."

Sylvester gripped the iron railing that ran along the edge of the terrace they were standing on. "When was the last time you know for sure the satellite was intact?"

"The morning your current party of guests arrived," Roberto said with certainty. "I was getting some tools to work on the boat before I went to collect your guests from Charlotte Harbor. I happened to look up at the tower and the transmitter was fine then. That day was also the last time I used the internet."

Sylvester's mind made the obvious link. So the damage to the satellite had to have been done since his guests arrived. Had it been done *by* one of them? "And there's also a problem with the boats?"

For the first time Roberto's professional mask slipped and anger showed through. "The engines on both the launch and your speedboat have been tampered with."

"How bad is it?"

"Bad." The curt word told Sylvester everything he needed to know. Roberto had never been one to overdramatize a situation.

"Can they be fixed?"

Roberto shrugged. "I'll try. But with no way of getting to the mainland for spare parts, it's a long shot."

Sylvester dropped a hand onto his shoulder. "See what you can do." He knew he could rely on Roberto. If anyone could repair the boats, he could.

When Roberto went away, Sylvester took a moment to assess the situation. Someone had cut off their means of communication and their only means of escape. They were trapped on the island. Surely even someone desperate to inherit his fortune would not go to such extremes? Anyway, the plan among his guests was to get rid of the competition, not keep everyone here. He shook his head slowly from side to side, trying to clear it. What was going on? What on earth did anyone stand to gain by keeping them all stranded here?

He was momentarily distracted from his thoughts as Connie came into view. She was walking barefoot along the water's edge, carrying her sandals. Sylvester only had to look at her to feel consumed with desire. But it wasn't just lust. His heart swelled in equal proportion to his erection whenever he was near her. It was the most bittersweet experience of his life. Sweet, because he had never expected to experience love like this. Bitter, because he knew it couldn't last.

As Connie drew closer, he saw that her expression was troubled. She had been looking down at the sand but, when she glanced up and saw him watching her, she left the beach and came straight to him. Not caring who could see them, he drew her into his arms and kissed her. They didn't have long enough together to worry about other people's opinions. The embrace quickly became heated and, when they pulled apart, they were both breathing a little bit faster.

"You look worried." Sylvester rubbed one finger over her forehead as though smoothing away imaginary frown lines.

She held up her hand, showing him the object she was holding. "I found it in the sand. It's Ellie's phone."

Guests and staff sat in a subdued group around the long table. Sylvester had called them all together in the dining room.

His face was grave as he bluntly outlined the situation. "Someone has deliberately sabotaged our means of communication and our transport off the island."

There was a general clamor of conversation, with everyone striving to be heard. Eventually, Lucinda managed to raise her voice above the others. "What are you going to do about it?"

"We are doing everything we can. Roberto is doing his best to repair the boats."

Lucinda rose. "I demand to leave this island immediately."

Sylvester's usual tolerance slipped slightly. "Believe

me, if you can find a way to get off the island, no one is going to stop you."

Guthrie caught hold of his sister's hand, pulling her back down beside him. "Don't you understand, Lou? We can't leave. There is no way off." In response, she burst into noisy sobs and buried her face in his shoulder.

"How are the phone signals being jammed?" Matt asked.

"It's likely someone is using a portable jammer," Sylvester said. "If we could find that, we would be able to unjam the signals."

Jonathan had been listening in silence but he regarded Sylvester with a frown at those words. "You mean someone in this room is using a phone jammer?"

"It's either that or there is someone hiding on the island that we have so far been unaware of."

"So let me get this straight—" Jonathan looked at each of them in turn "—unless there is a stranger at large, there are nine people on this island and one of them is deliberately imprisoning the other eight for some undisclosed reason?"

"That about sums it up." Sylvester nodded.

"Bastard."

"That also seems to sum it up."

Matt turned to Juan. "What about the kayaks?"

Juan shook his head. Connie remembered how cheerful he had been on the day she'd met him and he had discussed his plans to sail to Cuba in his Calusa canoe. Now his expression was glum. "All damaged. Someone has shoved a spike through the base of each of them. Even if they could be repaired, I wouldn't like our chances of taking one of them across to the nearest island. They're not built for distance."

"And your traditional Calusa canoe? You had plans to take that as far as Cuba," Matt reminded him.

Juan's face clouded over further. "Whoever did this knew about our project. They took a hammer and chisel to our canoe. I can repair it, but it'll take time, especially as Nicolás is away on the mainland and now I have no way of getting in touch with him."

Connie listened to them discussing the options for getting off the island with a sinking heart. It was wrong and selfish of her to imagine this was all about her, but that crawling feeling at the back of her neck had returned. As though she was being watched by invisible eyes.

Could the person who was doing this be *him*? Could the man who attacked her four years ago really be here on the island? She looked at the men in the room in turn. Sylvester? No, she shook her head. Of all of them, he was the one she knew for sure was not her stalker. Matt? He had risen from his seat and was pacing up and down, animatedly trying to come up with a solution to the problem. *He's my friend. He wouldn't hurt me.* Jonathan? She bit her lip. There was something about Jonathan, something that set him apart from other people. She wasn't sure she completely trusted him. Guthrie? Surely not. He seemed so jovial and helpless. Then there were the two members of staff. Roberto and Juan. What did she really know of either of them?

Apart from Sylvester, she couldn't really discount any of the men in this room. But, even if he was here on Corazón, was her attacker bold enough to do something like this? Surely his style was less about drama and more about lurking in the shadows? He would be more inclined to wait a few more weeks before getting her on her own. Unless he knew about her and Sylvester and had been tipped over the edge by their relationship…

"Are there any deliveries due?" Sylvester was talking to Vega.

She shook her head regretfully. "I had a big order of food delivered from the mainland two days ago, and the fresh water tanks are full."

"What about maintenance?" He turned to Roberto. "Are any of our contractors due on the island in the next few days?"

"I checked the schedule. The next person due is the electrical contractor. He will be coming to do a routine check, but his visit is not for another week."

Lucinda lifted her head from Guthrie's shoulder. "Are you telling me we are stuck here for seven days while someone—but we don't know who—has us at his mercy?"

Although Sylvester's face and voice were calm, they left everyone in no doubt of the seriousness of the situation. "I am, and while that's the case, we must all be very, very careful."

With the discovery of Ellie's phone, they had renewed their search for any other signs she might still be on the island.

"Nothing." Jonathan's expression was frustrated. "I suppose she could have left on a delivery boat and dropped her phone as she was going."

Connie, watching Sylvester's face closely, decided he knew something and followed him as he left the room and went up the stairs. He quirked a brow at her. "Are you trying to get me on my own?"

"Yes." She followed him into his bedroom and closed the door. "But not for the reason you think." She softened the words with a smile. "Not yet, anyway. What do you know about Ellie that you are not telling Jonathan?"

"Am I so easy to read?"

She stepped forward, sliding her arms around his waist and tilting her face up to his. "To me, you are. But that's because I've known you for a very long time. Five hundred years, to be exact."

He sighed. "There were no delivery boats that day. Ellie couldn't have left the island."

"My God, Sylvester, does that mean…?"

"That she's probably dead? I hope not. I hope there's a logical explanation that means she'll turn up safe and well. But when you've lived with the curse of Corazón for as long as I have, you tend to think the worst."

His face looked so lost and haunted that all she wanted to do was to reach out and comfort him. Resting her cheek against his chest, she tightened her arms around his waist. Sylvester's hands came up and slowly his fingertips moved up and down her spine, almost reverently, as if he couldn't quite believe she was there in his arms. They remained that way for a few, long minutes before their own special magic began to stir in the air.

"I thought I had this all planned. I hadn't counted on meeting you this way, Connie. Not now. Not ever." Sylvester's voice was a tortured groan.

"I'm sorry to be such an inconvenience." She lifted her head and kissed a line along his jaw.

"You are an inconvenience. A goddamned awkward, ill-timed, distracting…*wonderful* inconvenience."

He picked her up and carried her over to the bed. Impatience took over and their clothes were discarded in a blur of frantic movement.

Connie still had time to marvel that there was no

hesitation between them, that they could know each other so well, yet the passion they shared still burned as brightly as it had when Máximo and Cariña first ignited it five hundred years ago. It was a flame that would never be quenched. As soon as Sylvester's hands touched her body, she needed more from him. As soon as he kissed her, she was a trembling mass of sensation. She had never dreamed that desire like this existed, that she could want a man so much she would beg him to take her. That she would be able to tell him in intimate, erotic detail exactly what she wanted him to do to her. That minutes after she climaxed, she would want him inside her again. That her need for him would be an ever-present ache.

"Please." As soon as he lay next to her on the bed, she was arching her body up to his, her hands reaching down to guide him to her. There would be time for gentleness later, because they would never get enough of each other.

Sylvester ran his hand down over her stomach and she shivered a little as he moved it lower. His fingers roamed over her soft mound, stroking her outer lips, slipping between them to feel her arousal.

"So hot and wet," he murmured, his eyes bluer than ever as they probed hers.

Pushing his fingers up, he brushed over her throbbing clitoris, knowing the tiny nub would be begging for his touch. Connie tensed at the almost unbearable sensation of pleasure and anticipation that surged through her. Pulling back, Sylvester teasingly circled her snug entrance, making her lift her hips impatiently. Smiling into her eyes, he pressed his thumb into her, making her gasp and clench tightly around him. Using his fingertips, he reached for her clitoris, massaging firmly and coaxing a groan of pleasure from her.

Withdrawing his hand, he moved over her, holding his iron-hard cock against her, nudging the head in a little way. Connie went wild with need, pressing herself up against him as he teased her. Sylvester slid up and down, threatening to slip inside her but still holding back. She shifted impatiently once more, murmuring his name, and he pushed forward. Both of them gasped as he penetrated her.

Connie locked her ankles around his hips, squeezing her muscles tight around him, drawing him in as deep as she could, exulting in his groan of surrender. Time melted away. She no longer cared if she was Connie or Cariña, if this man inside her was Sylvester or Máximo. All that mattered was this connection, these emotions, this wonderful friction as she rocked her hips in time with his.

She felt the first spasm of his climax jerk inside her and her own answering waves began to build. It was as if a giant had picked her up and flung her out to the furthest reaches of the cosmos and she was spinning wildly out of control, floating high above the heavens. The fire that burned inside stars crackled in her, punching its way through her body with raw, molten energy and she cried out the only words that would do. "I love you!"

His head dropped onto her shoulder as he gasped out in time with his release. "And I love you, my Cariña."

Chapter 11

Sylvester shifted his weight away from Connie and came crashing back to reality. *You fool. As if life wasn't complicated enough already, you had to add unprotected sex into the equation?* He gazed down at her, loving the look of tenderness in her eyes, even as he cursed his own carelessness.

"I'm sorry. I was so crazy with wanting you, I never stopped to think about protection."

"We were both reckless." She bit her lip and he sensed her hesitation, as though she was wondering whether to continue. "We might not be ready for a child, Sylvester, but won't you explain to me why, when we love each other so much, we can't be together forever?"

He drew her into his arms and she rested her head on his chest, naturally and comfortably. It felt good. His throat constricted. She was right to ask. Why couldn't this be their future? Could he tell her? Was it something he could explain to another person without the risk of making the situation sound even more bizarre? Didn't he owe Connie an explanation? She had placed her trust in him, offered him her unconditional love.

When he walked out on her, didn't she deserve to know why? He came to a decision. He had to try to find the words to tell her the secret he'd kept to himself for his whole, long life.

He thought carefully about his words. "I don't pretend to understand how reincarnation works. If you believe humans are just a bunch of atoms, then we die and that's the end of us. But if you believe we have a soul, then you may also believe this is not our first life on this earth. It may also not be our last. Most people will never know the details of their previous lives. They may have occasional dreams or feelings of déjà vu, but otherwise, the past will not affect them. It's only in cases like ours, when fate conspires to cause our paths to cross again, that vivid memories will resurface."

Connie lifted her head to look at him. "But surely the fact that I was Cariña and you were Máximo only makes what we feel for each other stronger?"

He shook his head. "We can only go as far as our destiny will allow us. You were Cariña in a past life, but I wasn't Máximo."

"No. That's not true." Determinedly she shook her head. "I saw you in my dreams. When we make love, I know it's happened before. I'm not wrong about that."

"No, you're not wrong." He cupped her cheek with one hand. "But you don't understand. I wasn't Máximo in a past life...I *am* Máximo."

She frowned. "You're right, I don't understand."

This was the hard part. He found it difficult enough to understand it himself. "Máximo de León y Soledad did not exist before his thirtieth birthday. There are no records of him prior to that date. It was as if he came from nowhere. In a sense, he did. That happened because we are the same person." He took a deep breath.

"On my thirtieth birthday, I have to fulfill my destiny and go back in time to Spain in the year 1521. I have to pick up the pieces of my life as Máximo."

She was quiet for so long he thought he must have blown it. The only thing that gave him hope was the fact that she didn't pull away from him. Eventually, she drew in a shuddering breath. "Have you always known you would have to go back?"

Sylvester swallowed that strange obstruction that still persisted in his throat. "I wasn't born knowing it, if that's what you mean. Because I wasn't born in any conventional sense of the word. My life has existed on this loop, this immortal cycle. As Máximo, I was the first head of the house of de León. I have been the head of this house ever since. Knowing I must go back was more a realization that came to me gradually over the years."

"What do you suppose would happen if you stayed here?" Connie's voice was small and sad.

He stared over her head, out the window at the blue sky. The same sky he'd stared at five hundred years ago and every day ever since then. "If I don't go back, history would look very different. Máximo would not exist. He wouldn't have been there when Ponce de León landed in Florida. The history of these islands would have looked very different. Even leaving that aside—" he laughed slightly "—if anything as momentous can be dismissed so lightly. Máximo and Cariña would not have met and fallen in love. They would not have founded the house of de León. All that I am now would not have happened."

"Are you going back because you must go to her… because of your love for Cariña?" Connie bent her head over the coverlet, tracing the embroidered pattern with one fingertip.

Placing a hand under her chin, he lifted her face so she was forced to look at him. Although Connie blinked rapidly, a single tear escaped and slid down her cheek. Sylvester smoothed it away with the pad of his thumb. "Connie, I said I don't understand any of this. You know how stunned I was when I first saw you. That was because I *recognized* you. In that instant, I knew who you were. I didn't fall in love with you there and then. I couldn't, because I was already in love with you."

Her lip trembled. "Cariña will come to you in Valladolid. She will share your life from then on. Even though my own life will not have begun, I envy her because she can be with you and I can't."

He drew her close, wishing he had some words of comfort to offer her, wishing there was some way he could stop time, change the past, make things turn out differently. He had wished the same thing many times in his life, but never with such a strong reason.

Sylvester didn't know if the cycle was repeated. If these five hundred years happened over and over. If this was the first or one of many times in the supernatural loop that represented his immortality. He had found that questioning could lead him onto a downward slope of gloom and depression from which it was hard to clamber back. All he knew for sure about his questions was there were no answers.

It would be different if Connie, or Cariña, had shared his immortality. But that wasn't the case. She had not been alive for five hundred years the way he had. Cariña had been mortal. She had died when she reached old age. It was only now that she had come back again as Connie.

The supernatural world became even stranger here on Corazón. Immortality and reincarnation, although different, had collided with a force so powerful it had rocked their lives off course. Even though Sylvester had lived for five hundred years, the chances of his dead love being reborn had to be nonexistent. Unless Corazón was added into the equation. Here, all things became possible.

Some time later, Connie lifted her head again. "How will you go back? Do you know, or will you just vanish?" Her eyes widened. "Tell me I will be able to say goodbye to you."

"I will take the same route so many people on this island have taken over the years." She looked confused. "The Salto de Fe."

"No, Sylvester. You can't." Connie raised a shaking hand to her lips, her eyes wide with panic. "How do you know it will work? You could just die on those rocks for nothing. How can you be sure it will lead you back to Valladolid and to your life as Máximo?"

"I just know. For as long as I have known I must do this, I have known *how* I must do it. I know that when I step over that edge, it will take me to the exact point in time that I need to go to. It will take me to the precise point at which Máximo joins Ponce de León on his journey. The Salto de Fe is the leap of faith. Trust me, Connie."

She surprised him by starting to laugh. There was no trace of hysteria or disbelief, only genuine amusement in her expression. "I am lying in bed in the middle of the day with a man who tells me his island is cursed, that we knew each other in a past life, and he must jump into a ravine next week so he can resume his life as a sixteenth-century conquistador. I have no reason to trust you, Sylvester de León, but, for some strange reason, I do."

He lay back, smiling into her eyes and pulling her down on top of him. "In that case, perhaps you might consider trusting me one more time?"

In her dreaming state, Connie shivers and tries to cry out. The sense of menace is strong but she can't pinpoint its source. The Calusa braves stand proud and tall. Nearby, the voices of the maidens chant their sweet songs. Overhead, the sky is clear and the lightest of breezes ruffles the surface of the water. Her eyes seek out Máximo and find him among the ranks of the braves. His blue eyes hold hers briefly, warming and reassuring her.

Her father, the chief, steps forward, taking her hand. Beside him, her grandmother's face glows with pride. The Calusa king is coming to claim his bride. If she pleases him, one of their own will be the new queen of Shell Indians. Through her, their family will become all powerful.

I cannot do this. I love Máximo.

Her knees tremble as she walks with her father to the water's edge to meet the ceremonial canoe. Slowly she raises her eyes to the face of the man who holds her destiny in his hands...

"No!" Connie jerked bolt upright in the darkness, sweat cooling on her limbs while her heart raced wildly.

Strong arms were around her instantly and, with relief, she remembered Sylvester's presence. Leaning against him, she allowed reality to wash away the horror of the nightmare.

"What scared you so much?"

"It was another of those vivid dreams. I can't explain how real they are. It's as if my senses are more heightened than they are in reality. This time, King Yargua was arriving on this island—before it was known as Corazón, of course—to decide if he wished to take me—take Cariña—to be his bride." She shuddered. "My father, the chief, led me down to the water's edge to greet the royal canoe. I didn't want to go. By then Cariña was already in love with Máximo."

Sylvester's arms tightened around her. "I know. I was there."

Connie gave a shaky laugh. "Of course you were. When we reached the water, the king stood up and I forced myself to look up at him." She felt the words freeze in her throat, remembering the sheer terror she had felt, and forced herself onward. "I knew him, Sylvester. He is my stalker."

"What?" Sylvester sounded stunned. His hand fumbled for the lamp next to the bed so he could look at her. "Are you sure? You said you've never seen your stalker's face."

"I just knew. The same way you recognized me when you first saw me." She lifted a hand to touch her scars. "Even though I never saw the face of the man who slashed my throat, I know with absolute certainty he was the Calusa king in the past life we shared."

"My God." Sylvester was silent for several minutes, allowing the meaning of what she had just said to sink in. "Do you realize what this means? He never targeted you because of anything that happened in this life."

She nodded. "He came after me to get his revenge on Cariña. Because she left him for Máximo."

"But how did he know who you were?"

"The same way you did. He recognized me. I was

a model, remember? I was becoming successful, so my pictures were in magazines that were widely distributed."

Sylvester nodded. "If he saw your picture and identified who you are, he could easily have tracked you down. Or perhaps he was always looking for you?"

Connie plunged on. "When I first came to Corazón, I sensed he might be here, but I told myself I was being overimaginative. Everything on this island felt strange. There was the story of the curse, the things that were happening to the guests…how I felt about you."

"That wasn't strange." He kissed the top of her head. "That was wonderful."

She managed a smile. "Strangely wonderful. Nevertheless, I blamed all of those things for my perception of danger being thrown off balance. I'm so used to being scared, I decided I didn't know how *not* to be scared. Does that make sense?"

She raised her eyes to his face and the flame of love and sympathy she saw in their blue depths almost made her cry out. "I wish it wasn't true for you, but, yes, it makes sense."

"Now, after that dream I had just now, I know I was right. He is here on Corazón."

"Do you know who he is?"

"I wish I did, but I don't. I feel his malignancy, his evil intent, his hatred toward me. All of those things. I just don't get any feel for him as an individual. But this doesn't make sense. I know how Yargua looked back then. So do you. We'd both know him in an instant if he was here on Corazón today." She frowned fretfully. "Why doesn't he look the way he did back then? You are Máximo. You haven't changed over time. I am Cariña born again. I look like her. I get that. But this man looks nothing like the Calusa king. There is no one on the island who even remotely resembles him."

"As I've said, my credentials as a reincarnation expert aren't proven, Connie, but I don't think it works that way. It's the soul that survives to the next incarnation. The body dies. What body the soul inhabits when a person is born again is immaterial. The chances of you looking exactly like Cariña are, I think, remote and rare. Your looks seem to be one catalyst for why ours has become such a dramatic situation." Sylvester seemed to be following a particular train of thought. "Whoever this man is, I wonder if he even knows why he has these feelings of hatred and revenge toward you. Does he know who he was and who you were, or did he see your picture one day and just feel compelled to hurt you?"

"Dear Lord, that's a scary thought." Connie shivered. "How many stalkers and killers have a motive that has nothing to do with this life? How many people are committing horrible crimes to avenge a wrong that happened centuries ago without even knowing it?" The trembling intensified. "Did my mother die because you and I fell in love all those years ago?"

Sylvester held her, warming her with his body, running his hands up and down her arms and shoulders until the tremors ceased. "At least we now know why we are stranded on this island."

"He means to kill me this time." Connie knew it with a fierce certainty. "Will he also try and kill you?"

"He can try." Sylvester's mouth was grim. "Immortality doesn't have many compensations, but defeating this bastard is the one I plan on enjoying the most."

The atmosphere on the island, already tense, was now like a rubber band pulled so taut it was ready to snap. It was evident in the sidelong glances they sent each other. Every comment, no matter how minor, was analyzed and assessed for a double meaning. If one person wandered off alone, the others immediately became suspicious. If two people had a private conversation, everyone else in the group suspected a plot. Connie could feel the hostility toward her mounting because of her closeness to Sylvester. It was the reason she suggested they should try to keep their relationship low-key.

"Why?" Since Sylvester had responded by pulling her into his arms and kissing her, she sensed he might not be in favor of this proposal.

"Because if people are noticing, it will infuriate *him* even more."

"Connie, he is going to come after you, anyway. He knows you love me." His face had softened as he looked down at her. "Pretending you don't isn't going to fool him."

"Well, it might at least lighten Lucinda's mood," she suggested.

"Nothing is going to lighten Lucinda's mood."

It was true. Doubt and mistrust were like a silent alarm ringing constantly in the air and Lucinda seemed more in tune with its resonance than anyone else. This was evident just after Connie's conversation with Sylvester when, bursting in on her as Connie sat in her favorite chair in the den, Lucinda looked around wildly. "How can you sit there reading as though nothing has happened?"

Connie placed her book aside. She thought back to the first time she had seen Lucinda. To the glamorous, groomed, petulant woman on the quayside at Charlotte Harbor. This wild-eyed, distraught figure with the unkempt hair bore no resemblance to the person Lucinda had been back then.

"It takes my mind off things."

"How can it?" Lucinda's eyes seemed incapable of settling on one thing. It was as if, even in this quiet refuge, she was seeking the source of their troubles, trying to discover the hiding place of the person who had trapped them all here. "How can you think of anything else? We are stuck here and we have no idea what this maniac will do to us."

Connie felt sorry for her. She might be spoiled and demanding, but she didn't deserve this. None of them did. "Why don't we do something together? How about a walk? We could follow the shoreline. Who knows, we might see a boat or even a helicopter. Maybe we could attract its attention."

For a moment she thought Lucinda was going to refuse. Or perhaps, as the other woman stared off into space, she just hadn't heard. Then, gathering her thoughts, Lucinda nodded. "Yes. A walk. Give me a minute while I change my shoes."

Connie rose and wandered out into the hall to wait for her. The house was quiet. Vega was doing a stock take of the food supplies, although she was fairly sure there was enough to last until the electrical contractor's visit, which would happen on Sylvester's birthday next week. Roberto was working on the repairs to the launch while Juan was attempting to restore his beloved canoe. Sylvester, Matt, Jonathan and Guthrie were trying to track down the phone-jamming equipment, although Roberto had warned them looking for a small box on an island this size was like looking for a needle in a haystack. At the same time, they were also seeking any signs a stranger might be hiding out on the island.

The first scream made Connie freeze. It was the high-pitched, agonized sound of an animal in fear of its life, and it was coming from upstairs. It was quickly followed by a series of other screams and she recognized Lucinda's voice. Connie ran for the stairs at the same time Vega emerged from the kitchen.

"Find Sylvester," she called over her shoulder to Vega as she took the stairs two at a time.

Her heart was hammering wildly as she reached the top of the stairs. What would she find when she reached Lucinda's room? Would it be something as awful as those bloodcurdling screams promised or had Lucinda's frayed nerves been tipped over the edge of hysteria by something minor?

The door was open and Connie hurried inside. Lucinda was huddled in a corner, pointing at the bed.

With a feeling of dread, Connie turned to follow the direction of the other woman's shaking finger. The reason for the screams was immediately all too horribly clear.

Fully-clothed and facedown, Ellie's dead body was lying spread-eagled on the bed.

The guests gathered in the dining room and, for once, everyone was in agreement with Guthrie's suggestion they needed a drink. Vega brought cognac and Guthrie handed around glasses of the fine spirit. These were accepted with real gratitude. Connie was seriously concerned about Lucinda, whose hand was shaking so violently that Connie had to help her lift the glass to her lips so she could take a sip of the amber-colored liquor.

"How did she die?" Connie asked, looking up from her kneeling position in front of Lucinda's chair.

"Obviously there will need to be an autopsy, but it appears she was strangled," Sylvester said.

Lucinda gave a stifled sob and Vega exclaimed, "Such wickedness! Whatever is going on?"

"I wish I knew." Sylvester's expression was grave. "From the sand on her clothing and in her hair, I would guess she was killed on a beach."

Jonathan had been standing close to the window with his head bent. He looked up now, his green eyes glittering in a face that was too pale. "Someone in this room killed her and then thought it would be amusing to put her body in Lucinda's room this morning. Whoever did this, I want you to know you won't get away with it. I'm going to make you pay."

"When we are able to contact the police, you can rest assured they will do everything they can." Matt placed a hand on his shoulder but Jonathan flung furiously away from him.

"Don't touch me." Jonathan held up a shaking hand. "Don't you understand? I don't trust you. Any of you." With a sound like a wounded animal, he threw himself out of the room.

Matt turned to Sylvester. "Shall I go after him?"

Sylvester shook his head. "Give him some time alone. What's puzzling me is *why* Ellie was killed. Could she have seen or heard something she wasn't supposed to?"

"My God, Sylvester." Guthrie's hand shook as he poured himself another drink. "It's clear there's a madman—" he cast a suspicious glance in Connie's direction "—or woman in our midst, and you're trying to apply reason to what he's doing?"

"Mad or not, there has to be an explanation for all of this." Sylvester frowned, clearly making an effort to concentrate. "When Ellie disappeared, we were still able to communicate with the world outside of this island, so whoever killed her went to great trouble to make it look like she had left so the police wouldn't be called, even going to the trouble of hiding all of her belongings. To me, that suggests her death wasn't planned. She had to be disposed of in a hurry."

Matt nodded his head in agreement. "Now we can no longer contact the police, it doesn't matter. Whoever killed her doesn't care anymore. Displaying the body on Lucinda's bed looks like a deliberate attempt to scare us."

Lucinda gave a sob. "Or me. It could have been meant to frighten just me." Tears spilled over and began to trickle down her cheeks. "And it worked."

"She's going to need to change rooms." Connie spoke quietly to Vega. Although Sylvester and Roberto had covered Ellie's body in a sheet and moved it into an empty meat locker, there was no way Lucinda could be expected to return to the room where she had sustained such a shock.

"I'll see to it." Vega left the room.

Guthrie took Lucinda's arm. "Come with me. We'll go to my room until yours is ready." Slowly, with his arm around her shoulder, he led his sister from the room.

When they had gone, Sylvester sat at the table, his expression still deeply preoccupied. "I'm struggling to make any sense of this. I can't believe whoever is doing these things came to Corazón with a plan. It seems to me the plan developed after he or she arrived here."

"What makes you say that?" Connie came to sit opposite him.

"It's hard to explain. It's more a feeling than a certainty. If someone had come to Corazón with a plan to trap us all here, I just think he would have been better prepared. This feels like something that came into his mind once he was here."

"I'm not following you, Sylvester." Matt joined them at the table.

"I'm not sure I'm clear about it myself." Sylvester shook his head in frustration. "If you had arrived on Corazón with the intention of imprisoning us all here, would you have waited almost three weeks to jam the phone signals?"

"No, I suppose not." Matt looked surprised. "Or, for that matter, would I have waited and sabotaged all the means of transport at the same time? What you're saying is it almost seems like an idea that came to him once he was here on Corazón. The curse strikes again."

"Don't say that," Connie begged. Any mention of the curse sent cold fingers of dread trailing down her spine, reminding her of the malignant presence and grasping features of Sinapa, the woman who had blighted Cariña's life.

"Why not? It's true. We have a dead body, a maniac on the loose and no way of getting off this island." Matt gave a bitter laugh. "Unless one of us decides to swim more than five miles to reach the next island."

Connie gasped, raising a hand to cover her mouth. "That's it. That's why Ellie was killed." Both men looked at her in confusion. "She was a long-distance swimmer. Ellie was the one person among us who *could* have swum to the next island."

Chapter 12

Sylvester found Roberto working on the launch. "When you took the guests over to Charlotte Harbor the other day, what did they do?"

Roberto wiped his oily hands on a cloth. "They split up and went their separate ways. Lucinda went shopping, but she said she didn't buy anything interesting. She complained the shops were provincial and boring. I think Guthrie found a bar. Jonathan and Matt both wandered around and did their own thing."

"Did either of them mention what their own thing might have been?"

Roberto shook his head. "No. Jonathan never says much, anyway, but I did think he was even more quiet than usual that day. It was just after Ellie had gone missing, so it wasn't surprising. On the way back, Matt was asking me about fishing. Neither of them mentioned what they'd been doing in Charlotte Harbor. Why?"

Roberto might be an employee, but he'd worked for Sylvester for long enough, and knew him well enough, to be able to ask that question. "Just wondering if any of them could have purchased a cell phone jammer in that time."

He whistled. "I'm not sure it's the sort of thing you could just walk into a store and pick up over the counter. Not a decent one, anyway. Not that I've ever tried. But if someone had ordered one in advance, by phone or internet, to be delivered to a specific address in Charlotte Harbor, then he or she could have collected it that day. It's a small, portable item. I don't imagine he or she would have had any trouble organizing it at short notice."

"Was anyone carrying anything that could have been the jammer?"

"Sorry, boss. It could have been any one of them. They were all carrying bags with them on the way back, but I can't remember the names of the stores they'd been to. What makes you think they bought it that day?"

"Maybe I'm wrong and whoever is using it had it with them all along, but the jammer has only been used since that trip to Charlotte Harbor. And the other things—the damage to the boats and the satellite dish—all happened at the same time. I'm working on the theory this is something that came to him while he was here, rather than something he intended to do all along."

"And does that matter?" Roberto picked up a screwdriver, preparing to get back to work.

Sylvester shrugged. "Maybe not."

In many ways, it didn't matter. In any conventional sense, it made no difference at all. But this was Corazón, and Sylvester was a de León, so it mattered to him on a fundamental, primeval level. Because it meant whoever was doing this might have arrived on Corazón with no evil intentions. It meant that, over time, the curse had worked its dark magic yet again.

Corazón de Malicia. Heart of Malice.

As he walked back to the house, he drank in the tranquil beauty of his tropical island paradise. He didn't see the white sands, turquoise seas and waving palms. Instead he saw the mother of the Calusa king, her face twisted into a mask of venom as she poured out her words of hatred all those years ago. Although the image was faint, like an old black-and-white movie, he saw Cariña facing her bravely, their child on her hip, pressing the baby's face into her side so he couldn't hear the words. He saw himself—Máximo—arm outstretched, banishing the old witch from these shores. Too late. All too late. The curse was laid. The shadow of the past lay forever over this idyllic place.

Which heart have you blackened? Which troubled soul have you preyed upon?

If he was right and Connie's stalker had no idea about why he harbored feelings of rage and revenge toward her, then whoever it was would have been locked in his own special hell before he'd even arrived here. Tortured beyond belief and trying to make sense of what was going on inside his head. Bringing someone in that mental state to Corazón with all its potential for destruction… Sylvester's lips thinned at the thought.

There were two sides to his Corazón. There was the side that kept him coming back. The place he loved. The home he and Cariña had built up all those years ago. His memories of that time weren't clear, but he knew they were happy. That Corazón was a place of light and love. There had been great joy here, and there would be again when the cycle started once more. But there was also a dark underside. The bottomless darkness that opened over the pit of hell itself. It was this that had allowed the curse to thrive. This that had enabled the wreckers to take over his home and murder so many helpless souls, despite his attempts to stop them. It was this foul Corazón that, like a wild animal after prey, sensed weakness and hunted it down without mercy.

A muffled voice calling his name interrupted his thoughts. Turning his head, Sylvester looked away from the water toward the mangrove trees where he thought he had heard the sound. The noise came again, slightly louder this time. He made his way toward it just as a man stumbled out of the trees.

"Matt? My God, what the hell has happened?"

Although he said Matt's name, his friend was barely recognizable in the bloodied and bedraggled figure who fell to his knees as he reached him. Matt's clothes were torn and dirtied, his feet bare and his face and arms a mass of scratches. His left eye was swollen closed above a deep cut on his left cheekbone and his lip was split.

"Who did this to you?" Sylvester gripped Matt by his upper arm, supporting him to his feet.

"Didn't see him." The words came out stiffly through Matt's injured lip. "He came at me from behind, but even when I did get a glimpse of him, he was wearing some sort of mask."

Connie's description of her attacker came back to Sylvester. *He wore a mask.* His grip on Matt's arm must have tightened because the other man let out a yelp.

"Sorry. Why would anyone do this to you? What was the point of this attack?"

Matt attempted a laugh but it came out as a groan. "We didn't exchange pleasantries. In fact, he never said a word the whole time he was smashing his fist into my face and whipping me with a palm branch."

Sylvester still couldn't make any sense of what Matt was telling him had happened. His brain whirled with questions, but Matt needed care, not interrogation. "Let's get you back to the house. Can you walk?"

"I can try."

Refusing Sylvester's arm, Matt made his way slowly back to the house. Sylvester was pleased to observe he seemed more shaken up than badly injured. Nevertheless, as they entered the house through the open glass doors, his appearance was greeted with exclamations of horror by the other guests.

"It looks worse than it is," Matt assured Connie, who hurried forward, wrapping an arm around his waist and assisting him to a chair.

In spite of the seriousness of the situation, and the fact that the madman who had them imprisoned had struck again, Sylvester couldn't help noticing the look in Matt's eyes as Connie smoothed his hair back from his brow. *He's in love with her.* The thought struck him like a punch in the gut from a heavyweight fighter. *What am I doing, screwing with her life when she has a chance at a future with one of the best men I know?*

The clouds were like gray mountains looming large and mushroom-like on the horizon and the oppressive heat spiraled ever upward during the day. There was no breeze and the sea was unnaturally calm.

"Storm brewing," Vega warned, shaking her head. "And it looks like a bad one."

By late afternoon the sky was black and the wind had risen from nowhere. Lightning danced out from a dangerously low cloud and thunder was an ominous, continuous drumroll. When the rain came, it was almost horizontal, slapping against the palm trees, attempting to wash away the sand from the beach and bouncing straight up from the patio.

Watching from the sliding-glass door, Connie thought the sea appeared to be boiling. The pressure in the atmosphere was relentless, matching that inside the house. Nature seemed to be trying to do her best to replicate or even outdo the human drama. Somehow this wildness was more fitted to the mood than the brilliant sunshine and calm skies of the past few days.

Connie gazed at the lightning as it lit up the darkened heavens, revealing ghostly shapes within the rolling clouds. If only she could blame those imaginary beings for what was happening here on Corazón. It wouldn't be as scary as believing someone inside this house was responsible for what was going on. That someone they sat and ate dinner with had killed Ellie and was plotting more deaths.

There was a certain inevitability about the moment when the electricity failed. Connie recalled Ellie's comments about 1930s detective novels. *Of course the lights have to go out. We need to be plunged into darkness. The mood isn't eerie enough. Candlelight is exactly what is needed to add to the suspenseful ambience.* Satire didn't help. Like the lamps themselves, her thoughts refused to brighten.

She remained by the door until Vega bustled into the room carrying a lit candle and bearing several unlit ones. "This happens every time there is a storm," the housekeeper said in a long-suffering voice, setting out candle holders around the room. "Roberto will be working on the generator already, I'm sure."

Vega used the candle she was holding to light the others and a warm, flickering glow suffused the room. Connie wished she could have found it comforting. Her low mood had nothing to do with the storm or even the bizarre events of the last few days. She had the strangest feeling Sylvester was avoiding her. It wasn't anything she could be specific about. Instead, it was a slight distance, a withdrawal from her that was more intuitive than physical. She was concerned that, with less than a week before his birthday, he was preparing for the time when he must leave her in reality. Her heart, already just about as heavy as it could get, was weighed down with grief and pain. Losing Sylvester before she needed to would turn it to lead.

A sound inside the room made her turn away from her contemplation of the turbulent view beyond the window to find Sylvester regarding her. His expression was inscrutable.

"Corazón knows how to throw a party." He nodded as the skies lit up with another wild streak of lightning and thunder rumbled its ominous warning.

"It's beautiful in a raw, savage way. Nature is showing us how insignificant we are." He came to stand next to her and Connie leaned her head against his shoulder. Sylvester remained still, and fear struck her again. She was so in tune with him, she could sense his turmoil.

"Everyone else is taking refuge in their rooms."

"How is he?" She knew he had been to check on Matt, even though his friend seemed to be fine. Matt had been right about his injuries looking worse than they were. Once he'd cleaned himself up and changed out of his ruined clothes, the marks on his body were mostly deep scratches to the left side. His face, although bruised and cut, had escaped any broken bones. He seemed reluctant to discuss the matter, something Connie put down to that unfathomable thing known as masculine pride.

Sylvester didn't answer immediately. When he did,

it was with another question. "Does anything about the attack on Matt strike you as strange, Connie?"

She lifted her head to look at him, but the light from the candles gave her only an outline of his features. "What do you mean?"

He lifted one shoulder in an impatient gesture. "Maybe I'm letting this whole thing get to me. It just doesn't add up. Even masked, this attacker was taking a huge risk going after one of us in broad daylight. What if Matt had been able to fight him off or pull the mask off? The game would have been up immediately. And I can't see why Matt couldn't identify him even with the mask. Jonathan is tall and slim. I'm a similar height, but more muscular. Guthrie is short and stocky."

"You think Matt could be lying?" Connie asked.

"I'm not going that far, but there are other things that puzzle me. What did the attacker gain from this? Matt isn't seriously hurt. He's not even particularly alarmed. I think his pride has taken more of a beating than anything else. What did the attacker hope to gain?"

Connie considered the question. "Maybe to warn us he can hurt any of us anytime he chooses?"

"If that's the case, wouldn't you think he has subtler and more effective means at his disposal?" They remained silent for a few moments, both trying to probe the mind of the man who had them at his mercy. Sylvester's next words were murmured into Connie's hair. "Matt is in love with you. Did you know that?"

"I know he is attracted to me. I'm not sure it's love. He barely knows me."

He slid his fingertips under her chin, tilting her face up to his. "It's love. Could this attack have been his way of shifting your attention from me to him?"

She frowned. "You think he faked the attack to get my sympathy? That doesn't sound like Matt."

"You're right. He's not an attention seeker. This whole situation is making me crazy."

Connie drew a breath. It was time to confront the real issue between them. "Is that why you've been so remote with me?"

His face was illuminated by a brilliant flash of lightning and she caught a glimpse of the anguish in his expression before the darkness engulfed him once more. "Connie, trying to remain remote from you would be like trying to keep myself apart from my own soul. But by being with you, am I being fair to you? I'll be gone from here soon. Nothing can stop that happening. Maybe you should think about what happens after I've left." The next words were wrenched from him. "Perhaps your future includes someone like Matt."

Connie reached up and placed her hands on each side of his face. The electrical charge in the atmosphere was nothing to the spark that flashed through her body every time she touched Sylvester. "We didn't choose this magic we have, Sylvester. It chose us. I love you and I can't turn off or redirect those feelings just because there might be an easier way. I can't…and I don't want to. I know my heart will be broken in a few days' time. It breaks every time I think of losing you, but I would rather have a few precious hours with you than a lifetime with someone else."

With a sound close to a sob, Sylvester hauled her into his arms, fitting her body so tight against his that not even a pinprick of light could slide between them.

The dawn light showed the aftermath of the storm and Connie stood beside Sylvester on the balcony outside his room, surveying the damage. Corazón had withstood much worse and, although a few palm trees had snapped in two like matchsticks, the tranquility of the island was otherwise undisturbed.

"The house itself has only ever taken a direct hit once. That was during Emilio's time, when a fierce storm damaged part of the roof. It took a lot of work to restore it."

Connie was wearing just his shirt and nothing else, and the sight of her long, bare legs as she leaned over the balustrade was distracting Sylvester. Her next words drew his attention back to her face. There was a slight frown in the golden depths of her eyes. "Were you Emilio?"

"I was." He took her hand in his. "I have been here since Máximo bought this island from the Calusa king in the 1520s. Not King Yargua, of course. I doubt he would have been willing to sell me the island. But, when Cariña and I returned to Florida after we were married, Yargua was dead and his successor was happy to take Spanish gold in exchange for the most remote of his islands. I have been the head of the house of de León since that date, Connie. I have had different names, of course, but I have been the same person throughout the centuries."

The frown deepened. "But Emilio was evil."

"No. People *said* Emilio was evil. There is a difference."

"So, the lighthouse, the wreckers…that was all just a story? But I could feel the emotion of what happened when we were at the lighthouse."

"Oh, it happened. Just not the way history paints it. There was a time when these islands—the chain known as Corona de Perlas—although geographically miles apart, were more closely linked. The families who lived on them formed a political alliance against any outside attack. Corazón, as the largest and most strategically placed, was highly prized. As a group, the families collaborated on the building of the lighthouse. It was to serve two purposes. It would warn sailors about the treacherous rocks here on Corazón and also act as an early warning if ever the islands came under attack." Sylvester allowed his mind to take him back to a time he preferred not to think about. The darkest time in Corazón's dark history.

"There was a very ambitious leader on one of the other islands, a man called Marco Alvarez. I—Emilio—fell ill. It was smallpox and I wasn't expected to live." He laughed. "Of course I was going to live. But I was the only person who knew that.

"With no wife to nurse me, my recovery was a long and difficult one. Alvarez offered to help by assisting with the running of Corazón. I had no choice but to accept his offer. When I was well enough to take control of my own affairs, I discovered what was going on at the lighthouse.

"He had used my absence to bring a team of wreckers onto Corazón. They had already murdered hundreds of innocent people in my name. To ensure my silence, Alvarez had been placing large sums of money, spoils from the wrecks, in the Corazón coffers. It looked as though Emilio was the instigator of the wrecking activity. They were difficult times. If I spoke out against Alvarez, I allowed others to see that I wasn't strong enough to run my own affairs. I risked a possible invasion of Corazón by one of the other de Perlas leaders. All I could do was close down the lighthouse as fast as I could. From then on, Corazón had little to do with the other islands." His face hardened at the memory. "And nothing at all to do with Siguiente, the island home of Marco Alvarez."

"It's been bothering me ever since you said you had always been the head of the house of de León. I knew you must have been Emilio, yet I knew you couldn't be evil." Connie slid her arms around his waist. "You said Emilio had no wife?"

"Having found perfection with Cariña, I never married again." Sylvester gave a soft laugh. "It wasn't as if I needed an heir. I always knew who the next head of the house would be."

When Connie lifted her face to his, her eyes were filled with tears. "So you have been alone all this time?"

"I could never replicate what we had. And I had my memories of my life with Cariña—with you."

"But you've been lonely."

He looked down into those shimmering dark eyes. Eyes that seemed to draw his soul into their golden depths. "Yes, I've been lonely." He had never known how much until now.

Connie rose on the tips of her toes, wrapping her arms around his neck and pressing herself flush against him.

Sylvester shuddered, grinding his mouth down on hers as he crushed her even tighter against him. Holding her like this stripped him of every defense, of his power to think. When he could taste her and feel her, she pounded in his blood, his heart, his brain and his cock. And the centuries melted away. The hurt, the loneliness, the longing, the pain. All of those things ceased to matter. The fear of what was to come, the unknown, that step into the void, only affected him because it must tear him away from this perfection.

"God, Connie." He lifted her, feeling the silken warmth of her buttocks beneath his fingertips, and she wrapped her legs around his waist.

He knew there was no way he could take those few steps to the bedroom. Not with only his zipper between her soft, wet warmth and his throbbing erection. Connie rocked impatiently against him as he fumbled himself free, found a condom in his pocket and managed—despite his overwhelming need—to hold on to her and get it on before pushing inside her. And then he was lost in a rush of sweet sensation.

Throwing his head back, he murmured a soft curse. Being inside her was always incredible, overwhelming. Nothing mattered except this, here, now. The point where their bodies connected and the wild stream of heat that thrilled through him. A flood of pleasure so intense it was painful. Holding her against him, he thrust into her, losing himself in her as deep and as hard as he could. Over and over. Never enough.

Connie nuzzled his neck, murmuring his name as the first waves of orgasm hit her, and Sylvester felt his climax wash over him, taking him, claiming him, drowning him. It took forever to come back down from that high. Still inside her, he carried Connie through to the bedroom. Lowering her to the bed, he eased himself down on top of her and held her there.

"What you said just now—" her voice was husky "—was that true? There has been no one else in five hundred years? Not one of those women in the newspapers?"

Keeping his weight on one elbow, he brushed her hair back from her brow with his other hand. "Not one of them."

"My God, Sylvester." She reached up a hand and

cupped his face, her eyes darkening with emotion. Her delicate lips were parted, her hair wild, her cheeks still flushed. She flipped his world upside down every time he looked at her. Celibacy had been an easy choice for a man who had never wanted anyone else. There had only been her for him.

"After I lost Cariña, it was as if there was a huge weight pressing down on my chest. As if from then on I carried a giant stone around with me everywhere in place of my heart. Everything was an effort. It was as if I had to remind myself to take my next breath. And the worst part of all was that I knew I would have to go on endlessly without her. I wouldn't have just one lifetime to miss her, but so many. Those fresh waves of grief that hit you over and over? I've had five hundred years' worth of them."

"The things you did years ago, the daredevil, dangerous things...were they your way of trying to join her?" Connie placed her head on his chest, exactly where that imaginary stone had been. Except, with her soft cheek there, the centuries-old agony was magically erased.

"It sounds foolish now, doesn't it? Climbing Everest, trekking to the North Pole, flying single-handed around the world, climbing the sheer face of El Sendero Luminoso without a rope, using just my bare hands..." He listed some of his exploits. "I was challenging fate. Pushing this immortality thing to its limits. Seeing if I could overthrow it. There are people who spend fortunes larger than mine chasing everlasting life. But all I have ever wanted was to be a normal person. To live a normal life. Die a natural death." His chest expanded painfully as he stroked her hair. "Without Cariña, I wasn't alive. I was merely existing."

Connie lifted her head, the light from her eyes pouring into his, her whole heart in her gaze. Those eyes saw everything. They knew him, understood him, empathized with all that he was and all that he'd been through. The intensity of her feelings stripped Sylvester of everything, leaving him shaking and raw, leaving him feeling as though they had both walked over hot coals to reach this moment. All he could do was cling to her, murmuring her name over and over.

Gradually the storm of emotion subsided, but before either of them could do or say anything more, there was a furious pounding on the door and Matt's voice, higher pitched than usual and slightly panicky, reached them.

"Sylvester, come quick. It's Jonathan."

Chapter 13

Jonathan lay unconscious near the door of his room. His bed hadn't been slept in and he was still dressed in the same clothes he'd been wearing at dinner the night before. He appeared to have sustained a brutal and bloody beating. The windows to the balcony were open, the curtains blowing slightly in the breeze.

Roberto, having been roused from his bed, checked him over where he lay. "He's been battered about the head and body. I'm no expert, but I'd say with something other than fists, some sort of blunt object. It looks like he's taken several blows to the head," he told Sylvester. "His vital signs, pulse and heart rate, appear to be fine, but I don't know what internal damage has been done. Under normal circumstances, I'd say let's get him to a hospital, but, since that bastard has us trapped here..."

"What can we do for him?" After exchanging Sylvester's shirt for her own clothes, Connie had made her way to Jonathan's room.

"Let's make him as comfortable as we can." Roberto set about removing Jonathan's shoes, tie, jacket and trousers. Then, between them, he and Sylvester lifted the other man, dressed only in his underwear, onto the bed. Connie arranged the bedclothes over him and fetched a wet cloth from the bathroom. She thought his eyelids flickered slightly when she placed it on his forehead. When he showed no further signs of coming around, she decided it must be her imagination and didn't mention it to her companions.

"What made you come to his room?" Sylvester asked Matt.

"My own room is next door. I'd just woken up when I heard a noise—a sort of loud thud—and, after everything that's happened, I was suspicious. I knocked on Jonathan's door. When I didn't get an answer after knocking a few times, I decided I'd rather barge in and risk annoying him than leave it and find out later that something awful had happened."

"It's a good thing you did," Connie said with a shudder. "Just imagine if you'd gone away and he'd been lying here even longer."

Sylvester frowned. "But he must have been attacked last night. He was still fully dressed and he hadn't been to bed. If he's been lying here unconscious all night, what was the thud you heard?"

"I don't know. Maybe he regained consciousness, was trying to get help and fell again?" Matt suggested.

"Is that possible?" Sylvester turned to Roberto.

"From his injuries, I'd have said not, but I suppose anything is possible."

Connie had a horrible thought. "Sylvester, you don't suppose the attacker came back again? Maybe he attacked Jonathan last night and returned this morning but Matt disturbed him?"

She had a mental image of her stalker, masked and

silent. For once, she didn't picture him attacking her. Instead he was beating Jonathan into unconsciousness. Maybe he thought he had killed him? Had he gone away, been unsure and come back to check? Finding him still alive, had he intended to finish the job but been driven out onto the balcony and into jumping over when Matt began pounding on the door?

Her skin prickled, then cooled with the sickly sweat of nausea. Her pulse seemed to take over her body, sending the blood pounding too quickly to her head, so she had to lean forward to get rid of the sudden dizzy feeling. *I will not let him do this to me. He is not in control of my life.* The unspoken words steadied her and she was able to look up again. When she did, Matt's eyes were on her face and she met them squarely. *Don't you dare ask if I'm okay.* He must have seen the flash of fire in her expression because he quickly looked away again.

"Has anyone checked on Guthrie and Lucinda?" Sylvester's words raised the prospect of a new specter. What if Jonathan wasn't the only person the attacker had visited in the night?

"I'll go." Matt hurried away. Seconds later they heard him knocking on doors.

When he returned a few minutes later, it was with good news. "They both slept soundly once the storm was over and didn't hear anything unusual last night."

With a feeling of relief, Connie turned back to Jonathan. As she ran the cool cloth over his brow again, his eyelids fluttered and he gave a soft groan. "He's coming around!"

"Thank God." Sylvester hurried to her side.

"What the—?" Jonathan opened his eyes, groaned louder and closed them again.

"You were attacked," Connie told him. "Try to lie still."

"I don't think I can do anything else." He gave a shaky laugh. "My head hurts like hell."

"Can you remember what happened?" Sylvester asked.

Jonathan opened his eyes again. "I remember coming up here with Matt after dinner—"

He was interrupted as Matt gave a sudden shout and ran toward the balcony. This action drew everyone's attention away from what Jonathan was saying.

"Stay here." Sylvester spoke urgently over his shoulder to Connie as he and Roberto followed Matt.

That familiar prickle started to work its way up from the base of her spine, heating her flesh. *He is here and he's playing his games.* She could hear the three men talking on the balcony, but couldn't quite catch what they were saying. There was clearly no big altercation going on. They hadn't captured any intruder.

"I don't remember anything more," Jonathan said. "Nothing at all."

When the others returned, Matt looked sheepish. "I'm sure I saw a shadow on the balcony. An outline of a man's shape. If he was there at all, he was too fast for me."

Sylvester looked slightly skeptical, as though he thought Matt might have been jumping at shadows.

Connie gripped her hands tightly together. Whatever Matt had seen when he'd dashed toward the balcony, she had felt the stalker's presence in that instant. It was hard to believe he would be bold enough to come back again, climbing onto the balcony in broad daylight, knowing there could be other people in Jonathan's room.

Dear Lord, could he have been here all the time, listening to us, knowing what we were doing and saying? The thought sent a fresh wave of fear thrilling through her and only Sylvester's clear blue eyes, steady on her face, anchored her, grounded her and allowed her to continue with some pretense of normality.

With the immediate drama over, attention switched back to Jonathan. He was a pitiful sight, the unbruised areas of his face as white as the sheets he lay on. "I can't remember a damn thing after I came into my room." He winced as he tried to turn his head to look at Matt. "I can't even remember what we were talking about before we said good-night."

"Nor can I. It was idle chitchat, I think."

Sylvester drew Connie and Matt aside while Roberto checked Jonathan over more thoroughly. Matt ran a hand through his already disordered hair. "Is he picking us off one by one? What's the point of that? To frighten us, enrage us, drive us crazy?"

"All of those," Sylvester said. "This attack was worse than the one on you, so maybe we can expect the next one, if it comes, to be worse again. We have to put a stop to his games."

"That's exactly what he does. He plays games." Connie gave a soft moan and he slid an arm around her waist. "But he won't stop until he gets to me."

Sylvester's fingers tightened, gripping her hard against him. "He'll have to go through me before he can get to you."

Even though neither of them said it aloud, Connie knew they were both thinking the same thing. Sylvester would be gone in four days.

Despite everything that was going on, there were aspects of the de León family history that fascinated and puzzled Connie. She supposed it was because, through Cariña, she was caught up in it now.

"Did you have to reinvent a new identity for yourself each lifetime so that no one became suspicious of you?" she asked Sylvester as they walked along the edge of the water watching the moonlight dance on the waves.

"Yes," Sylvester said. "I haven't been reborn each time. I have simply lived on…and on. But, I reasoned that I couldn't always be Máximo de León. Instead, every seventy years or so, I changed my name. I didn't just do it on a whim. I would change my servants, go off on a voyage for a while. Return as the new head of the family. It was easier in a world where there was no record-keeping or regulation. This time, it has been harder. Sylvester de León will disappear soon, and that will cause problems. Particularly as Sylvester de León has never actually existed. I'm trusting Arthur Reynolds to make everything right."

"If you have always been the head of the house, what happened to Máximo and Cariña's children?"

"Máximo became very wealthy. Through him, the de León fortune extended beyond Corazón to the other de Perlas islands. His children went on to found their own dynasties."

"I wonder if they ever questioned why their father never aged."

"I guess they put it down to good genes." Sylvester laughed. "And the magic of Corazón." His face became serious. "Once they were adults, they didn't remain on the island, so none of them was around long enough to question why I didn't age."

Connie frowned. "Didn't it become strange for you when Cariña *did* age? When you were still a young man but she was an old woman?"

"My memories of that time aren't clear enough for me to answer that. Apart from the lifetime I am living now, I have only vague recollections, snippets of what has happened during the many years of my life. I remember everything that has happened to Sylvester, but my life as Máximo or Emilio is less clear. Sometimes it gets annoying, like when you try to remember the name of a film or a song title and it just won't come to you. When you try to force it, it becomes more elusive." He stopped, catching her by the hand, so she turned to face him. "I know how much I loved Cariña...loved you, love you still. I never dreamed that I would see you again. Not until I returned to Valladolid. These few weeks, having you here, having love in my life again after so long, has been the most amazing gift. Many men have older wives, and it would have been a gradual change, something that crept up on us. What I know for sure is the hardest part was losing her."

The hurt in his eyes when he spoke of losing Cariña told her all she needed to know about the end of the first part of their love story. They might never know why she had been reborn now and not at any other time during the last five hundred years. Perhaps it was part of some plan Corazón had for them, or maybe it was an accident of time and fate. Puzzling over these things only seemed to create more questions. It was a timely reminder that this part of their story was drawing to a close. Each time she thought about it, the hurt was as fresh and raw as the first time. *I will never grow used to this pain. Never accept that he must be taken from me this way. Even when I am old and gray, I will never say, "It was meant to be."*

"If we had stayed in Valladolid..." She wasn't sure where the words came from, or even what they meant.

She couldn't see Sylvester's eyes because the moonlight shadowed his features, but she sensed their warmth on her face.

"You sound just like her. Even though Florida was her home, Cariña loved the old house at Valladolid. But, for so many reasons, staying there wasn't an option. Firstly, it was as if we were always meant to return here. The pull of Corazón was too strong for us to resist. And, in spite of everything, this has been my home for a very long time." He turned and they both looked up at the beautiful, golden building. It looked like a house of happy endings. How could it lie to them? How could it let things turn out so badly?

"Secondly, there was danger for Cariña in Valladolid. It was the capital of Castile, home of the Spanish Inquisition. Although she attended Mass, she was an outsider and the strange story of her traveling across the world to join Máximo attracted attention. It only needed a wrong word and trouble, greater than a Calusa curse, would have been headed her way."

Connie smiled. "And let's not forget the third reason."

"Third reason?"

"That you, Máximo de León y Soledad—" calling him by that name sent a frisson of pleasure down her spine "—are an adventurer. One who couldn't resist the lure of this 'new world.'"

"Ah, yes. *That* reason. I'd almost forgotten about that." He gave a soft laugh. "And we returned with Spanish gold. It enabled us to buy this island, and later others in the de Perlas chain, from the Calusa. As the Calusa numbers dwindled, the king who followed Yargua withdrew his chiefs from this part of his realm. He was glad to receive our money in return for these lands."

"You built up quite an empire in those early days."

"All for nothing. Although Máximo and Cariña's children each inherited their own islands, their descendants traveled farther afield, to Spain and Cuba. The curse took everything over time. Gradually the old woman's words took shape. None of them were bad people, but their hearts weren't pure enough to withstand the curse. We had everything except good fortune." His voice was hollow. "That's why the de León family dwindled over the centuries and I'm forced now to turn to strangers when I make my will."

"Where did your immortality come from?" It was a question Connie had wondered about ever since he had told her.

"I don't know. I wondered if Sinapa cursed me with immortality when she cursed the de León family. But I will disappear on Sylvester's thirtieth birthday and turn up on Máximo's thirtieth birthday in 1521. Sylvester doesn't exist after that and Máximo doesn't exist before that. I'm not born and I don't die. I don't see how Yargua's mother could have worked her magic on me to make that happen when she hadn't met Máximo until he arrived here."

"So you could lose this memory of our time together once you return to Valladolid?" Connie said. "In the same way you have lost parts of the last five hundred years."

His face was sad. "I hope the magic allows me to capture at least something of this time. As for the rest, I don't understand any of it. I just know how it is meant to be."

Connie stood on the tips of her toes to brush his lips with hers. "That's the point of magic. You don't get to understand it."

His hands on her waist were warm and firm through the thin cotton of her dress. "There is magic every time I look at you and I understand that. It's called love."

"Charmer." She teased her tongue along his lower lip, delighting in his indrawn breath and the tensing of his muscles.

They turned and walked back the way they had come. Dinner had been a subdued meal. After the attack on Jonathan, Guthrie had insisted he and Lucinda eat in his room. They would not be leaving its safety, he had informed Sylvester, until a boat arrived that could take them off the island.

Jonathan had sustained two broken ribs in the attack, but it was his head injuries that worried Roberto most.

"This wasn't like the attack on Matt. Jonathan wasn't meant to recover from this," Roberto had said, his usually pleasant face serious, after he had finished examining Jonathan. "And I don't think he's out of trouble yet."

Roberto had moved into Jonathan's room to care for him and had joined Sylvester, Connie and Matt at dinner. Juan had declined an invitation, choosing to eat in the kitchen with Vega instead.

"There must be someone hiding on the island." Roberto had been insistent. "It's the only possible explanation."

"We've searched everywhere," Sylvester had said.

"That just means we haven't found his hiding place. Yet."

The house was silent now as they entered, even though it was still early. It would be easy to follow Guthrie and Lucinda's example and remain locked away until they were able to leave the island. But Connie refused to spend her last few days with Sylvester in hiding.

She headed toward the stairs, but Sylvester took her hand and turned toward a room she hadn't been in until now. "This is my study." He opened the door and flicked on the light. "I don't pretend to be an artist, but I painted this many years ago from memory."

He stepped back so she could view the picture on the wall. Set in a plain wooden frame, it depicted a very old, very beautiful, house built of rose-colored brick. Fading sunlight just touched the terra-cotta roof tiles and the wrought-iron rails of the uppermost balconies. Although this house was the grandest, it clearly formed part of a square of other homes, and Connie glimpsed the spire of a church in the background.

That tingling feeling of a memory that was more than remembrance came back to her again. This time it was like a warm embrace. Briefly, she heard the cries of street vendors in the town square, felt the dusty Spanish heat and smelled the scent of the orange groves. She turned to Sylvester with shining eyes.

"It's the old house at Valladolid."

"In a few days' time, when I am gone, I want you to have this picture."

Unable to speak, she crossed the distance between them and was swept into his arms.

Connie opened her eyes, unsure what had woken her. All she knew was that it wasn't a dream this time. She had been sleeping soundly when her eyes flew suddenly open. Used to sensing danger, she had never before woken so abruptly or with such certainty that there was someone in the room.

She was so sure menace lurked in the dark corners of Sylvester's bedroom that she didn't even allow the gasp that rose in her throat to escape her lips. Instead, barely breathing, she tamped down the panic that threatened to consume her and lay still, allowing her eyes to roam over the shapes and shadows.

There! Near the open balcony door…the door that had been closed when she'd fallen asleep in Sylvester's arms. The slightest shift, so subtle it was barely a movement at all, caught her eye. Her instinct for peril had been right. Someone was in the room. Tired of haunting her dreams, her stalker had returned to her reality at last.

Inching her fingertips across the space toward to Sylvester, she reached for his hand, intending to wake him. Relief flooded through her when he lightly gripped her fingers with his, warning and reassuring her at the same time. He was awake and as aware of the intruder as she was.

When the stalker sprang, it was fast, and it wasn't in the direction Connie expected. He didn't come for her. Fluid, merging with the darkness, the attacker launched himself at Sylvester. By the light of a thin streak of moonlight sneaking through a gap in the drapes, Connie caught a glimpse of a knife blade and cried out in terror.

Around her the shadows erupted and Connie strained her eyes to make out what was happening. Her hand hovered over the lamp switch. If she illuminated the scene, would she help Sylvester or risk giving the advantage to the stalker? He was the one with a weapon; if he could see, it would make Sylvester an easier target. In the end, she decided darkness might work in Sylvester's favor. All she could do was hope she was right. That, and try to get to the door so she could raise the alarm.

Sliding from the bed, she crouched low, grateful she had fallen asleep wearing a tank top and her underwear. Perhaps modesty wasn't important at a time like this, but she was glad she didn't have to knock on doors and attempt to cover her nakedness while she asked Matt or Roberto for help.

Her eyes were growing more accustomed to the darkness now and she could make out two distinct figures engaged in a desperate fight. As she made a dive for the door, one of the men turned his head and looked her way with a snarling sound. Although she couldn't see his face, she knew who he was. He had been her constant companion for the last four years. The thought caused her to freeze.

"Run, Connie." Sylvester's words brought the stalker's attention back to him and the knife gleamed briefly in the attacker's hand before making a deadly downward arc.

Sylvester's guttural cry told Connie the worst had happened. He had been stabbed. She had no idea how bad it was. Her impulse was to go to him, no matter what danger might be waiting for her. Her own safety didn't matter. She couldn't leave Sylvester, not if he was hurt.

"Connie, go..." Sylvester's voice was breathless, urgent.

With a strangled sob, she reached for the handle, just as the door flew open. Light flooded the room and Roberto was framed in the doorway, clad only in sweatpants. His black hair stood up in every direction as though he had just woken.

"Something woke me, almost like someone shaking me awake. Then I heard a noise. Someone cried out..."

Before Connie could move, the masked intruder covered the distance between them. His hand drew back and the knife, already red with Sylvester's blood, plunged hilt-deep into Roberto's stomach.

Roberto crumpled in a helpless heap on the floor.

Sylvester, his shoulder and arm drenched with blood, staggered forward and swung the bedside lamp with both hands. It crashed into the stalker's back, toppling him forward on top of Roberto.

"Get his mask off." Swaying on the spot, Sylvester's complexion was gray, his features etched with pain and shock. He was clearly having trouble staying upright, let alone speaking.

"I can't." The words came out as a terrified whisper. After all this time, she couldn't touch him, couldn't bear to look into his eyes. She dreaded learning the final, awful truth of who he was. This man had controlled her life for so long. He controlled it still. Her body refused to make a move in his direction, urging her instead to follow her instincts and flee from him once more. Four years of conditioning were too much to overcome. Her natural motion was away from him not toward him.

As Sylvester lost consciousness, Connie ran from the room, attempting to call out for Matt and Guthrie. No matter how hard she tried, the sound that left her lips was no more than a croak. After a few attempts, she caught her breath, her desperate footsteps slowing to a halt. *Wait. What am I doing?* No matter how afraid she was, she had left Sylvester and Roberto while they were helpless with the stalker...and the knife.

She had no more than a split second to think. Keep going and get help or go back? Did she choose fear or love? Taking a deep breath, she turned around, making her way back along the corridor to Sylvester's room. Fear, cold and visceral, held her tightly in its grip, but she remembered all the times she had told herself she wouldn't allow *him* to defeat her. That she would rather be dead. A tiny moan escaped her. *Me. Not Sylvester. Don't let Sylvester be dead.*

Almost afraid to look, she pressed her shoulders to the wall, risking a swift glance around the door frame. Roberto lay still, exactly as he had fallen, the knife still protruding from his stomach. He didn't appear to be breathing. Sylvester was on his hands and knees, slowly attempting to get to his feet.

The stalker was gone.

Chapter 14

The world swam dangerously out of focus as Sylvester leaned heavily on Connie and they made their way to the bathroom. He eased himself down onto the commode, his good hand flat against the tiled wall for support.

"Roberto?" If he could find the energy, he'd have cursed the weak note in his voice.

"He's dead, Sylvester." Her voice broke on a tiny sob and he sensed the effort it was taking her to hold herself together.

He bowed his head, thinking of the man who had worked for him for the last twenty years. The man who had been more friend than employee. "Are you sure?"

"I'm sure. You blacked out again as you tried to get to your feet. I knew that at least you were alive then, so I left you for a few minutes while I checked on Roberto. He has no pulse." She swallowed hard, clearly fighting back the memory. Bending her head, she examined the deep gash that ran from the shoulder to the elbow of his left arm. "I don't want to leave you alone, but I need more than just water to tend to this. I need to get Roberto's medical kit from Jonathan's room."

"Can you clean me up for now, then we can go together to Jonathan's room?"

She nodded. Opening the medicine cabinet, she found painkillers and shook two out of the bottle. Pouring water into a glass, she held the pills out to him. "Take these."

His hand shook as he accepted the water from her and Connie closed her fingers around his, lifting the glass with him so he could drink without spilling the cold liquid all over himself. He swallowed the pills, leaning his head back against the tiles as Connie took the glass away. The bathroom he knew so well kept swimming out of focus. Shock or blood loss? He wasn't sure which. Maybe it was a combination of both.

"I heal fast," he said as Connie soaked a washcloth and, kneeling between his knees, began to clean the blood from his torso. He attempted a smile. "Immortality has its compensations."

The tears she'd been trying so hard to keep in check began to roll down her cheeks at those words. "When I thought I'd lost you just now, it hurt more than anything I could ever have imagined. And in a few days' time, I get to do it all again for real."

She rested her forehead on his now-clean chest, and he brought his good arm up to stroke her hair. After a few moments of this indulgence, Connie seemed refreshed and returned to her task. "Did you get any sense of who he was?"

Sylvester hissed a sharp breath in as she began to clean the wound itself. The action gave him a moment to collect his thoughts. Had he recognized his attacker? No. Did he know who he was? *Know* was too strong.

Did he have an idea? Yes. Was he ready to share it? That was a whole other question. "It all happened so fast. I just wish I'd been able to knock him out with that lamp."

"I couldn't take his mask off when you asked me to." Her voice was low and anguished. "I couldn't touch him."

He ducked his head, attempting to look at her face. "I understand, Connie. Really, I do."

"Each of the men on the island, except Juan, has been attacked now," she said as she continued to thoroughly swab the gash.

"So we have."

"Don't you think that makes it more likely it is a stranger? Someone, as Roberto said, who is hiding on the island. *Not* one of us?"

Sylvester could tell how desperately she wanted it not to be someone she knew. He wished she was right. His own gut feeling was telling him she wasn't. Since all he had right now was a hunch and a tingling down his spine, he remained silent.

"This will need stitches." Connie studied his arm, her usually golden complexion appearing pale under the overhead lighting.

"It may not." At her look of inquiry, he explained. "My healing powers really are remarkable." When he pushed himself up from the commode, he was pleased to find his knees were steady. He glanced down at his blood-soaked boxer briefs. "Maybe I should change out of these and then we'll disturb Jonathan so you can dress this injury."

They made their way through to the bedroom, pausing beside Roberto's body. Connie fetched a throw from the bed and covered Roberto with it.

"He only came to see if he could help." Her lower lip trembled at the memory. "He didn't stand a chance."

Sylvester welcomed the rush of anger he felt, because in its wake it brought a return of his strength. Whoever had tortured Connie for the last four years clearly thought he could use the same cowardly tactics against them all. He thought of the proud Calusa king. Hiding behind a mask while terrorizing a lone woman? Holding a group of helpless people hostage to get his revenge? Was that really the style of a fearsome warrior? They might have crossed several centuries to get to this point, but he didn't believe Yargua, the Calusa ruler he had encountered all those years ago, would stoop to this. If he could appeal to the Calusa behind the modern-day man, could he put an end to this insanity? He would relish the chance to try.

Connie helped him remove his bloodstained underwear and slip on a pair of sweatpants. Jonathan was sleeping soundly when they crept into his room, but he woke when Sylvester switched on the light. Although he was disoriented, Jonathan struggled into a sitting position and exclaimed in horror at Sylvester's injury.

"I can't believe this is happening." Jonathan's face was swollen and bruised beyond recognition. "We've joked about detective stories and horror films, but what we are living through is scarier than any plot I've ever heard of."

And the truth behind it all is stranger than any fiction. "It's even worse," Sylvester said. "Roberto is dead."

"What?" Matt appeared in the doorway, his own face registering shock. "I heard voices and came to see if I could help. My God, Sylvester, what the hell has been going on here?"

"Before I explain anything, can you fetch Guthrie and Juan?" Despite the horrified expressions of those around him, Sylvester did his best to keep his voice steady. "They are the only able-bodied men here right now."

Connie helped him into Jonathan's bathroom. "You can't seriously think Guthrie or Juan did this?"

"I don't know what to think." It was true. His suspicions couldn't be true. "But I said he would have to go through me to get to you, and that's exactly what he just tried to do. We need to put a guard around you, Connie."

She looked slightly queasy, but didn't answer him. Instead she found Roberto's medical kit. "This is going to hurt," she warned.

Sylvester gripped the sink hard as she poured antiseptic onto a washcloth and swabbed the wound. Beads of sweat broke out on his brow and he jerked violently at the stinging sensation.

Connie bit her lip, clearly distressed at having to cause him pain. The knife had penetrated deep, tearing through flesh and muscle as his assailant ripped into his arm with full force. It was a devastating injury. On any other man, it would need extensive medical care and might even lead to permanent damage to the nerves in that arm. For Sylvester, it would mean a few days of pain before he healed fully.

Having thoroughly cleaned the wound to prevent any infection, Connie put dressings in place, securing them with medical tape.

"You would make a very good nurse," Sylvester told her, flexing his arm, when she had finished.

"Don't make jokes. When I think about how close you came…" Her eyes filled with tears again.

He drew her into the crook of his good arm, holding

her against the warmth of his body. They had both sustained a severe shock, but it was worse for Connie, because this was all about her. Even though she had lived with this nightmare for so long, the bottom line was that this madman wanted her. But he wanted to watch her suffer before he killed her. The stalker might tell himself this was about past life revenge, and maybe that was how it had started. Somewhere along the way, this twisted game had become something else. Something he was enjoying. Not anymore. Sylvester held Connie's trembling body close to his side and inhaled the clean, fresh scent of her hair. *This ends*, he vowed. *Before I leave here, this game will be over.*

The fear that had pulsed in the air before the attack on Sylvester and Roberto had been cranked up to fever pitch. The stalker had led them to the abyss of his obsession and left them staring over the edge. Corazón, the paradise island, had become their prison. Everything about it was tainted. Even the early morning sunlight rising over the golden sands seemed sinister; the birds appeared to be singing a song of warning, and the scent of the flowers was sickly and poisonous.

They sat huddled together in Jonathan's room listening as Sylvester and Connie told the story of what had happened during the night. The awful truth had to be faced. One by one, they were being hunted by a madman. At least they knew for certain now that it *was* a man. Sylvester was positive, from his height and strength, that his attacker was male.

Most of the group was inclined to agree with the theory Roberto had put forward the night before.

"There has to be someone else on the island." Guthrie turned away from where he had been gazing out the window as he spoke. "We must have missed him last time we searched. Don't you have any guns on the island, Sylvester?"

"They have never been needed. Until now." Sylvester looked weary. Unsurprisingly, Connie decided, after what he had just been through.

"Then we'll have to get together whatever weapons we can and search the island again." Guthrie sounded strong, determined and ruthless. Completely unlike his usual self. As if he had shed his slightly comic persona and underneath there was a different person, one who was unrecognizable.

"No." Despite his fatigue, Sylvester's voice remained firm. "Jonathan, Matt and I are injured. Even you took a nasty blow to your head not so long ago, Guthrie. That only leaves Juan." His eyes found Connie's. "We believe the person behind this is the man who attacked Connie four years ago, and that he's come for her again. The important thing is to make sure she is well guarded. No one is above suspicion. There must be two of us around at all times."

"I'm not so badly hurt I can't make myself useful," Matt said. "I could search with Guthrie and Juan while you stay with Connie, Lucinda, Jonathan and Vega."

"We all need to stay together from now on. I don't mean we have to be in the same room at all times, but if we split up as you suggest, we make ourselves vulnerable."

Watching Sylvester's face, Connie was gripped by a sudden awareness. He wasn't being stubborn or refusing to listen to other opinions for no reason. Sylvester knew something. Her stomach gave a sudden downward lurch. When she had suggested the person who attacked them must be a stranger, Sylvester hadn't answered. Now, he was vetoing Guthrie's suggestions with a hard look in his eyes. *Guthrie?* She turned to look at him, trying to see him with fresh eyes, attempting to see beyond the cheerful, slightly clownlike exterior. Could he be the stalker?

Guthrie was blustering now, attempting to prove he was right and Sylvester was wrong. Connie thought of the first night here at Corazón and how she had sat next to him at dinner. Guthrie's stories had been entertaining, but all about his misfortunes. How everything that went wrong in his life was someone else's fault, never Guthrie's. Yes, that could be her stalker, she supposed. All those centuries ago King Yargua had blamed Cariña and Máximo for the way the island chiefs had begun to plot against him. Her hand stole to her throat as she thought about it. Could the answer have been so glaringly obvious all along? But if Sylvester suspected Guthrie, surely he would have warned Connie and put her on her guard?

This whole situation was making her crazy, making her look at everyone through suspiciously narrowed eyes. *Next I'll be wondering if Jonathan really is as badly injured as he looks! Or if the person in that room could have been a woman, after all...*

Lucinda, a pale shadow of her former self, had sobbed quietly for some time before falling silent. Now she raised her head to show eyes that were red and swollen. "We must be able to do something. We can't just wait in turn to be attacked or killed. What about the lighthouse?"

"It doesn't work." Sylvester's voice was gentle, his former impatience toward her vanished now. "The light was decommissioned centuries ago."

"But Lucinda has a point." It was the first ray of hope Connie had found in anything that had been said over the last few days. She seized it desperately. "If we could find a way to get the light working—or get some sort of alternative in place—we might be able to attract attention. You said some of the other islanders use helicopters."

"I'll take a look at it. I'm not as mechanically minded as Roberto—" Juan paused as emotion threatened to overcome him "—but I might be able to fix something up."

"I repeat what I said. No one goes anywhere alone."

"What are you suggesting?" Guthrie's voice was scathing. "We all go down to the lighthouse together, and stand around in a group while Juan tries to get an eighteenth-century gaslight working?"

Sylvester's blue gaze could have cut diamonds. "If that's what it takes."

Guthrie's jaw dropped comically. "You still think it's one of us, don't you?"

"I'm not prepared to take the chance it isn't."

As Sylvester let his words sink in, Connie watched their impact on the faces around the room. The prospect of getting the lighthouse to work had given them a tiny slither of rosy optimism. Like a child's balloon it had swayed and bobbed before their eyes for a few tantalizing seconds. Then, with a few curt words, Sylvester had taken out a pin and popped it.

To Connie, it felt like the prison doors were clanging closed once more. She trusted Sylvester implicitly. If he thought it was someone in this room, then she couldn't see how it could be otherwise. She scanned each face one final time, willing the stalker to slip up, to give her a clue.

Who are you?

He flexed his shoulders, feeling sharp pain flare right up the center of his back. That bastard Sylvester had hit him hard with the heavy brass lamp. He would have one hell of a bruise to show for it tomorrow. Not that he would be showing anyone, of course. He would keep covered up, act normal, hide any stiffness or pain. Play a part, fit in, pretend…all of those things he did so well. Ever since the day he'd seen Connie Lacey's picture in that magazine, he had been living a double life.

To his friends and family, he was the same person he had always been. Nothing had changed. But inside him, everything was different. He hadn't known why, back then. He just knew, as he stared at the perfect oval of her face, the flawless gold of her skin, the blue-black gloss of her hair and the honey-brown depths of those remarkable, almond-shaped eyes, that he had to hurt her. Killing her outright wouldn't be enough. Connie Lacey was going to suffer for a very long time before she died. So far his tactics had proved successful. He knew he had made her life hell. She had been cowering in fear of him ever since the night he had attacked her and killed her mother.

It was her fault. All of it. It had all become clear when he came to Corazón. The memories had come back slowly. In a trickle rather than a flood. Now he knew exactly who she was and why she—and that arrogant Spanish bastard—must be made to pay for what they had done to him.

Why the hell did Roberto have to come in just at the point when he had Sylvester at his mercy? It was almost as if something on this island was working against him, preventing him from getting to Connie. Every time he did get close to her, someone, or something, conveniently got in his way, keeping her safe. It was like the curse of Corazón was working in reverse where she was concerned, as if fate was wrapping her in a protective blanket.

He allowed himself a smile. She couldn't escape forever. She was going to pay. He would make sure of it. But for now, how about a little twist of the knife? Something to make those pretty eyes a little bit sadder? Something that would turn her gaze away from Sylvester for once? He paused for a moment, lost in thought, before nodding to himself in quiet satisfaction.

She liked the Calusa books in Sylvester's precious collection, didn't she? This would be easy. Everyone was getting ready for breakfast, licking their wounds, trying to work out what was going on. They'd never figure it out, of course. He was too smart for that.

Sneaking into the den, he found the books about the Calusa easily. They were where Connie had left them in a pile on a side table. There were logs and kindling in the fireplace and matches on the mantelpiece above. Kneeling, he struck a match and held it to the kindling. It caught immediately and he grinned delightedly.

Reaching for the first book on the pile, he started systematically ripping out the pages and feeding them into the blaze. There was something satisfying and mesmerizing about the action and he had to remind himself he didn't have long to spend on this. Rising to his feet, he was just about to start on the next book when Vega, humming quietly under her breath, walked into the room.

He paused and she looked from the blaze in the grate to the book in his hand. Her dark eyes were grave as she raised them to his face.

"What are you doing?" She looked confused. "Those are the master's treasured books."

His mind froze. *Why did it have to be Vega?* His

brain refused to allow any other thoughts to intrude. In that instant, he had a horrible premonition that everything—every detail—was reflected in his face, and this sweet, harmless woman would be able to read his guilt and see him for what he really was. Her eyes widened as she took in the change in his expression.

"Oh, no." Her hand flew up, covering her mouth. "Not you. Tell me it's not you."

He had to act fast. Grabbing her, he hauled her into the room, kicking the door shut behind her. Cursing the misfortune that meant he didn't have his knife with him, he kept a hand over her mouth as he dragged her closer to the fire. He already knew the poker was a useful weapon. He'd used it once before, quite successfully, on that idiot Guthrie.

The first blow was messy. Vega tried to run when he released her, so the poker came down on her shoulder, felling her but not knocking her out. She cried out, infuriating him. He brought the poker down wildly after that, finishing the job quickly, efficiently and brutally. When he was done, he was breathing hard and his clothes were a mess.

"What the hell were you thinking of?" He spoke to the body on the floor. "You and Roberto? You weren't meant to be part of this. Why couldn't you mind your own goddamn business?"

Regret, sharp and dangerous, flooded through him. It was always the same. Being two people was such a fucking nightmare. Fighting this battle with himself was too hard. His rational self stared at Vega's body, at his bloodied hands, and recoiled in horror. The monster inside him, with its powerful instinct for self-preservation, drove him swiftly out through the glass doors, onto the patio and down the steps to the beach.

Fully clothed, he kept walking until he was up to his neck in the calm, blue waters. Striking out with a powerful stroke, he swam into the deeper waters until he was out of sight of the house and he could tread water while he stripped off his outer clothing.

Chapter 15

"Vega?" Connie had called the housekeeper's name a few times and not gotten any reply. She decided the time for formality was long gone and was heading toward the kitchen to help with breakfast when a faint smell assailed her nostrils. Was it smoke? She turned her head, sniffing the air. It definitely was, but it wasn't coming from the kitchen.

"You remind me of something." Matt was coming down the stairs. "I know. It's a sniffer dog."

"Can't you smell it? It's smoke." She moved toward the den. "It's coming from in here."

He was before her in one swift movement. "Let me go first."

Matt opened the door just wide enough to see inside and paused on the doorstep. Unable to see what he was looking at, Connie could only judge the scene by Matt's expression. She could tell it must be bad. Shock registered in the rigidity of his facial muscles and made his fine gray eyes widen. He remained immobile for a moment before he stepped back and closed the door.

"Fetch Sylvester." His voice wasn't quite steady.

Connie knew it was serious enough not to try to ask questions. Running swiftly up the stairs, she found Sylvester emerging from the shower. He had insisted he would be able to manage to wash on his own. His prediction about how well he'd heal seemed to be coming true. Although he wasn't using his injured arm, his strength was returning. Now, with one towel wrapped around his waist and another slung around his shoulders, there was no sign, other than the waterproof dressing on his arm, that he had been attacked.

His smile of greeting quickly faded when he saw Connie's face. "What is it?"

"I don't know, but it's bad." Her mind had already made the worst possible connection. Her sixth sense was working overtime. Vega hadn't answered when she'd called her name… *Please don't let whatever Matt saw in the den have anything to do with Vega.*

Sylvester dressed quickly. When they reached the foot of the stairs, Matt was standing exactly where Connie had left him, with one hand still on the door handle. His eyes went to Sylvester's face and he seemed momentarily incapable of speech.

"I…"

Sylvester placed his hand over Matt's. "Let me look." He spoke over his shoulder. "Wait here, Connie."

The two men went into the den together. There was a horrible fraught silence that seemed to last forever, then Matt lurched out of the room again. Doubling over, he didn't quite make it outside before his stomach surrendered its contents. Sliding down the wall, he sat on the floor with his knees drawn up and his head bent between them.

When Sylvester appeared in the doorway, his face was a pale mask of grief and pain.

"Please tell me it's not Vega." Connie knew before she said them that the words were futile.

He drew her into his arms and, cradling her head against his chest, slid his hand down the length of her hair. "I'm sorry."

They stood locked together for long, anguished minutes and, when she finally raised her head, Connie wasn't sure whether the tears that dampened her face were hers or Sylvester's.

"Why?" She knew the same question could have applied to any of these senseless acts. The answer was always the same. *Because a madman is out to get his revenge on me for something that happened five hundred years ago.* But this time the question had more poignancy. Why Vega? Out of everyone on this island, she was the one who should have been the safest. What possible threat could she pose? What sense of power or enjoyment could anyone have gained from harming the sweet, kindly little housekeeper?

"It looks like she disturbed him while he was burning books about the Calusa."

Connie's brow wrinkled. "So he stabbed her?"

"No, he beat her to death." As Sylvester spoke, she started to understand Matt's reaction. "With the poker."

She raised a hand to cover her mouth, staring at him in horror. "No, Sylvester! How could anyone do that? The other things he's done were evil…but this…"

He nodded. "This takes it to a whole new level."

Matt made a strangled sound. "Don't. Please stop. It's bad enough I had to see it. I'm not ready to analyze it. Not yet."

Breakfast didn't happen. Not surprisingly, no one felt like eating. Reactions to the news of Vega's murder varied from Juan's deep sorrow, and spitting rage from Guthrie, to Lucinda's increased hysteria.

"This is all your fault!" She turned on Connie, her eyes wild, her lips white and flecked with spittle. Connie took a step back, fearful for a moment that Lucinda might be about to physically attack her. "It's you he wants, not us. Why don't you give yourself up so he'll leave the rest of us in peace?"

Jonathan had managed to drag himself down the stairs and was stretched out on one of the sofas. He spoke up sharply before anyone else could intervene. "You're talking crap, Lucinda. He didn't kill Vega to get to Connie. He killed her because she caught him burning those books. He killed Roberto because he interrupted him as he was trying to kill Sylvester. And how is Connie meant to *give herself up* to a coward who doesn't show himself? Even if she did—and why the hell should any of us make this easy for him?—there's no guarantee he'd leave the rest of us alone."

Lucinda stared at him for a second, her facial muscles working, her fists clenching and unclenching at her sides. Then she hurled herself facedown onto another sofa, giving way to tears.

"Thank you." Connie bit back her tears as she turned to Jonathan. "But she's not thinking straight. She's frightened."

"We all are, but we have to stick together. If we start turning on each other, this bastard will get even more sadistic pleasure from it."

Guthrie had been pacing the length of the salon, but he paused now, swinging around to face Sylvester. "You have to agree to another search of the island."

Sylvester regarded him calmly. "Very well. You, Matt and I will undertake the search."

The words deflated Guthrie's rage slightly. "What are we waiting for? Let's get going."

"I need to talk to Juan and Connie in my study before I go anywhere."

"Why?" Guthrie's expression was a combination of belligerence and suspicion.

"It's personal." No one could pull off haughty quite like Sylvester. Even in these circumstances his manner was enough to put a halt to any further questions. Connie bit back a smile. That note in his voice, that proud expression, the set to his shoulders all harked back to his conquistador heritage. He had led men across oceans and into foreign lands. He could silence Guthrie's blustering protests with a look.

Once inside the study, Sylvester spoke quietly but urgently. "I lied when I told Guthrie there are no guns on Corazón." He unlocked the top drawer of his desk, revealing a revolver. "I loaded it myself last night. It was in the drawer next to my bed—" he cast Connie an apologetic glance "—but I didn't have time to reach for it when I realized there was an intruder in the room. It was too dark and he came at me too fast."

Connie felt her face pale. "I've never fired a gun." She had thought about buying a weapon after the attack, but the constant moving around and lack of cash meant she never got around to doing anything about it. And she had never been sure she could pull the trigger, even if she came face-to-face with the stalker.

"That's why Juan is here. You know how to use this, right?"

Juan nodded, his usually pleasant face grim. "After what happened to Vega and Roberto, it will be my pleasure."

Because of the high temperatures Sylvester had been

forced into an unpleasant decision. He had decided they would have to store the bodies in empty meat lockers in the basement where they had already placed Ellie. Although moving them meant valuable evidence might be lost once the police did get involved, the alternative was unthinkable. Juan had helped to transport the bodies of his friends that morning. It was no wonder he was angry and eager for revenge.

"This is important." Sylvester looked from Connie to Juan, holding their attention. "No matter who comes to you and what message they bring you, you two are to stay together and keep this gun with you at all times. Is that clear?"

Connie swallowed hard. There was a deeper message behind those words. It was hidden in the endless blue depths of his eyes. She tried to read them. *No matter who comes to you?* Was he expecting something to happen while he was out searching? Was this about Guthrie again?

"Must you go?" She had to swallow the obstruction in her throat to get the words out.

He drew her to him, pressing a kiss onto her forehead. Even during this, the culmination of the darkest time of her life, his touch exerted a magical force over her. When Sylvester's arms were around her, she felt as though nothing could harm her. It was as though he managed to instill some of his own immortality into her. "It's time to force a confrontation. Make sure you, and the others, stay inside the house."

He was gone before she could begin to unpack his meaning. How was he going to force a confrontation? The words implied he really did have an idea of who the stalker was. So would the showdown come during the search? Would Sylvester, Matt and Guthrie find the stranger's hiding place and finally hold him to account for what he had done? Or was Connie's horrible premonition correct, and was Sylvester planning to trick Guthrie into exposing himself as the stalker? Neither idea was comforting.

One thing was certain: Sylvester believed she could trust Juan. "We should go back to Jonathan and Lucinda," she said. "It's best if we stick together."

Juan nodded. Removing the gun from the drawer, he did something to it that Connie assumed made it safe. Tucking it his waistband, he pulled his shirt so it hung outside his pants. "I'm ready."

The words made her feel queasy. He was ready to blow someone's brains out. Was Lucinda right? *Should I try to find the stalker? If he killed me, would this nightmare finally end for all of us? Would he leave the others alone?* It had crossed her mind even before Lucinda had uttered those spiteful words. But Connie knew that, even though the stalker's goal was to kill her, he wanted to torture her by harming the people around her along the way. She had been given enough glimpses into his twisted mind to know she would be the last one left. He intended to keep her alive until the end.

"You know the island best, Sylvester. Where should we start?" Guthrie asked.

The three men had climbed to the point that was roughly the center of the island. It was a raised mound, one of the artificial sites created centuries earlier by the Calusa out of discarded shells and fish bones that was now covered with vegetation. From this point, they could see most of the island.

To the far west, there was the lighthouse, standing tall, proud and slightly sinister on its rocky promontory.

Beyond that point there was nothing except the Gulf of Mexico. On the opposite side of the island, the house nestled into the encircling arms of its protective golden bay. Nearby, the staff quarters clung to the shores of another, smaller bay.

Dotted around the edges of the island were several other tiny inlets, each offering a glimpse of a perfect, white-sand and palm-fringed beach. Despite the trees and brush that decorated the island's interior, the heart-shaped coastline was obvious from this angle. On a clear day such as this, it was just possible to glimpse the distant, shimmering outline of Siguiente, the nearest island in the de Perlas chain, once the home of Marco Alvarez, sworn enemy of the de León family.

Even though this island was his home, and he knew it like the back of his own hand, searching it wasn't going to be easy. Last time there had been six of them. They had split into pairs with Sylvester, Roberto and Juan—as the people who knew the island best—each leading a partner on the search. Even then, it had been a cursory hunt, time-wasting and unproductive. It had been more to satisfy everyone else's fears than with any real expectation on Sylvester's part of finding a hidden fugitive. There were just too many hiding places. It might be a small island, but it was still big enough for a man to remain concealed if he chose. Now, with Roberto dead, Jonathan incapacitated and Juan needed to guard Connie, it would be just the three of them searching. Even someone with no idea of the geography of the island could easily stay several steps ahead of them.

Sylvester did his best to keep these thoughts hidden from his companions. He didn't believe there was a stranger on the island. He still believed the search was futile, but he had his own reasons for agreeing to Guthrie's suggestion.

"We should do this systematically, starting from here and taking a path toward each of the bays in turn, returning to this point each time."

"Won't we keep doubling back on ourselves if we come back here each time?" Matt asked with a frown.

"Yes, but from this vantage point we should be able to see if there is any movement. I told the others to stay in the house. If there is someone else on this island, and our searching disturbs him, then coming back to this point each time should give us an idea of his location."

There followed a frustrating and tiring few hours of trekking back and forth down to each of the little bays and back up to the mound in the brutal heat. Even though they had brought plenty of water with them, they were soon feeling the effects. Sylvester was more accustomed to Florida's punishing heat and humidity, but before long Guthrie and Matt were sweat-soaked and struggling.

Red-faced and panting, Guthrie looked like he had just emerged from a steam room. "There has to be a better way. How much of the island can be seen from the lighthouse?"

"Not as much as from here," Sylvester said. "That's because this mound blocks the view of the east side of the island. The lighthouse wasn't built for looking at the island. It was built to warn ships, so the viewing platform overlooks the sea and the nearby rocks."

"Aren't there dungeons beneath the old fortress?" Matt had been shielding his eyes from the sun as he looked across at the lighthouse. He turned back now to look at Sylvester, a gleam of excitement dawning. "That would be the perfect hiding place."

Guthrie's eyes narrowed suspiciously. "You never mentioned this, Sylvester."

"That's because no one in their right mind would go down there. It's too dangerous."

Guthrie snorted. "And you think the guy we're looking for *is* in his right mind?" He tipped his water bottle to his lips, emptying it. "What are we waiting for?"

Sylvester gritted his teeth. The lighthouse, with all its potential hazards, was not the place he would have chosen for a confrontation. But he had been outmaneuvered. He consoled himself with the thought that at least the lighthouse was on the opposite side of the island from Connie. "What indeed?"

He gestured for Matt and Guthrie to go ahead of him along the narrow track their feet had made over the last few hours across the vegetation. It occurred to him, as it had several times already, that he could just act on his hunch and end this now. Creep up on the person he suspected and take him down with a blow to the back of the head. *But what if I'm wrong?* Because hunches were all he had. That was why he'd been cryptic in his warning to Connie. If he told her what he was thinking and was proved wrong, he'd look as crazy as the person doing all of this. That was the point of this senseless search. He intended to force the stalker into the open. All he had to do now was to find the right way.

When they reached the rocks, Sylvester had to call out to Guthrie, who was in the lead. "You can't walk across here." He gestured to the Salto de Fe, where the spray was just visible above the cleft in the rocks. "We have to walk around the ravine." He and Guthrie started to walk away, taking the circuitous route toward the lighthouse. "Matt?" Sylvester called to the other man to come with them.

"Sorry." Matt roused himself and followed them. "It's a force of nature, isn't it?" He glanced back at the Salto de Fe, a hint of nerves and fascination mingling together on his face.

"A dangerous one. Like so many things on this island." Grim-faced, Sylvester kept walking.

When they reached the rocky point where the lighthouse stood, Matt went over to the ruined walls of the fortress. Sylvester dredged up his long-ago memories of the old building. Although Máximo and Cariña had made their home on the other side of the island, where the modern-day house stood, when they'd first arrived there had been a need to repel invaders. When Máximo had bought the island from the Calusa king who succeeded Yargua, there were other adventurers who saw its potential and sought to take it from him by force. Several Calusa braves, unnerved by the changes taking place, had chosen to stay on the island when their chief left and stayed loyal to Máximo. They had proved to be his most valuable asset, both in building this fortified keep, in protecting his island and family from invasion and as guards when they were forced to take prisoners.

As Matt and Guthrie stood over one of the stone circles that marked the entrance to the dungeons, the sense of foreboding that had been with Sylvester all day grew stronger. It wasn't just the sensation of someone walking over his grave; it was a black cat prowling over it while the devil watched and chuckled.

"This has been moved recently." Matt pointed to the evidence the stone had been shifted. Sure enough, after centuries of disuse, the area around the rock was lighter and brighter with loose, chalky pieces that had been dislodged and spread over a few feet in a circle around it.

As Guthrie reached out a hand for the rusted iron

ring that held the stone in place, Sylvester experienced a violent flashback to the dank darkness that lurked beneath that stone. To the catacombs that led in one direction only. Out into that final plunge from the sheer rock face to the hungry sea below.

"We can't go down there." Sylvester was starting feel as though he might be invisible. As though his voice, usually so authoritative, was having no impact.

"If he's down there, we need to know."

"If he's down there, he's dead." *But he's not down there. He's right here next to me.*

With a huge effort, Guthrie hauled the stone to one side. Sylvester made a move to turn away but it was too late. The shove in the small of his back toppled him off balance and he found himself tumbling down into that gaping darkness before he even had time to comprehend what was happening.

The morning dragged endlessly on. Somehow the minutes crawled into hours. Connie dipped in and out of that strange feeling, that uniquely Corazón experience. As if competing forces were tugging at the edges of her subconscious. This island was an intricate, beautiful tapestry, woven by the delicate hand of an artist. The threads had been selected with care, each color chosen to match the tropical shades of the natural environment. From a distance, the fibers came together to form a picture so perfect it made your breath catch in your throat. It was only when you stepped up close that you could see beneath the surface layer. Underlying the glorious, shimmering threads, there was a hidden web of decay.

There was evil here, and it had allowed the curse to thrive. It had taken the sick mind of her stalker and distorted it further. It had magnified the worst character traits of each of the guests, making them into sad caricatures of their true selves. It was older than Sinapa, the Calusa wise woman who, in her hatred of Cariña, had uttered the words of the curse, as old as the magic behind Sylvester's immortality, older than time. Yet there was another enchantment to Corazón. Something good and pure. Something that didn't want this festering wickedness to thrive. And it was that which Connie tried so desperately to reach out to as she waited, because she felt strangely that it was being drawn to *her*.

Juan accompanied Connie into the kitchen as she made sandwiches and coffee. She carried them back into the salon on a tray and they made listless conversation as they ate. Just as she was about to return the plates to the kitchen, Matt burst through the door.

His clothing was disheveled, his eyes wild. He looked like a man who had gazed into the eyes of the devil and only just survived.

"Sylvester and Guthrie…the lighthouse…come quick!" Before he had even finished gasping out the words, he set off again at a run.

Juan leaped to his feet, preparing to follow him. "No, wait." Connie placed a hand on his arm. "Remember what Sylvester said? We mustn't leave the house and we have to stick together."

"Then let's go."

Connie hesitated. *No matter who comes to you and what message they bring.* Those words of Sylvester's had resonated with her when he'd spoken them and they came back to her now. Suddenly she could see it all. She knew everything Sylvester knew. It was all perfectly, horribly, clear. Her hand went to her throat.

"Jonathan can't go anywhere."

"I'm not waiting around here if Guthrie is in danger." Without pausing to debate the matter, Lucinda marched out the door. Juan faltered, clearly uncertain about what to do next.

"Go after her." Connie nodded to him, amazed at how calmly she was able to speak considering the revelation that had just come to her. "I'll follow you."

After a second or two of looking at her with uncertainty in his eyes, Juan dashed after Lucinda.

Jonathan kept his eyes fixed on Connie's face. "Are you okay?"

She nodded, even though she felt far from okay. A laugh tried to rise in her throat and she shoved it down. How could the word *okay* possibly be applied to this situation? She forced herself to focus. Jonathan's safety was important now. He couldn't come with her and he would find it difficult to defend himself once he was left alone.

"I need to help you into Sylvester's study, even though I don't think the attacker will come after you. If I'm right, he'll be too busy at the lighthouse. That seems to be where the action is. But you'll be safer there than in this room. There is only one way in, so you'll see him coming more easily, and I'll bring you Vega's biggest knife."

Jonathan placed his arm around her shoulders as she helped him to his feet. "You know who it is, don't you?"

"I think so."

"Be careful, Connie." He leaned heavily on her.

Her voice was bleak. "It may already be too late for that."

Once she was sure Jonathan was comfortable in the study, and she had given him the knife to keep at his side, Connie faced up to the prospect of leaving the house. She was certain she was right to leave him. Although he was alone, Jonathan would be the safest person on the island. She, on the other hand, had done the very thing Sylvester had warned her against. She had separated herself from Juan. The minute she left the house, she would be alone, exposed and completely at the mercy of the stalker. Exactly what he wanted.

Curiously, she no longer felt afraid. As she stepped onto the patio and looked swiftly around, she took a moment to analyze her feelings. There was impatience to get this over with, nervousness at what she might find when she reached the lighthouse, and a curious feeling of exhilaration that it would soon be finished. All of these were underpinned by a strong undercurrent of anger. She had allowed herself to be duped for too long. *No more.*

Taking the route toward the lighthouse, she had the oddest feeling she wasn't alone. Yet her unseen companion wasn't the stalker. She knew, with a fierce certainty, he wasn't following her. He would be waiting for her at the lighthouse. That was where he wanted her. She knew his intention was to draw her toward the Salto de Fe.

No, the invisible presence she could feel was benign. More than that... It was comforting. Connie had never believed in ghosts, but this was a spiritual experience, soothing and tranquil. On a soul-deep level, this silent being who walked beside her was taking her hand and reassuring her everything was going to turn out fine.

Connie turned her head, trying to get a sense for who it was. This time when she asked the question, "Who are you?" her voice was filled with wonder instead of terror.

As Connie approached the lighthouse, the feelings of trepidation grew stronger than those of serenity. Why was she doing this? If she was right, she was walking into a trap. If she was wrong…

"Then I'm wrong and it's just another one of my stupid feelings," she muttered, using her voice to spur herself on. Closing the final few yards across the rocks, she knew she wasn't wrong. The watchful presence of the lighthouse was more sinister than ever.

The raw beauty of this part of the island stung her again in its contrast to the lush splendor of the habitable side. It was a metaphor for Corazón itself. On the surface so idyllic, but beneath the tropical perfection was that primal pulse that couldn't be hidden. Not for the first time, Connie pictured this island as a living thing. A sleeping beast. Once stirred from slumber, Corazón was a powerful force, relentless and unstoppable, its heartbeat right here in the pounding waves of the Salto de Fe.

And Corazón had been stirred into life. She and Sylvester had awakened the island's memories. Or Corazón had revived theirs. Connie wasn't certain which way around it worked. She wasn't sure it mattered. Corazón was the key, drawing them in, bringing them together. Some compelling magic must be at work to make this chain of events come about. Their centuries-old love triangle wasn't over yet. It had to reach its conclusion. Whatever that might be.

"Do you know?" Connie looked around her at the rocks, at the waves spraying up from the Salto de Fe. She shivered slightly as she got the feeling the island *did* know the answer.

Her fingertips hesitated on the lighthouse door. Going in here alone was madness. She should never have let Juan proceed ahead of her. If the stalker was here, she was dancing to his tune. *In a few days, Syl-*

vester will be gone forever. You will leave Corazón and have to take your chances alone once more. Trust your instincts again. Stop cowering in the shadows.

For four years this man had dominated her life. He was the reason eight other people had been left stranded and cringing in fear on this island. Ellie, Roberto and Vega had died at his hands. No more.

Gripping the door handle, she turned it and determinedly walked inside.

Only silence and dusty disuse greeted her, making her immediately decide her intuition had betrayed her. This didn't have the feel of a place that had been visited recently. *You can go. There's no one here.* She knew her terrified nerves were trying to seize on an opt-out clause. But if she left now, she would be facing this situation again soon. And if the stalker was here, was leaving going to be a choice at all?

Connie's body was offering her conflicting options. Her pounding heart was telling her to get out of there, to run as fast and as far as she could. But she couldn't move. Her nervous system had shut down so her limbs were frozen in place. Something deeper than her rational mind had taken charge, lifting the hairs on the back of her neck, widening her eyes and driving the blood from her hands and face. All the while, in the background, her brain was telling her she could do this. Relaying pieces of information. *Sylvester said it is time to force a confrontation. Juan must be close. He has the gun. And where are the others? Sylvester? Matt? Guthrie? Lucinda?*

Her eyes went to the spiral staircase. If she was going to do this properly, she had to go up there. Her mind went back to the scene in Sylvester's bedroom when Roberto lay dead on the floor and the attacker was momentarily stunned. In that instant she had been unable to summon the courage to remove his mask. Such was the power he had wielded over her for so long. Now she was certain she knew whose face she would see. She knew who had been hiding behind that mask. A surge of anger stiffened her spine. *I want to look you in the eye.* Steeling her nerves, she placed her foot on the first rung.

She had forgotten how much the staircase creaked. Biting her lip, she attempted to make herself lighter as she climbed, easing her weight to different sides of each step to see if it made a difference. Deciding it didn't, she gave up. Whoever was at the top—if there was anyone there at all—would have been warned by now that she was on her way up.

When she stepped into the cramped space of the circular lamp room, her worst fears were immediately realized. Guthrie lay on his side, his hands and feet bound. Although he was conscious, his face was badly bruised. Next him, Lucinda was in a sitting position. She was also tied up. Unlike Guthrie, she had been gagged, but she didn't appear to have been beaten. When she saw Connie, she moaned slightly around the cloth that had been stuffed into her mouth. Her eyes, huge and terrified, flew to the tall figure who lounged against the glass dome of the lamp.

"What kept you?" He swung the knife slowly back and forth between his fingers as he spoke.

Connie drew in a deep breath. Somehow, now she knew she was right, her nerves had vanished.

"I didn't want it to be you, Matt."

Chapter 16

"*You* didn't want it to be me?" A note of bitterness showed through as some of Matt's former nonchalance deserted him. "How the fuck do you think I feel?"

Connie desperately needed to know where Sylvester was, if he was all right. When she suspected Guthrie might be the stalker, she had believed Sylvester wanted to stick close to him so he knew what Guthrie was doing. *But it was Matt. All the time, Sylvester thought I was safe as long as* he *was with Matt.* Somehow Matt must have given Sylvester the slip. When he'd burst into the house and gasped out his frantic message, it was exactly what Sylvester had tried to warn her about. *He was trying to warn me to trust no one. Not even my friend Matt.*

"How did you get away from Sylvester?"

"You can thank Guthrie here for that." Matt prodded the bound figure on the floor with the tip of his sneaker. Even though Guthrie was hurt, Connie saw a flash of anger light his eyes. *Good.* Guthrie was her best chance of an ally. "I tricked him into believing there was someone hiding in the dungeons under the old fortress. Sylvester wasn't happy, but Guthrie fell for it, so it was two against one."

Did she want to ask the next question? She decided she had to hear it all. "So where is Sylvester now?"

Matt jerked a careless thumb in the direction of the rocks. "Where he belongs. In the Salto de Fe."

Connie gave a little cry of horror, her stomach recoiling at the smile of enjoyment in Matt's eyes as he feasted on her pain. As she bent her head, she risked a brief glance at Guthrie. He moved his head ever so slightly from side to side in a negative movement. Could Matt be lying? Telling her that Sylvester was in the Salto de Fe to torture her? That seemed to be what Guthrie was attempting to tell her.

Trying not to let him see the hope on her face, she lifted her gaze to his face. She didn't have to pretend to be frightened by the smile in his eyes.

"And what about Juan? He came after Lucinda."

"You don't seem to understand the rules of murder, Connie. You don't get to interview me before I slit your throat." The smile widened. "Again."

She took a steadying breath. She had already decided the best chance of getting out of this was to keep him talking. It was a slim chance, but she would take slim over none any day. "So I don't get to say 'why me'?"

The smile twisted again, turning into something other than a smile. Becoming a truly terrifying glimpse into the state of his mind. "You already know the answer to that. But, since we're having this conversation, picture how it feels to be a normal guy and then one day see a photograph in a magazine—*your* photograph—and have your whole world turned upside down."

"I would imagine it was fairly devastating." She

managed to keep the flare of her emotions in check. *Not as devastating as it turned out to be for me.*

He snorted. "You have no idea. You screwed up my life."

Did he want an apology? "When you first saw me, did you know who I was? Beyond that picture, did you get a feeling for our past lives?"

Matt shook his head. "I didn't know what the hell was going on. I'd never felt anything like it. It was this rage, tearing into me." He pressed his fist into his chest. "Here. I took a week off work. Stayed in bed, just trying to fight the impulse to come after you. I had all these images in my head of you—the girl in the magazine—of hurting you, making you suffer, making you pay for something. I didn't know what you had to pay for, I just knew it was bad. But I also knew I'd never met you. I thought I was going crazy." He gave a shaky laugh. "Turns out, I *was* going crazy."

"But you did come after me." Connie shuddered at the memory of that night.

"I couldn't fight it." Matt's voice became pleading, as if he needed her understanding. "It was too powerful."

"If it was me you were after, why did you kill my mother?" Behind her gag, Lucinda gave an anguished little moan at the words.

"It was all about hurting you, making you pay. Like I said, I didn't know then what it was you had to pay for. I just knew I had to make you suffer. When I had you both in my power, I knew it would hurt you more if I made you watch her die, left you with those scars and let you know I'd come back. Again and again." His face contorted into a grimace. "From then on, my life was ruled by you, Connie. I became two people. Trying to live a normal life being Matt Reynolds, stand-up guy, attorney by day and stalker, would-be killer, by night. I spent every spare minute tracking you down, following you around, letting you know I knew where you were and that I could come after you at any time I wanted."

"But you never questioned why you felt this way about me? You never tried to get help?"

He made a jerky movement and the knife trembled in his hand. "Don't you see? I couldn't accept what was going on myself? Inside here, I was a mess." He tapped his temple. "Couldn't believe it was me doing these things. How could I talk to someone else about it? Then, when Sylvester came up with this mad scheme of his, imagine how I felt when I was researching his relatives for my father and your name came up. Talk about coincidence!"

Connie almost laughed. There were no coincidences where Corazón was concerned. She knew that now. They were all meant to come together at this moment in time.

"You were a long shot. Not really a relative at all. The connection was so distant my father was going to cross you off the list, but I persuaded him to invite you. I wanted to be able to look into your eyes, to see if I could find out what this hold is that you have over me."

"You pretended to be my friend." She had been lonely for so long. The realization that the person she had believed was a friend had turned out to be her stalker all along was torture, like scalding steam held against her flesh. There were many things for which Connie would never forgive Matt, but that remained high on her list.

Matt shook his head. "That wasn't pretense. I liked you, Connie. It was unexpected, but the friendship was genuine. That was the real me. It was Matt Reynolds, not the monster that lives inside me."

Surprisingly, the distraught, pleading look in his eyes tugged at her heartstrings.

"Gradually, after I'd been on the island a few hours, I started to get strange flashbacks and dreams. The longer I was here, the stronger they became."

"You've been to Corazón before. Hadn't you felt you'd experienced them in the past?"

"No. They were all linked to you, almost like memories triggered by your nearness. In my mind, you were here on the island but you weren't *you*. And it wasn't now. It all started to make sense. I saw you for the first time in your Calusa dress. God, Connie, you looked amazing. I wanted you so badly. I had other wives, but with you, I was going to found this great dynasty. Then I discovered what you'd done. How you'd betrayed me." His face darkened. "It was him…Sylvester or Máximo, whatever the hell his name is. You chose him. Then and now. You made me look like a fool. That's why you have to pay. That's why he has to die."

Connie bit her lip, desperately trying to fight the flare of hope that kept trying to ignite inside her. *Sylvester can't die.* She was the only one in this room who knew that. *He can't die, but can he get here in time to save us?*

Sylvester moved slowly toward the circle of light, feeling his way along the rocky wall. The ten-foot fall into the dungeon had jarred him, leaving him dazed and bruised. But he was recovering now, becoming used to his surroundings. He remembered the stories. It was easy to become disoriented down here. There were hidden pitfalls, real ones, and uneven rocks that could trip a man up, leaving him crawling around in the darkness with broken bones. The dungeons weren't really dungeons at all. Once a prisoner was thrown down here, there was no need to lock him in a cell. There was only one way out and the end result wasn't pretty.

Climbing back out the way he had come wasn't an option. The drop from the opening in the rock was too far above his head. Even if he was able to find a way to climb up to it in the pitch darkness, there was no way he would be able to shift that heavy stone circle from below. The only way to go was toward the opening in the cliff face.

He had no way of knowing how many prisoners had stumbled to their deaths through these windows onto the ocean. Had any been mad enough to attempt to climb either up or down the sheer rock face? He wondered if any of those long-ago captives might even have made it to safety. There was no way of knowing.

But none of them had the preparation I have. Or the credentials. I am the man who climbed El Sendero Luminoso without a rope. Oh, and I'm immortal. Those things have to count for something. Don't they?

When he stood at the edge of the opening, the magnitude of the task facing him became clear. Going down toward the sea wasn't an option. The height wasn't a problem, nor was the sheer drop. Both were less dangerous and taxing than other climbs Sylvester had tackled before. But this rock face was slippery with bird guano and, closer to the water itself, seaweed. It made for a lethal combination. Even if he did succeed in climbing down and reaching water, he wouldn't be any better off. He would still have to find a way to get back onto the island and back to Connie.

Why the hell didn't I warn her about Matt while I had the chance? The simple answer was that he just hadn't been sure enough. But there was more to it than that. Sylvester remembered Matt Reynolds as a fresh-faced kid just out of college, starting out in his father's firm. Matt had been a conscientious, likable young man with a wicked sense of humor. He had been in awe of Arthur's most famous client, but that hadn't stopped them becoming friends. Sylvester liked Matt, had counted him among the very limited number of people he trusted. How could he reconcile what he knew of him with what was going on here? And how could he—even with everything he knew of reincarnation and the way the past could affect the present—possibly believe that Matt's body harbored the soul of King Yargua?

Yet Sylvester's suspicions had been aroused as soon as he'd seen Matt's injuries after he was supposedly attacked. Had he been mistrustful of him even before then? He wasn't sure. He had been so wrapped up in what was happening between him and Connie, he had barely spared a thought for anyone else. Looking back, he thought perhaps there had been some changes to Matt's behavior. He had seemed uncharacteristically quiet and introspective. But hindsight was a gift and Sylvester wasn't sure he had really noticed those signs at the time.

When Matt was attacked, the worst of his injuries had been on his left side and, while it was entirely plausible that his attacker might have come at him from that side, it had crossed Sylvester's mind that it was also possible the wounds had been self-inflicted.

At first he had gone with his theory that Matt was trying to arouse Connie's sympathy. It had seemed out of character, but men in love didn't always act rationally. Sylvester should know. There was another puzzling matter. Even if he was in shock, could Matt really claim not to know who had attacked him in broad daylight?

Sylvester had begun to watch his friend more closely after that, and had started noticing odd behaviors. That bizarre dash onto the balcony in Jonathan's room, occasional looks and comments that seemed unusual.

Last night, as he had grappled with the stalker in the darkness, Sylvester had become convinced he was right. The height and build of the man he was fighting could only have fitted one man on the island. He was sure it was Matt. That was why, in spite of everything else, his first thought had been to get Connie to remove the attacker's mask. Her understandable reluctance had been a missed opportunity.

Now Sylvester blamed himself for the chain of events that had brought him to this cliff edge. If he had spoken out sooner, could he have prevented Vega's death? Stopped Matt from bringing them to this point? He had hesitated for another reason, one he hated to admit, even to himself. *I wondered if my feelings toward Matt were changed by jealousy.*

When he had realized that Matt was in love with Connie, it had been like someone twisting a knife deep into his heart. For the first time he had faced the prospect that she might find someone else in the future. Even though he was going back in time to share his life with her as Cariña, he couldn't bear the idea of Connie—*my Connie*—with someone else in *this* life.

And in the middle of this whole mixed-up, unnatural, supernatural mess, what does that say about me?

It was time to stop prevaricating and start climbing. Introspection was a time-wasting indulgence he couldn't afford. Although the upward climb was shorter, it was no less challenging. He might have accomplished plenty of climbs without ropes or safety equipment, but he had always had the benefit of the best shoes and someone had gone ahead of him to clean the rock face of loose stones and other debris. Climbing in his sneakers would be dangerous, so he would have to go barefoot. And he was definitely on his own this time. Shrugging out of his T-shirt and kicking off his footwear, he took a few minutes to scan the rock, trying to plan a route in advance, before swinging out from the edge.

Climbing was as much a puzzle as a feat of strength and endurance. As he moved, he had to look ahead and decide where next to place his hands and feet. At each stage, he faced a series of minute cracks and holds, varying in size, shape and distance from each other. He urged himself on with a single thought. Connie's life depended on his ability to move quickly.

Sylvester contorted his body, twisting, stretching, lunging, swinging, dangling, pushing himself onward and upward inch by inch toward the top of the cliff. In a series of curiously balletic movements, ignoring the screaming of his muscles and the burning of his scraped-raw fingers and toes, he drove himself with equal measures of physical force and mental determination.

He had told Connie he had no idea where his immortality came from. It was true but, over the years, he had developed something that looked like a theory. It was linked to the Calusa legends surrounding the Corona de Perlas islands and their ancient spirits.

Sylvester had seen for himself the power that Corazón could exert. He didn't believe Sinapa's curse would have carried the same weight if it had been delivered anywhere else. He might have instigated the current house party, but he didn't believe the make-up of the group was a coincidence. Matt had been able to get away with his evil, daring schemes for a reason.

That was what this island could do. And Sylvester believed that, five hundred years ago, Corazón had also conjured up its own hero.

When Corazón's lifestyle, including the worship of the ancient spirits, was threatened by the conquistadors, a unique event had occurred. Its own hero had arrived. He not only became sympathetic to the Calusa way of life through his relationship with Cariña, but also remained to defend the island's interests throughout the ensuing centuries. Sylvester was flesh and blood, but the ancient spirits of this island had made sure his was a body that never died. A brave, heroic body that served them well. They continued to rule Corazón. His job was to protect it.

If that was true, and Sylvester believed it was, then he was Corazón's creation. Or puppet. Which of those he believed depended on Corazón's mood and Sylvester's point of view.

Right now, Sylvester's point of view was perilous. His left hand was less than a foot from the top of the cliff, but his body was stretched to the limit and he couldn't find anywhere to place his left foot. His injured arm was aching and his muscles were crying out in protest after the fall into the dungeon. He had probably been in a similar position a dozen times before, but the life of the woman he loved had never depended on his next move. Resting his cheek against the rock, he took a moment to think, to feel the island's pulse. It all came down to what Corazón wanted.

Risking a glance up by leaning away from the edge, he could see his next handhold. If he swung out now, he could reach it with his right hand, but it would mean hanging on by only his weakened left arm. If the muscles weren't strong enough, he would plunge onto the rocks below. *I won't die, but Connie sure as hell will... if she's not dead already.*

Mustering every bit of strength he had, Sylvester lunged for the handhold. The outcome hung in the balance. The muscles in his left arm screamed in agony and his bruised and bloodied fingers burned as they gripped the tiniest of ledges. His right hand clawed wildly above his head for the next hold, scrabbling to find it. Catching and missing it. *Fuck.* He wanted to scream the word aloud, but he couldn't spare the energy.

Sweat was pouring from him, greasing his whole body, coating his face, stinging his eyes and blinding him. He took a breath. *One more try. That's all I have in me.*

There was more desperation than finesse in his second attempt. He hurled himself out from the cliff face, swinging perilously as he went for the hold again. And missed again. A sound somewhere between a sob and a scream escaped his lips and was flung far above him, swept away on the slight sea breeze. *I'm so sorry, Connie...*

Even as the words formed in his mind, a hand gripped his left wrist. The person holding him wasn't strong, but it was enough. Enough for Sylvester to get his right hand onto that tiny ledge, to find his next foothold. Whoever his mystery rescuer was, he or she remained silent as Sylvester accomplished the rest of the climb. There was no cheering, no shouts of encouragement, no urging him on. Just that steady grip on his wrist. By the time Sylvester hauled himself over the top of the cliff and lay on his back, panting and looking up at the sky, his rescuer had disappeared.

Chapter 17

"If I'm the one who has to pay, why did you have to hurt so many other people on this island, Matt? They didn't do anything to you. Why not just come after me?" Again, the knife twitched nervously in his hand and Connie's heart leaped in time with it.

The question had an adverse effect on him. Connie knew she'd touched a nerve, almost as if he could justify his pursuit of her to himself, but the reminder of the others he'd killed and injured tugged at his inner self in a way he didn't like. Without warning, Matt's light-colored sneaker lashed out, connecting hard with Guthrie's ribs. Guthrie's body convulsed as he cried out in pain.

"That was the plan. I *was* coming after you. It was his fault. Guthrie stopped me. Stupid bastard. What made him come into the house right at that minute? You seem to have a guardian angel watching over you here on Corazón, Connie." Matt's eyes were wild as he looked at Connie. "He was focused on getting to the bar for a drink, but I couldn't risk him looking up and seeing me halfway up the stairs with the poker in my hand. So I hit him over the head instead, cleaned up the poker and put it back in its place, went out the doors from the den to the beach and pretended I hadn't come back to the house until much later."

Connie's hand stole to her throat and she swallowed hard to combat the nauseous feeling that rose in her throat. "You were on your way to my room that day… with the poker?"

She hadn't seen Vega's body, but horrible images had insisted on forcing themselves into her imagination. *That was what he planned to do to me. Only minutes after taking a walk together, after I was worried he might be falling for me, he was planning to bash my brains out with a poker.* Hysterical laughter started to bubble up inside her and it took every ounce of her self-control to contain it.

"Yes." He seemed pleased she understood. "If Guthrie hadn't interfered, it would have all been over then and no one else needed to get hurt." Matt turned his head as though sensing an invisible presence. "But then it was as though the island took over, the memories started to come back. Killing you wasn't going to be enough. You had to suffer more than that."

"So you decided to imprison us all on Corazón?"

He sighed. "That took some planning, I can tell you. You were the one who gave me the idea when you said you couldn't stay marooned here forever just because you didn't like boats. Once or twice I almost gave up and just decided to finish you off instead. Seeing you with Sylvester, that was what kept me going. It was like the two of you were laughing at me all over again. It gave me the incentive I needed to see it through."

"We never laughed at you, Matt. Not then. Not now."

For a moment she thought her words had penetrated

his mania. She saw a flicker of sadness in his eyes, but then the shutters came down again and he gave a hollow laugh. "Killing Ellie first was a stroke of genius, don't you think? You were absolutely right about her. She kept boasting about how far she could swim and, while I'm not sure she actually could have made it to one of the other islands, I wasn't prepared to take any chances. And she was starting to annoy me."

Connie's blood chilled even further. Was she really trying to reason with a man who could kill someone because they annoyed him? "But then you were attacked."

He grinned. "That was damn difficult. Smashing a rock into my own face hard enough to cause bruises, then hitting myself with one of those palm branches? I wasn't sure I could do it, but I wanted to be sure no one would suspect me." There was a genuine note of pride in his voice. "I'm pleased with the way it went, although—" the grin vanished "—I'm not sure Sylvester bought my story."

Connie remembered Sylvester's question on the night of the storm. *Does anything about the attack on Matt strike you as strange, Connie?* She wondered why he hadn't shared his doubts about Matt then. "And Jonathan? Why was he next?"

"He was another suspicious bastard. And he was supposed to die." His lips thinned into a hard line. "I hit him hard, and enough times, with a large, wooden statue that was in my room. He must have a skull made of iron."

Connie thought back to the morning Jonathan had been found lying on his bedroom floor, still in his clothes from the night before, his bed not slept in. "You attacked him the night before and pretended to find him the next morning. If he was meant to die, why didn't you make sure he was dead before you came to find Sylvester?"

"I panicked. Nobody's perfect, okay?" Matt shrugged impatiently. "I thought I *had* killed him. Then, the next morning, I really did hear a thud. I wasn't sure if it came from Jonathan's room or not, but I wasn't taking any chances. After I checked on him and found him still alive, I went back to get the statue, but Vega was around. I could hear her singing and realized she was going in and out of the linen cupboard on that corridor. She could have caused the thud I heard. By then, I couldn't see any way I could get from my room to Jonathan's with the statue, kill him and get back again in bloodstained clothes if Vega was around. But I also wasn't sure if she'd already seen me going into his room. I decided the only thing to do was to be the person who discovered him." He seemed to feel he should be congratulated for his quick thinking. "But then I had the whole nightmare of wondering whether he would come around and, if he did, how much he would remember."

Connie struggled to keep back the response that wanted to burst from her lips. *You had a nightmare? What about Jonathan? What about all of us? We didn't know who was next, what evil little plan you had in store for us.*

"So when he started to speak, you pretended to see someone on the balcony." Connie had sensed the presence of her stalker at that moment, stronger than ever. It was all so clear now. He *had* been there. Of course he had. Her instincts were right. Except he'd been there in the room with them, not on the balcony. *To think I was worried the stalker might be listening to our conversation, might know what we were thinking. And all the time, he was standing right next to me.*

"It bought me a little time, gave me a chance to listen in to what he was telling you. I could judge how good or bad his memory was and know how to act. When I heard him tell you he couldn't remember anything about what happened, I was able to breathe a sigh of relief."

"What made you think Jonathan was suspicious of you?" Connie asked. As far as she was aware, Jonathan had never given any indication he distrusted Matt.

"Just something he said. You seem very interested in Jonathan. Lining up your next lover now Sylvester is gone?" He gave her a nasty smile. "Of course, Sylvester would have been dead last night if Roberto hadn't got in the way."

Connie felt a flash of anger at the thought of Roberto's body. "He was trying to help. You didn't give him a chance."

"He should have kept his nose out."

"Like Vega?" She didn't care anymore that the knife was jittering wildly in his hand. He needed to hear the truth about what she thought of him. She wanted him to see the disgust in her eyes. "Did she deserve to die because she walked in on you at the wrong moment?"

"I don't want to talk about that." He seemed to shrivel before her eyes.

"I'll just bet you don't want to talk about how you beat a defenseless woman to death with a poker. Just like you stabbed my mother so you could hurt me. You say it's the spirit of the Calusa king that makes you do these things, but Yargua was a brave man, Matt. Killing Ellie, Roberto and Vega weren't acts of bravery."

He made a sound like a stifled sob. "I know what you're trying to do. Stop it."

Connie looked down at the two pitiful, bound figures at their feet. "None of this has anything to do with Lucinda and Guthrie. Can you show mercy, as the Calusa king would have done, and let them go?"

Matt followed her gaze with an absentminded frown, as though he had forgotten about his captives. "Why? So they can bring Sylvester to your rescue?"

Her heart gave a joyful bound at the words. He seemed to have forgotten he'd told her Sylvester had gone into the Salto de Fe. Was it her imagination or, with perfect timing, did she hear the faint creak of the spiral staircase? Was her overwrought mind making connections that weren't there? Was she longing for Sylvester so much she was imagining him coming to save her?

She took a chance and sneaked another quick look down at Guthrie and saw his eyes widen in a signal. He had heard it, too. She raised her voice, hoping to send a warning to the person on the stairs. "Let them go, Matt."

Guthrie started kicking his bound feet against the metal frame encasing the light. The noise echoed loudly around the small space. "She's right, you bastard. We're no use to you. Let us go!" He shouted the words at the top of his voice.

Connie felt an overwhelming sense of gratitude toward him. Guthrie was risking his own safety to give the person on the stairs a chance to get to the top without Matt hearing them.

With a furious exclamation, Matt leaned down and grabbed Guthrie by the hair, smashing his face into the metal casing.

"Shut up! I gagged your sister because she was hysterical. I thought I could trust you to keep quiet."

Blood immediately began to pour from Guthrie's nose. Lucinda started to sob, the sound stifled by the gag so it came out as a soft snuffling. Connie tried to bend in the cramped space to assist Guthrie, but Matt caught her by her upper arm and hauled her upright. "Before you die, answer me this. Was there ever any part of you that wanted me?"

She couldn't pretend. Wouldn't grovel to this man who thought torturing her for four years and murder were payback for her loving another man. Would never deny her love for Sylvester. Not even to save her life. Lifting her chin proudly, she shook her head. "No matter how many lifetimes I live through, I will always choose Sylvester."

"Then it's time you and I headed for the Salto de Fe." His face was wistful as he smoothed her hair back from her face and slowly raised the knife.

With a howl of fury, Sylvester swung around the door frame and hurled himself into Matt. Dressed only in jeans, his hands and feet were bloodied, his upper body and face streaked with sweat and dirt, his face contorted with rage.

Sylvester's body hit Matt so hard he was propelled away from Connie. Within the tiny space, the two men grappled against the huge glass light. As his hands came up around Matt's throat, Connie could see the determination on Sylvester's face. The knife went spinning out of Matt's grip and Connie pounced on it.

Crawling over to Guthrie, she started to cut through the bonds around his hands. Before she could finish, there was a dramatic shift in the balance of power in the fight. Sylvester might be stronger and more muscular than Matt, but he was hampered by his wounded arm and seemed weakened by new injuries. Looking up from her task, Connie saw to her horror that Matt had managed to free himself and was systematically punching Sylvester in the ribs.

"No!" Connie crawled over to the scene of the fight, holding the knife out in front of her in a shaking hand.

"Connie, stay away." Sylvester managed to gasp out the words of warning.

Ignoring him, she launched herself at Matt, sinking the knife into his thigh, twisting it deep and dragging it down almost to his knee before pulling it back out again. Blood gushed from the wound, staining his light-colored trousers.

Snarling with rage, Matt turned on her, bringing his knee up under her chin before she could plunge the knife into him again. Connie fell back, hitting her head against the metal casing so hard she saw stars. Sylvester dropped to his knees, cradling her in his arms.

"I'm okay," she murmured.

"Give me the knife." He took it from her. Getting up again, he swung around, preparing to face Matt.

It was too late. Matt had gone. They heard the final telltale creak of the spiral staircase as it bore his weight. Muttering a curse, Sylvester tossed the knife to Connie and dashed out onto the viewing platform.

Despite a horrible dizziness as she moved, Connie managed to finish freeing Guthrie before turning her attention to Lucinda. Even with the gag removed, Lucinda seemed incapable of speech and sat quietly hunched over, hugging her knees to her chest.

"You saved us all." Connie's eyes filled with tears as she hugged Guthrie.

"I think it came at the cost of a broken nose." He grimaced as he tenderly felt his damaged face. "Although I got off lightly when I think of what happened to other people. Did you see where he went?" He spoke to Sylvester, who had stepped back inside from the viewing platform.

"I can't be certain. I went out onto the ocean side first and, although I walked around the platform, there was no sign of him. If he was walking across the rocks, I should have seen him." He held out his hand and helped first Connie and then Lucinda to their feet. "Unless he went straight to the Salto de Fe."

Connie clung gratefully to him. "Could he have jumped into the Salto de Fe?"

"I don't know what to think about that. Rational, honorable Matt Reynolds might have killed himself out of remorse. But while you are still alive, I believe the spirit of Yargua inside him would want to keep coming after you, keep trying to make you pay for what Cariña did to him. What happened when Matt ran out of here just now will depend on who was in charge. Did he run to the edge of the Salto de Fe and throw himself in because he couldn't live with what he'd done? Or did he sneak away and hide, so he could come after you another day?"

Lucinda leaned against Guthrie. "You mean this nightmare might not be done, even now?"

"Let's hope it is," Sylvester said. "Even if Matt is still alive, that injury to his leg from the knife wound Connie inflicted is a bad one and he has no access to medical treatment. For now, let's get back to the house and report back to Jonathan." Sylvester slid an arm around Connie's waist. "Can you walk?"

"Yes." She smiled up at him. "Which is just as well, because you certainly can't carry me."

"Probably not, but I'm prepared to try." He kissed the top of her head. "Let's get away from this place." He looked over his shoulder at Guthrie. "Can you help Lucinda?"

Guthrie nodded and the little group made their way

slowly down the staircase and out into the bright sunlight.

As Sylvester turned to take the path across the rocks, Guthrie halted him. "Look." They followed the direction of his pointing finger. "Bloodstains. They lead toward the Salto de Fe."

Sylvester studied Connie's face, a silent question in his eyes. She considered the matter before nodding decisively. He turned to Guthrie. "We'll follow the stains. Although I don't know what, if anything, we'll see. It's like nature's version of the most intense white-water ride imaginable inside there."

The trail of blood, standing out harsh and dark in the bright sunlight, took them unerringly to the brink of the ravine.

Connie gripped Sylvester's hand tightly as the four of them stood at the very edge of the Salto de Fe. It was an awe-inspiring sensation. She felt as if she was standing on the edge of the world, preparing to step off. *I did this once. When I was Cariña, I went over this edge into that raging tumult below.* It was one of Cariña's memories she couldn't capture. Stubbornly, it eluded her. How had Cariña survived? *It's part of the magic of Corazón*, she reminded herself. No one could actually be thrown into that raging madness and live to tell the tale. *In a few days, Sylvester will leap into this ravine and be gone forever.* She briefly closed her eyes to ward off the pain caused by the thought.

"If Matt did throw himself over, he will have been swept up into those waves. There will be nothing to see here." Sylvester was already turning away.

"Wait." Connie pointed. To their right, a few feet down, there was a narrow ledge. A light-colored object splattered with red bloodstains was balanced on it.

Connie recognized it immediately. She had been there when—before it became splashed with blood—it had poked Guthrie in the ribs. "It's Matt's sneaker."

They found Juan tied to a tree in the pine forest near the little cottage. He was almost tearfully apologetic as Sylvester untied him. "He took me by surprise. I was looking for Lucinda. I couldn't find her after she ran out of the house."

"I got lost," Lucinda explained. "I'd never been to the lighthouse. When Matt ran in and said Guthrie was in trouble, I dashed out of the house without thinking. I had an idea of the general direction, but I wandered off the path. I blundered around a bit in the trees and that was when Matt found me." She shivered. "He grabbed me and marched me to the lighthouse with the knife against my throat."

"He must have taken care of Juan first, then come after Lucinda. She was unarmed, distressed and didn't know where she was going, so she was the easier target," Sylvester said. He turned back to Juan. "What happened to the gun?"

Juan hung his head. "Matt threw it in the river." He pointed to the little stream that ran beneath the bridge. "He told me he preferred knives. He said it was a Calusa thing. I thought he must be unhinged." As he rose he staggered. "Sorry, boss. He hit me a hell of a blow over the head from behind."

"We're the walking wounded." Guthrie chuckled then winced as the action hurt his injured nose.

"We are also the survivors," Connie said, and they were silent for the remainder of the walk back to the house, thinking of the others who had not been as fortunate.

When the house came into view, she experienced that uncanny sensation again. Watchfulness and watched-for-ness. As if she and the house were as one, completing each other. She had been the mistress here long ago, and the house had been waiting for her, needing her back once more. It was calling to her, giving her the strangest feeling. Her heart felt oh, so glad to be part of this glorious place, yet sorrowful that what she and the house both wanted could never be.

Because Sylvester leaves in two days. She thrust the thought aside. *There has been enough drama for one day. Time enough for sad thoughts when his birthday arrives.*

When they trouped into the house, Connie hurried straight to the study. Jonathan was where she had left him, stretched out on the sofa, reading one of the Calusa books that had survived Matt's onslaught earlier in the day.

She gave a cry of pleasure and relief when she saw he was safe and, abandoning the distance she had always felt from this deeply reserved man, ran to him and kissed his cheek. Although a faint flush stained his cheeks, she got the feeling he was not displeased by the gesture.

"Now that's out of the way, you have to tell me what happened."

"It's a very long story."

"I'm not going anywhere." Jonathan patted the sofa beside him. "What happened to Matt?"

Connie scanned his face in surprise. "How did you know it was him?"

"I've had plenty of thinking time while you were gone." He looked around the room. "But also—" he gave a slightly embarrassed laugh "—there's something about this place, isn't there? Something that makes you fanciful and imaginative. And my memory of the night I was attacked has started to come back. Not fully, but I can recall snippets of my conversation with Matt before I went into my room."

"Were you suspicious of him?"

His brow furrowed as he tried to concentrate. "I'm not sure it was even as strong as that. I think I said something like if we really were in Ellie's 1930s detective novel, the killer would turn out to be the most likable character. Then I laughed and said, 'That would be you, Matt.' We said good-night and, almost as soon as I went into my room, the door flew open again and I felt an almighty blow on the back of my head."

Connie bit her lip. "He said he thought he'd killed you."

Jonathan winced. Beneath the bruising, his handsome features were grim. "Why didn't he kill me when he found I was still alive?"

"Matt said Vega was up and about on that floor—she was going back and forth along the corridor outside your rooms. He was too scared to do anything in case she heard something or saw him, so he came to find Sylvester and said you'd been attacked. You can imagine his relief when you couldn't remember anything."

"Where is he now?"

Connie roused herself from her thoughts, aware she had not yet told him the full story. "Let's go through and join the others. This may take some time."

Chapter 18

There were six people at the dinner table that night. The empty seats were a reminder of why their numbers had dwindled. Despite his injuries, Jonathan proved to be adept in the kitchen with Connie assisting him. Lucinda washed dishes, swept the dining room and set the table. She seemed eager to put any past airs behind her and show her willingness to help. Guthrie slipped into his usual role of bartender and entertainer. There was a general air of sadness tinged with relief. Sylvester recalled Connie's comment that they were the survivors. It had affected them all deeply. *We might have survived, but we are not untouched.*

"Three people didn't survive." Jonathan echoed Sylvester's thoughts as they sat down to dinner.

"Four, if you count Matt," Sylvester reminded him. "Whatever was going on with him, my friend Matt Reynolds got destroyed along the way in all of this."

Lucinda shivered. "He seemed so normal."

"He *was* normal," Connie said quietly. "That's what makes it so hard to understand."

"But you're all sure of what you saw?" Jonathan

looked around the group for confirmation. "He did jump into this ravine you call the Salto de Fe?"

"As sure as we can be when none of us actually saw him," Sylvester said.

"But he must have. There was nowhere else for him to go." Lucinda shivered, even as she insisted. "Those rocks are exposed. There was no hiding place."

Sylvester noticed the way her words made Connie glance at the darkness outside as though it had become threatening again. "Even if Matt didn't jump, he was badly injured, with no access to any medical treatment." He kept his eyes on hers, hoping to reassure her. "And he's lost the element of surprise. If he tried anything now, we know who we're up against. We've stopped suspecting each other."

"That's right." Guthrie looked around the table with a smile. "We're in this together from now on."

"Let's hope there's nothing to be in it for. No excitement, no surprises. Just one more day before the delivery boat comes," Jonathan said.

"I'll drink to that." Guthrie raised his glass.

When dinner was over, Sylvester and Connie walked along the beach. He could already feel the weight of losing her even though she was right beside him. It was like hellfire scalding through his veins, making every inward breath feel like he was drawing broken glass into his lungs. Everything hurt. It stung his eyes to look at her, branded his flesh to touch her, burned his lips when he kissed her. Yet he couldn't get enough of her. All he wanted between now and the time when he had to go was the sweet, delicious agony of her in his arms.

I've lived with the knowledge that I must go for five hundred years. Now the time is almost here and it is torture. This was why he'd never allowed himself to get close to anyone else. This was what he'd dreaded throughout his long, lonely life. And the worst part of all was that he knew Connie was feeling the same way. He had the knowledge he would meet her again as Cariña. Connie had nothing to cling to. No future together to look forward to. The bleak expression in the dark depths of her eyes burned a path to his heart. *This is what I've put her through.* At least there was one final thing he could do for her.

They had discussed whether they should tell the others the whole story, including their past lives and the reason why Sylvester had to leave. In the end, they had decided the truth was too far-fetched. Sylvester would leave a letter that would explain as much as necessary to his heirs.

"There is something we need to talk about, no matter how painful it may be." Sylvester turned to look at her in the moonlight. Her beauty took his breath away and saddened him at the same time. "I want to know what your plans are after I am gone."

"Don't." Connie placed her hand on his chest as she shook her head.

He caught her wrist, lifting her hand to his lips. "I must. I said I would leave my fortune to those who were left. That means there will be four of you. You will be a wealthy woman, Connie. But I also said the island itself will go to the one I consider the most worthy. It's yours if you want it."

"If I want it?" Connie laughed softly as she gazed at the beautiful golden house. "Of course I want it. I love this island. Since I arrived here, I've felt a curious synergy with this place. An interdependence, as if we belong together." She rested her forehead against his chest with a sigh. "But I could never be here without you,

Sylvester. My heart would break every time I walked along this beach, or sat beside the fire in the den, or lay in the bed we shared. Your memory will never leave me, but somehow it is bound up in Corazón." She lifted her head. "Jonathan should have the island. He feels its pull, too, even though he doesn't seem like the sort of person to indulge in whimsical feelings."

"I don't think Corazón allows us to be cynical." Sylvester took her hand and, despite her reluctance, drew her back toward the house. If they succumbed to the night, then the dawn would inevitably follow. "It makes our decisions for us." He remembered the invisible hand that had helped him to climb the cliff. "Sometimes, when the outcome hangs in the balance, it steps in at just the right moment."

Connie leaned her head on his shoulder. "That sounds very specific."

"It is. When Matt pushed me into the dungeon, there was only one way out. I had to climb from the opening in the cliff face up to the lighthouse."

He felt the shiver that ran through her. "My God, Sylvester, I saw that cliff from the boat when we first arrived on the island. How on earth did you do it?"

"I'm a good climber, but right at the end I was struggling. Then—and this would sound strange to anyone who had never been to Corazón—just as I was about to fall, an invisible hand reached down and helped me climb the rest of the way." He laughed, a note of embarrassment in his voice as he realized how it sounded. "Does that make me sound crazy?"

"Yes. But this is Corazón and crazy is the norm here." They had reached the terrace and Connie turned, pressing a kiss onto his cheek. "Whoever it was who helped you, I'm very glad they happened to be passing, invisible or not."

Sylvester closed his eyes briefly as he held her closer. "What do you want to do tomorrow?"

He didn't want to say aloud what they were both thinking. It would be their last day together. The following day was his birthday and he had already decided to leave at dawn.

Connie didn't hesitate. "I want to go to our place."

Sylvester didn't need to ask what she meant. The little cottage by the lake Máximo had built with his own hands had been the scene of their secret meetings, the place where he and Cariña had first made love. He nodded, drawing her into his arms. Connie was right, of course. It was fitting that the cottage should be the place where they spent their last hours together.

The next day, they went to the cottage early, eager to spend as much time alone together as they could. Connie was determined that they should focus on the emotional intensity of the bond between them. There would be time for sorrow when he had gone. Nothing could tear their love apart. They had already proved that. Five hundred years had not dimmed their feelings; now they had one more day left to celebrate them.

Tomorrow, she would face the hardest challenge of her life. She would say goodbye to Sylvester. She was resolved to make every second until then count. The light in his blue eyes told her he understood and shared her determination.

Connie had never wanted him the way she did in that moment. Not even back in those heady days when he had first been hers. Even though he knew her body better than she knew it herself, there was a newness, an excitement, to this instant that was like a star exploding deep inside her.

Sylvester settled on top of her, keeping most of his weight on his elbows. It felt natural to be pinned down by him this way. Natural and very, very exciting. His lips met hers with tender strength, his tongue sweeping inside her mouth like it belonged there. His shoulder muscles bunched and relaxed beneath her fingers, his arm completely healed now, only a faint red scar to show for the trauma of a few days earlier. Immortality had worked its magic.

He shifted position, moving his mouth over her nipples, grazing lightly with his teeth, causing heat to roll through her, leaving her gasping and helpless. Kissing the swell of her breast, he moved downward, licking and kissing over her ribs and along her hipbone.

Connie lay back, feeling the hard wood of the bed through the softness of the blankets, remembering these sensations from other times. Impatience coursed through her. She wanted to lift her hips and demand he move that clever mouth to exactly the right spot, to where she burned for him. At the same time she wanted to relish every second. She wanted to enjoy the anticipation and feel the furnace building inside her.

Sylvester hooked his hands under her knees, spreading her legs wide and holding her open to his gaze. The look in his eyes made her limp and boneless with desire.

"So beautiful. So sweet and pink and ready." She knew he'd said those words to her before. In this place. In another time.

He took one long, slow lick upward to her clitoris, stealing the last remnants of her breath. Pulling back, he looked up at her face, enjoying the effect he had on her.

"Please, Sylvester." Connie arched her back, offering

herself to him. He lowered his head again and, without warning, slid his tongue right up into her. She arched further, releasing a tormented gasp. His hand moved under her buttocks, gripping and raising her so he could hold her open to his mouth. All the while he continued to feast on her, devastating her with his mouth and tongue. He found her nub, teasing the bundle of sensitized nerves by alternately swirling then sucking until Connie was writhing and bucking in a frenzy against the restraints of his hands.

Orgasm engulfed her, drowning her, pulling her down into a swirling vortex of pleasure that went on and on. Even as she thrashed and cried his name, Sylvester kept his mouth on her, heightening the sensations, keeping her on the crest of the wave before gentling his movements, guiding her down from the peak, then slowly, slowly, bringing the tremors to a standstill. With a kiss on her inner thigh, he pulled her close and settled next to her.

"For someone who hasn't done that for five hundred years, you haven't forgotten any of the moves," Connie murmured when she finally regained control over her voice.

"If I remember rightly, I had plenty of practice." He kissed her forehead. "You kept me on my toes." He grinned. "Or should I say, on my elbows?"

"You know what they say. Practice makes perfect." She pushed him back with the heels of her hands against his shoulders, straddling his waist, her hair tumbling forward to curtain their faces as she kissed him. "I'm in charge this time."

"Yes, ma'am." The submissive note in his voice was at odds with the decidedly mischievous twinkle in his eyes.

Shifting position slightly, Connie leaned down to

get a condom from the back pocket of Sylvester's jeans. Moving so she was astride his thighs, she paused to caress him—enjoying the soft groan that reverberated through him at her touch—before sheathing him.

"Now you're all mine."

Those blue eyes darkened with an intensity that tugged at a point deep in her chest. "Always have been." His voice was husky with emotion.

She held him to her, sliding straight down onto him, squeezing him with her muscles as she took him all the way into her.

Sylvester sucked in a breath. "So good." The words were forced out through his clenched jaw.

A burst of intense pleasure exploded somewhere deep and low inside Connie, sending sparks shimmering through her whole body. She gripped Sylvester's hips, digging her nails into him, hanging on for the ride as she began to move. Keeping him in deep, she moved slowly back and forth, rubbing herself against him. Tipping her head back, she lifted his hands to her breasts. Her hard nipples rubbed against his palms as her breasts swayed in time with her movements.

Sylvester's expression was pure ecstasy as he watched her undulating above him. "I love seeing my cock slide in and out of you."

He knew exactly what those words would do to her. Raw heat flared up in her belly, making the heavy ache in her sex almost unbearable. Slow and steady weren't good enough anymore. "I need you on top."

He rolled, staying fully inside her. Connie wrapped her legs around his waist and held on tight as he plunged into her. Deep. Hard. Fast. Giving her exactly what she needed. She arched up to him, digging her nails in his back, rolling her hips to meet him as he slid back into her. She cried out each time he slammed all the way in.

"Make yourself come while I fuck you." His voice was raw with passion.

Still with him buried deep inside her, she reached down and stroked her clitoris with her middle finger, jerking wildly at her own touch. It felt amazing, bold and daring, incredibly sexy to be touching herself at the same time Sylvester thrust into her.

"Your face… God, Connie, watching you come is amazing." He angled himself so he could watch her fingers. "I'm so close. Go first for me."

She moved faster, at the same time tightening her muscles around him. Every feeling was heightened. She was so full of Sylvester, while at the same time her own caresses delivered an injection of raw heat straight to her nerve endings.

Sylvester thrust once more, tipping her over the precipice into a climax that stripped her of every last defense and had her crying out his name as she writhed and jerked beneath him. Sylvester drove deep several times more before coming to a shuddering stop, remaining inside her as he kissed her neck and murmured something incoherent.

Sometime later, when he had managed to regain his breath and shift his weight to one side, Connie turned in his arms, tilting her face so she could look at him. "How did the Calusa king find out about Máximo and Cariña? Did someone betray them…us?"

"There was a game among the Calusa braves and I defeated one of them in a feat of strength contest. He was jealous and decided to stage an impromptu rematch. He was going to lie in wait for me at dawn. Instead he saw Cariña leaving the cottage. He couldn't wait to take the news of what he'd seen to the king and be rewarded for his loyalty. Sadly, his little plan backfired."

Connie winced. "Yargua didn't reward him?"

"No, he stabbed him through the heart. As Matt said to Juan, knives were his thing even then. Unfortunately, the brave had already made his announcement in front of witnesses, so the news couldn't be hushed up. The king had been publicly humiliated. The bride he had chosen had been lying with a blue-eyed Spanish devil."

Connie sighed. "I might not remember the details of Cariña's life, but I do know from my own experiences that lying with the Spanish devil must have been fun."

"Fun?" Sylvester pretended to be hurt. "Is that the best you can do?"

She started to laugh. "Okay. It must have been miraculous. Is that better?"

"It was miraculous every time." He drew her closer. "And we still have plenty of time for it to be miraculous again…and again."

Sylvester eased Connie's sleeping form gently out of his arms. Dawn was just beginning to light the sky. It was time for him to go. Even though he knew she wanted him to wake her so she could say goodbye, he couldn't do it. He would never be able to say the word *goodbye* to Connie. This way was better. He had said it the best way he knew how, by loving her and holding her, by worshipping her with his body. Over and over until they had both tumbled into a deep sleep of exhaustion.

As he hurriedly dressed, he watched her sleep, managing to see the outline of her features in the half light. Not because he needed to imprint her on his memory. Her image had been at the forefront of his mind for five hundred years. He just enjoyed looking at her. Watching the steady rise and fall of her breath, the dark crescents of her eyelashes on her cheeks, the soft cushion of her lips.

Sylvester remembered a similar Corazón dawn, five hundred years ago. It was one of Máximo's memories that had stayed with him, leaving a permanent scar on his mind like a mark carved into the bark of a tree. It was the day he and Cariña should have been leaving together to start their new life in Spain. The little rowboat had been ready for the journey to the mainland. From there they would purchase passage to Spain. He had enough gold to make a good life for them in Valladolid, home of the de León family.

The feeling of exhilaration he had felt then came back to him now. It was tangible. *Just the two of us from now on.* He had smiled at the thought. Not for much longer. The news that Yargua had found out about them had coincided neatly with Cariña's news about the baby. *No more hiding, no more fear.* The brooding, shadowy figure of Yargua would no longer have the power to threaten their happiness. He couldn't wait to get going, to start this next chapter of their lives together.

But Cariña had been late. She was supposed to meet him before the sun came up…

When the two Calusa braves had come to him, their faces told him it was bad news before they spoke. He had picked up enough of their language to grasp the gist of what they were saying. Cariña was dead. Thrown into the ravine, they gave it a Calusa name meaning the Leap of Faith, and which Máximo called the Salto de Fe.

"¿Cómo?" he asked, his voice no more than a croak. Then, frustrated with himself for not being able to find

the right word in their language, he forced himself to concentrate. "How?"

Desperately he tried to follow their explanation. Something to do with death, disgrace and her grandmother. Yargua was coming for Máximo. The king would kill him when he found him.

"Let him come." His lip curled. What was the point of living without her? He would welcome the Calusa king's blade into his heart. Yet hadn't he already known he was different? That Yargua couldn't kill him?

No. The braves had hustled him into his boat. He must go and go now. If Yargua suspected they had seen him, warned him, his friends would feel the force of his wrath. They had pushed his little craft out to sea and slunk away into the mangroves as he started to row. Before long Corazón had become a speck on the horizon, an ache in his chest.

Sylvester remembered nothing more of Máximo's journey. It was just as well, he decided, since the voyage had been accomplished by a man with a damaged soul, a tortured mind and a heart that was in smithereens.

Forcing himself back to the present, he wondered at his lack of feeling. He had expected to endure more than this when the moment of parting came. Had expected to be stretched out on the rack of grief, punched in the gut by sorrow in the same way he had been back then. Instead he felt numb. There was no searing pain; he wasn't doubled over with grief. He was cold from the inside out, as if someone had poured iced water into his veins. As if he would never properly feel again.

Connie had asked him what would happen if he didn't go back, and Sylvester had considered it. Had seriously thought about it. But he knew it wasn't an option. *I don't exist outside of this crazy immortal loop.*

There can be no happy ending for us. I will go back and have a happy ending of sorts. Meanwhile, the ending of Connie's story isn't written yet.

Be happy, my love. He didn't dare whisper the words aloud for fear of waking her. As he left the room, the ice in his veins began to melt. The pain came in a rush and he welcomed it, needed the soul-crushing, heart-breaking, life-ending tragedy of it to propel his feet onward. To keep him moving and breathing, because without it he really might have just frozen and waited for Corazón to do its worst. To punish him for not taking the final step.

People who used the phrase "what's the worst that could happen?" had never lived on Corazón. Its beautiful darkness had never shaped their lives. Sylvester had had five hundred years in which to appreciate its force. In so many ways he was Corazón, or part of it, at least. He understood this island; his heart beat in time with its rhythms; he had been born—created—out of its energy and fire. Corazón had made him and Corazón could break him. Sylvester knew that was exactly what would happen if he didn't step into the Salto de Fe of his own free will today.

Even so, he walked slowly across the island. His feet dragged like those of a reluctant child. The familiar sights looked different this time. He reminded himself he wasn't seeing them for the last time, that he would be back again soon. No one knew the story of Máximo de León better than he did. If he hadn't met Connie, he would have been looking forward to the adventure with a thrill of anticipation. *How can my heart be torn in half by my love for two women who are the same person?*

When he felt the rocks beneath his feet, he paused. The memory of his climb two days ago coming back to him, sharp and clear. He had thought about it several times since, replaying the dramatic ending to his climb over and over in his mind. He had not imagined that helping hand. He had made light of it when he'd told Connie, feeling embarrassed at the idea, even though he was used to Corazón and its secrets. But someone had leaned down from the top of the cliff and assisted him. If that had not happened, Sylvester would have plummeted onto the rocks below. Did that person know that, although Sylvester couldn't be killed, it was only by saving him that Connie—and with her, Guthrie and Lucinda—could be saved? Who was the mysterious person who, having helped him climb those last few feet, had vanished without a trace?

The Calusa had lived on these islands, but they had always respected the ancient spirits who were the first inhabitants of the Corona de Perlas. The Calusa priests would perform elaborate ceremonies and offer up gifts of shells and fish to the spirits. At the heart of the superstitions, legends and ceremonies was the fearsome Salto de Fe. It had a different name in the Calusa language, of course, but its reputation was the same. Many souls perished in its depths, but many others rose again from within that wild ravine. The Calusa believed the waves within the Salto de Fe captured the energy of the ancient spirits. That they could cleanse a heart of evil and reenergize a body, giving a person new life. There were ghosts on Corazón, many of them survivors of the Salto de Fe. Had one of them assisted Sylvester on his climb? He shrugged. It was destined to remain yet another of the many mysteries Corazón kept in its secret store.

He paused at the edge of the Salto de Fe, collecting his thoughts. He had always imagined he would keep on walking, just step right over the precipice and into the past. Now he found he needed time to think, to almost savor the moment. He gazed into the swirling depths. *I have waited five hundred years for this. What do a few more minutes matter?*

Chapter 19

Connie can feel Cariña's fear as she struggles against the strong arms that hold her. Like a hunted animal, she can taste her own terror, can sense it in her panting breath, her widened eyes, her trembling limbs. Her heart is pounding so hard she can feel it trying to escape through her throat. Hauled out of her bed in the middle of the night by Yargua, she is being dragged across the beach in the darkness.

Her grandmother tries to pry the Calusa king away from Cariña, but receives a backhanded blow across the face that sends her reeling. As Sota falls to the ground, she hits her head on a rock. Her neck is twisted at a grotesque angle and she doesn't move. Giving a strangled sob, Cariña tries harder to get away, to go the old woman, but she is pulled relentlessly on.

Máximo!

She attempts to scream his name, but the rough hand across her mouth means the sound is a muffled gurgle. When she takes the opportunity to bite down on Yargua's fingertips, she hears him curse and feels a brief moment of triumph when he is forced to uncover her mouth. As he lifts her onto his shoulder and carries her away from the beach, she knows where he intends to take her and her triumph is short-lived.

"You thought you could betray me and live to boast of it?" The king's voice is hoarse with anger, his grip on her unrelenting.

"We never meant you any harm, mighty one." If she pleads with him, grovels to him, maybe she can make him understand. "We fell in love before my father made the marriage pact."

"Love?" The word seems to fuel his rage and he grabs a handful of her hair, pulling it so hard she sees stars. "You think this is about your puny affair? This is not about you. This is about me, about my pride, my position. I was ready to bestow the highest of honors upon you. You were to be my bride. Once the rumors started you had given yourself to another man—and not just any man. No, you had to choose the Spaniard!—you undermined me as your sovereign, as a Calusa and as a man. Now I see the island chiefs eying my throne, wondering how easy it will be to topple me from it. If a mere girl can defy him, why can't we? *That is what they are thinking. I see it in their eyes. For that, you will pay...you and your Spanish lover. No one questions my position. No one can expect to make their king look foolish and survive."*

It doesn't matter what she says from then on, what promises she makes. They will leave here... He will never see her or Máximo again after this day... They will go to Spain. He will never hear of them again... Yargua ignores her, marching relentlessly on.

When he places her on her feet and she feels the rocks and hears the waves crashing into the ravine, she renews her attempts to fight him. It is no good. He laughs as he hauls her the final few yards to the edge of the precipice.

Bravely, she faces him. "This is not the end. You know what the legend says. If you throw me into this chasm, I will begin a new life as soon as my body hits the rocks."

He presses his face close to hers and she feels the sharp blade of his shell dagger between her breasts. Too late, she realizes his intention...and her mistake.

"No, you won't. You can't begin a new life, because you will already be dead when I toss you over the edge. Don't worry—you will have company. Your beloved grandmother and your Spanish lover will be joining you very soon."

Connie jerked awake from the nightmare. Except she knew now what she saw wasn't a dream. She was reliving parts of her former life as Cariña. And now she knew the real story. History had it all wrong. Connie had been right to feel uneasy about the story of how Cariña had been killed when her grandmother threw her into the Salto de Fe. Just as she had known all along, Sota loved Cariña and would never have harmed her. The truth was, Cariña had been murdered by the Calusa king, who threw her dead body over the edge of the precipice after he stabbed her.

Connie sat straighter, turning to where Sylvester should be, wanting to tell him this momentous news. He was gone. Pressing her hand to his pillow, she found it still warm. He must have only just left. *My worst nightmare wasn't what I just saw in that dream. It's what is happening to me right now. Today is Sylvester's thirtieth birthday. He has gone.* Another thought swept over her, bringing a wave of sadness sweeping in its wake. *He didn't say goodbye.*

The sweet, tender ache of her whole body was a reminder he *had* said goodbye to her. After they had returned to the main house from their private cottage, he had spent all night long holding her, loving her and showing her in a hundred different ways that, if he could, he would have stayed here in this life with her. Her immortal billionaire had gone to meet his destiny. A destiny that included her but which she could never share. What sort of cruel fate could dream up a torture so surreal?

It's over. He has gone to the Salto de Fe. By now he will be five hundred years away from me. He will be coming to this land with Ponce de León.

Pain came, sudden, overwhelming and unbearable. It punched her, tore at her, ripped a gaping hole in the middle of her body. She gasped, her thoughts flailing wildly as she tried to deal with the intensity of it. *I can't feel like this. I knew he was going to leave me. I knew I would grieve for him, but I can't do it this violently.*

Shakily, she rose to her feet. She had to get a grip. Even as she told herself all of this, the tears began to fall. As she pushed open the doors to balcony, she couldn't see the view. She couldn't think of anything other than that Sylvester had gone. She would never see him again. Never hold him again. Never touch him or kiss him. She would leave Corazón when the supply boat arrived today and it would be as if their love had never existed. *He* had never existed. Wrapping her arms around her waist, she bent her head and sobbed until her throat was raw and her body had nothing left to give.

When it felt like she had no more tears to cry, her thoughts gradually returned to the dream. A sudden jarring question forced its way to the surface. If Cariña was murdered back in 1521, who was the woman who'd traveled across the world to be with Máximo? Someone made that hazardous journey. Whoever she was had married him, bore his children, returned here and built a life with him on Corazón. It was all well-documented. It *happened.*

Connie started to laugh through her tears as the answer came to her. It was so simple. So wonderfully, perfectly, easy.

Why did we never see it? We have been fooled all this time because we believed that woman was Cariña.

Like she was on a roller-coaster ride, her emotions had gone from misery to euphoria in seconds. Shaking her head, still barely able to comprehend the truth, she ran from the balcony back into the bedroom, throwing on underwear, shorts and tank top. Impatiently pulling on her sneakers, she dashed out of the room and hurried through the silent house.

Hold on, Sylvester—or should I get used to calling you Máximo from now on? I'm coming with you, my love.

Questions crowded in on her. Sylvester had said the woman who arrived in Valladolid didn't get there until many months after Máximo had left Corazón. How could she be sure that, if she followed Sylvester into the Salto de Fe now, she would go back to the right point in time? *Trust me.* Connie heard Sylvester's voice saying the words. He had known that the Salto de Fe—the Leap of Faith—would take him back to the exact point where Máximo joined Ponce de León's expedition. Connie would have to trust that she could go back in time to the exact point where she would meet up with Máximo in Valladolid. *I will be Cariña again. Once I jump into that chasm, Connie Lacey will cease to exist.* The thought made her shiver with a combination of apprehension and anticipation. *Nothing matters except that I will be with Sylvester.*

Sylvester had said something else about that woman. *She was heavily pregnant, barefoot, and dressed in rags.* Her hand slid down over her flat stomach. Could it be true? There had been that one time when they had been driven so wild with desire they had forgotten to use protection. Was it possible the future de León heir was already growing in her belly? If it was true, a scarier thought followed hard on its heels. Cariña was *heavily* pregnant by the time she arrived in Valladolid. Why did her journey take so long? None of these questions had answers. In the end, it came down to one simple question. Was Connie prepared to take the ultimate leap of faith? That one was easy. For Sylvester, the answer to that question would always be "yes."

As she raced across the island, she could sense that invisible protective presence alongside her. Whatever—whoever—it was, this unknown being wanted her to succeed. She knew it without understanding how she knew. Something on this island was sheltering her. It had been with her all along.

Connie neared the rocky part of the island and the lighthouse came into view. Her footsteps slowed. There was a figure standing at the edge of the Salto de Fe. Her heart gave a leap so violent she felt it in her throat. *He is still here!* Sylvester was poised dangerously close to the brink of the ravine, his head bent as he gazed into the churning depths. He was too far away to hear her above the roar of the crashing waves if she called out his name. With a soft cry of relief, Connie began to break into a run once more.

She was prevented by a hand closing tightly around her upper arm.

"Not so fast." Matt snarled the words as he swung her around to face him. His eyes glittered with triumph as she struggled wildly in his grasp. "This is like old times, Connie. Very old times. Remember the last time we were here together? Just you and me…Cariña and Yargua." He held up a knife. This one had a blade made of a giant sharpened shell, similar to the ones used by the Calusa to spear their fish.

No. Connie shook her head. Fate couldn't be this cruel. She had escaped him once. Twice, if she counted the time four years ago when he had cut her throat. Surely, when she was so close, just feet away from Sylvester and their happy ending, the past was not about to rise up and intervene again? She had believed Corazón was going to let them go. *Don't let me be wrong.*

"You jumped into the Salto de Fe," Connie panted the words as she tried to jerk her arm free.

Sylvester was focused on the ravine, his back still to them. The waves splashed up between the crevices in the rocks, spraying water into the air around him. If only he would just turn around!

"Did you really think it was going to end so easily?" Matt looked ill. Worse than ill, he looked close to death. His face was corpse-like in its paleness, his eyes sunken hollows, his lips colorless. "This is Corazón. If you believe in the ancient Calusa spirits, you could say they were on my side that day. While you were still inside the lighthouse, I managed to plant one of my sneakers on that ledge just inside the Salto de Fe—" Connie glanced down and saw he was still wearing the other one "—and dashed back to hide at the other side of the lighthouse while you were all hobbling down the stairs. If you don't believe in the ancient spirits, then you have nothing but your own stupidity to blame for the fact you fell for it."

The leg of his trousers was black with dried blood and his bloodless lips were flecked with spittle. A dank, stale smell rose up from him. It was the scent of the grave, mixed with something older and more deadly. Connie shrank away from him. There was very little of Matt Reynolds left now.

"Remember what you said to me all those years ago? About how you would start a new life after you jumped into the void?" Matt leaned closer, his fetid breath scalding her cheek. "I took it from you then by slitting your throat. Guess what, Connie?" He started to laugh, a high-pitched, maniacal sound that scraped her nerves raw. "I'm going to do it all over again, and that poor fool over there doesn't even know."

Connie began to struggle in earnest, kicking out at his injured leg and screaming for Sylvester to help. As Matt raised the knife to shoulder height, his hand halted and a look of dismay came over his features. He muttered a curse and cast a glance over his shoulder as though expecting to see someone standing behind him. His arm appeared to be locked in position, almost as though an invisible hand was holding it there, preventing him from lowering it.

Frowning, he tried again. And again. His whole body started to shake with the effort, but he couldn't bring the knife down. Weakened by his injury, holding on to a squirming Connie with one hand, he didn't have the strength to fight off whatever force was being exerted against him. Realization dawned on Connie. Matt was fighting an invisible assailant. And she knew, in that instant, who was stopping him from bringing that knife down.

The truth came to her in a sudden rush of awareness and tears filled her eyes. She knew who her ghostly protector was. Throughout the centuries, the woman maligned as Cariña's murderer had been waiting for her chance to put things right. Ever since Connie's arrival on Corazón, Cariña's grandmother, Sota, had been at her side, guarding and defending her. The woman who, when Cariña's mother died in childbirth, had raised her as her own child, who had showed her nothing but love and devotion throughout her life, had continued in that role, even after her death.

Snippets of conversations came back to Connie. Even Matt had commented on it. *You seem to have a guardian angel watching over you here on Corazón, Connie.* She recalled Roberto bursting through the bedroom door as Sylvester was grappling with the attacker in the darkness. Roberto's words echoed in her mind. *Something woke me, almost like someone was shaking me awake.* Then there had been that invisible hand helping Sylvester just as he was about to fall from the cliff in the last stages of his near-impossible climb.

The thought of everything Cariña's grandmother had done for her gave Connie the injection of strength she needed. With a final tug, she wrenched herself free of Matt.

His stream of curses followed Connie as, with a renewed burst of speed, she darted across the rocks. Although she sensed Matt coming after her, he was slowed by the spirit of Sota, who retained her ghostly grip on him. The old woman would not be able to hold him for long, but she was doing all she could to give Connie a chance to get away.

"Sylvester!" Connie called his name, but she was too late. Just before she reached him, Sylvester executed a perfect swallow dive straight into the raging torrent of the Salto de Fe.

Shock made her pause, a sob rising in her chest. She didn't know if Matt really was right behind her, or if it was her overactive imagination that made her sense him reaching out for her, his fingers grasping at her tank top, snagging the thin material but not quite getting a strong enough grip. Not giving herself a chance to find out if his touch was real or imaginary, Connie threw herself forward, hurtling over the edge of the precipice and into oblivion.

Chapter 20

She stumbled along the rutted track, her bare feet bloodied and blistered. The once-elegant velvet dress she'd discovered in a chest on board the ship flapped, torn and ragged, around her calves. The bodice and sleeves hung loose because she had lost so much weight. Although she had scavenged what food she could along the way, it had never been enough. In contrast, the waist was strained over her swollen belly like skin over a drum. The noonday sun beat relentlessly down on her uncovered head. She should seek shelter, but she was so close now. So close after all these months, after facing death so many times.

The steady clip-clop of hoofbeats and rumbling cart wheels on the hard-packed, red earth sounded like the sweetest music and she paused, shielding her eyes with one hand. When the farm cart came into view, she risked her safety by placing herself firmly in its path.

With a curse, the farmer halted his horse. *"¿Qué pasa?"*

When Connie had first stepped onto Spanish soil after the long months of being marooned on the island following the shipwreck, she had been afraid she would not be able to communicate. Close proximity with the Spanish sailors and this long journey on foot into the interior of the country had taught her enough to get by. This was not the language she had learned in school, but there were similarities.

She pressed a hand to her stomach, outlining her pregnancy bulge while miming exhaustion. She pointed hopefully at the cart. "Valladolid?"

He rolled his eyes and jerked a finger toward the rear of the vehicle. *"Sí."*

Eagerly, she hurried to the back of the cart, managing to scramble clumsily into it before he set the horse in motion once more. It was thankfully free of livestock, but their odor lingered. Pigs, Connie decided as she stretched full-length on the rough boards. *I don't care. I'm almost there.*

Despite the lurching of the cart and the scorching sun, she must have dozed because she was awakened by the cart clattering over cobbles, competing shouts and the sensation of alternating light and shade playing over her closed eyelids. She sat up, taking in the scene with wide eyes. She had been dreaming of this for so long, it was hard to believe she was here in Valladolid at last.

Even by the standards of the busiest cities in the modern world she had left behind her, the bustling square where the farmer halted his cart was crowded to the point of insanity. Market stalls selling every imaginable ware had been crammed onto the cobblestones. Customers and traders were rushing in every direction, waving and yelling at each other.

Although her Spanish couldn't cope with this, they spoke with an inflection that made her think of her dreams and of Máximo. It gave her the strength to force her tired limbs onward as she clambered down from the cart. She pushed her way through the crowd, looking neither left nor right, her eyes fixed on the building she had glimpsed. As she drew closer, she saw it really was the house she had seen in the painting in Sylvester's study at Corazón. Hardly daring to believe the evidence of her own eyes, she kept going.

It was this image that had been before her through it all. As she had broken free of Matt and stepped into the Salto de Fe. As she had tumbled into the abyss and darkness engulfed her. When she had opened her eyes to find herself aboard a wooden galleon, she became the object of strange glances from her sixteenth-century companions because of her modern-day clothing. When the ship had run aground on rocks and she, with the handful of other survivors, had been washed ashore on a tiny island, clinging to the wreckage. Even as, during the dark days of surviving on the meager rations from the ship, supplemented by berries, leaves and the occasional fish and rabbit, she had realized Sylvester's child really was growing inside her.

During the wild, swooping hope when, after months on the island, sailors from another ship saw their fire one night and came to investigate. And, finally, she had kept the thought of this house before her as, alone, penniless, pregnant and five hundred years before she had actually been born, she had set out to walk the four hundred miles from the Port of Palos on the Spanish coast to the Castilian city of Valladolid.

Not concentrating, she stumbled on the uneven paving stones and an elderly woman caught her by the arm, helping her to a stone bench in a shady corner of the square. The woman gestured to a nearby stall holder to fetch water and, when it was brought in an earthenware cup, Connie sipped the cool liquid gratefully. The old woman pointed to Connie's swollen belly, clearly asking a question about the baby's arrival. Connie smiled, shaking her head. *Not yet, but very soon.*

She pointed at the grand house across the square. "Máximo de León y Soledad."

The old woman and the stall holder regarded her dubiously. It was hardly surprising. She was as out of place here in this square as Máximo had been when he'd first arrived on Corazón. She looked like a beggar. In her rags and with her gaunt appearance, these people must wonder what she wanted with a member of the noble house of de León.

"Máximo." Connie lifted her chin proudly. She had not come all this way to be denied.

"Sí. Él está aquí." She heaved a sigh of relief. They were confirming that Máximo was here. Her worst nightmare had been the prospect of arriving in Valladolid to find her timing was all wrong and he had already left on another expedition.

Helping her to her feet, the old woman escorted her across the square to the house. Supporting Connie with one hand, she rapped loudly on the door knocker with the other. After a minute or two, an impatient voice could be heard and then the door swung open. A woman, obviously a servant, stood in the doorway, hands on her hips and a frown on her face. She looked Connie up and down in disgust before the two women engaged in a heated conversation, none of which Connie understood. The woman inside the house was clearly ordering them to be on their way. As she attempted to close the door on them, Connie stumbled, falling to her knees just inside the entrance.

"Máximo." She murmured the word as she lost consciousness.

When she came around, she was lying on a bed and someone was applying a cool, scented salve to her brow. She decided she must be dreaming and closed her eyes again. Then she sensed a movement beside her and knew without turning her head who it was. A warm sense of well-being washed over her before she finally heard *his* voice close to her ear. "Connie…my God."

When she opened her eyes, Sylvester's blue eyes were filled with tears. She struggled to sit up, but he kept his hands on her shoulders, pressing his lips to her forehead. "I was expecting Cariña." His voice was husky as he traced the scar on her neck with one finger. "But it all makes sense now. You came after me?"

She felt a single tear, the first since she had started her long journey, slide down her cheek. Her hand moved down to her belly. "I wasn't alone."

He covered her hand with his. "I noticed."

"I left the same day as you. I had another dream. Yargua murdered Cariña. He stabbed her before he threw her into the Salto de Fe. I knew then she couldn't have been the one who followed you. I realized it had to be me. I ran after you, I even saw you jump into the Salto de Fe. I tried to call out to you, but Matt caught hold of me—" She gasped as a sharp pain tore through her abdomen.

"Explanations can wait. You are here. We are together again, that's all that matters."

"No, you don't understand. The baby is coming." Connie started to laugh at the shock on his face. "We conceived this child on an island called Corazón. Now he is eager to make his appearance here in Valladolid in 1521."

* * *

Despite Connie's emaciated state, the birth was easy and young Roberto made his way into the world several hours later, startling his father with the power and ferocity of his cries.

Máximo had been banished from the room by the outraged women of his household.

"¡Mi señor!" Sofía, his housekeeper, had exclaimed in horror at his suggestion he should be allowed to stay for the birth. "Such wickedness is unheard of."

Connie, meeting his eyes over Sofía's head, had smiled reassuringly. "Go. This is a different world. I'll be fine."

"What language is this she speaks?" Sofia asked, frowning in an effort to understand.

"It is the language of Corazón," Máximo told her as he pressed a kiss onto Connie's hand before reluctantly leaving her to his housekeeper's ministrations.

Now, summoned to view his son and heir for the first time, he could only gaze in wonder at the sight of the two of them. At his beloved Connie who had made this incredible journey to be with him and at this tiny, crumpled being they had made between them. His heart expanded with so much emotion he thought it might explode. Sitting next to Connie, he slid an arm around her shoulders so they could gloat together over their son's perfection while he took his first meal.

"Sofía is determined to fatten me up." Connie pointed to the remnants of her own dinner.

"I should think so." Sylvester could feel the bones of her shoulder under his hand. It was a harrowing reminder of what she had been through, and also of how strong she was. To have endured that journey into the unknown and to have kept going despite everything that had been thrown at her. He shook his head. "You are remarkable, do you know that?"

She tilted her head to smile up at him. "I have no problem with you telling me that every now and then." A slight frown clouded her brow. "But what will other people think, Sylvester—I mean, Máximo? You have a reputation to uphold. There will already be talk about my arrival, about the baby."

"I've been thinking about that. Not because I want to protect my reputation, but because I want us—the three of us—to be able to live happily in this world. The biggest change will be for you, Connie." He smoothed her hair back from her brow. "It means you will have to become Cariña."

She nodded. "Our story was already told, wasn't it? From the moment we met, this was our destiny."

"It looks that way. The truth is too incredible for anyone to believe. If we try to tell the real story, we risk being laughed at, or worse, accused of sorcery. This is sixteenth-century Castile. Ferdinand and Isabella may be dead, but the Spanish Inquisition they created lives on. I can't imagine the suggestion of time travel would go down well."

Connie drew Roberto a little closer to her, shivering slightly at the implication of his words. "Will anyone believe the alternative version? That I am a Calusa princess, who traveled from the new world to find my Spanish husband? Even that sounds incredible."

"Believe it or not, there is a precedent. You've heard of the twelfth-century English priest Thomas Becket?" Connie nodded. "Legend says his father was a crusader who was captured by the Saracens. When he was released, Becket's mother, a Saracen princess, followed him from the Holy Land. They had fallen in love while he was imprisoned in her homeland. She wandered around Europe repeating the only English words she knew, *London* and *Becket*, until she found him."

"Becket was canonized as a martyr, so the priests of the Inquisition cannot doubt our story if they believe that of one of their own saints."

"That's true, but we will have to be careful. You must go to Mass and take care not to do anything that draws attention to you. You are different. The Inquisitors would label you an infidel."

"By drawing attention to myself, you mean I shouldn't sing pop songs or talk about my favorite movies?" Connie laughed as she leaned her head into the curve of Sylvester's neck. "Can it be true? Are we really safe at last?"

"We are safe, but there is one more thing I need to do." Sliding from the bed, but keeping hold of her hand, he went down on one knee. "For this, I will call you Connie one last time." He looked up into her shining eyes. "When I saw you there on Corazón that first time, my heart shattered into a thousand pieces because I knew I was looking at the love of my life and I thought I could never have you. Never touch you, never kiss you, never tell you what I was feeling. Never look into your eyes as we made love. I knew my destiny was to leave you and come back here. Yet, all the time we were suffering, Corazón had its own plans for us." He pressed his lips to her hand. "Now I do have you, Connie, I'm never letting you go again. I love you with all my heart. Will you marry me?"

"Of course I will! Why do you think I followed you across time and space?" Bright tears spilled over and she blinked them away. "The day I was attacked, I stopped living and started existing. My only emotions were fear and despair. That changed when I arrived on Corazón, the day I met you. I didn't understand it at first, but suddenly this raw energy took over my life. I became alive again. Every step I took on this mad journey was worth it because I wasn't scared anymore. I was running *to* someone instead of *from* someone. That was what you did for me, Sylvester. You gave me hope as well as love." She smiled through the tears. "Now come back here and help me place this young gentleman in the cradle Sofía found for him in the attic. Then you can kiss me."

Obligingly, he followed her instructions. "You will have to remember to start calling me Máximo," he reminded her. "People will think it odd if you keep getting your husband's name wrong."

"If I forget in future, you can tell them we Calusa are hopeless with names." She covered her mouth apologetically, stifling a yawn. "It's been a long day."

"You need to get some sleep."

"Maybe a bath first?"

"For you, my Cariña, anything."

Chapter 21

"You survived the journey, just as I said you would." Máximo lifted Cariña out of the rowboat and set her down on the white-gold sand before handing Roberto to her. Out in the bay, the Spanish galleon they had just left bobbed and danced in time with the current.

"Survived, yes. But the anxiety of being on board a ship once again, so soon after the shipwreck, has added to my stock of gray hairs."

He laughed, running his hand down her glossy black locks. "Your hair is untainted, my love. And, don't forget, there are those of us who would love to experience the joy of finding a single gray hair. Aging is not the nightmare you imagine it to be."

She bit her lip. "I'm sorry."

Shifting Roberto's weight to her other hip, Cariña gazed around her. Last time she had been here, her name had been Connie Lacey. There had been a beautiful golden mansion on this beach with every modern convenience. But Corazón had not delivered the paradise it promised. There had been a killer on her tail. This time, she had everything she wanted with her husband at her side and her child in her arms. They had another chance, and she was determined to grasp it, to fight for it with everything she had. They had been through too much to leave their new future to fate.

She recalled the day they had decided to return. The old house in Valladolid, its façade grand and imposing from the square, was a comfortable family home inside, and Cariña—the name still tripped her up from time to time, but she was growing accustomed to it—had soon come to love it. Her convalescence and their honeymoon had been rolled into one, and the beautiful house would forever hold happy memories for her. But she was fully restored to health, and Roberto was six months old. She had known the inevitable conversation was overdue. They had both been postponing it.

Máximo had led her to the shady stone bench overlooking the four hexagonal fountains with the mosaic tiles of green, white and blue decorating their bases. The fragrance of the blue sage flowers lining the walkway between had been particularly strong that day. It was Cariña's favorite place. She had made herself a promise. *Wherever I live, I will have a corner in my garden just like this.* It had taken the sting out of Máximo's next words.

"We always knew the day would come when we would have to go back."

And now they were here on Corazón once more. But it felt different. Was it because of everything they had been through? Because of everything she now knew about this island? Or simply because of the five hundred years' time difference? No. It *was* different, but Cariña wasn't sure why.

Máximo slid an arm around her waist and she leaned gratefully against him. As always, his touch soothed her. "Yargua is dead. There is nothing to fear from him anymore."

"There is still the curse. When you first spoke of it at that long-ago dinner party on Corazón, it was just a story, a nasty fairy tale happening in someone else's life. But now it's about my life and my family." Cariña turned her face up to his, her eyes troubled. "I've been thinking about it a lot. Do you think what happens to us next is carved in stone? Must it be exactly the same again this time as it was last time?"

"You mean, could the course of history be changed?" Máximo frowned.

"Is there anything we could offer Sinapa as an inducement *not* to place a curse on us?"

The sudden flare of hope in his eyes was painful to see. Only a man who had experienced the misery of centuries of the curse of Corazón could wear that look. "What do the Calusa need that they don't already have?"

"It's not exactly something she needs, but I saw in my dreams how much she liked the gold coins when she saw them. Her eyes gleamed with pleasure when they brought the caskets ashore after they raided the galleons."

"You think we should bribe her?"

"I think we have nothing to lose by trying." She kissed him. "And a whole future to gain if we succeed."

Máximo took Roberto from her, lifting his son into the air, laughing as the baby gurgled and waved his plump arms. "If we could lift the curse of Corazón, there would be only one other thing that I would wish for."

Cariña shielded her eyes from the sun as she looked up at him. "What would that be?"

"Maybe I'm being greedy, but this time around I would like to grow old alongside you, my love."

In many ways, coming back here and playing the part of Cariña was harder than turning up in Valladolid. There, she had been a stranger, a novelty. No one had expected her to speak their language or to know their customs. Now, she was back on the island where Cariña had been born, but she didn't speak the language of the Calusa. She didn't know the names of the people Cariña had grown up with. She didn't even know how to address Cariña's father, who greeted her with a combination of fear and delight. Fear because he had believed her to be dead. Delight that she wasn't.

Máximo, who had picked up a smattering of the Calusa language during the months he'd lived among them, communicated the information that Cariña had lost her memory when she fell into the Salto de Fe. He pointed to the scars on her neck. She was lucky to be alive. It was only half a lie, and Cariña swallowed any guilt she might have felt when she witnessed the chief's delight at the sight of Roberto. The Calusa regarded her with wonder from then on and she made a vow to herself—this self and the one who had died at Yargua's hand—that she would learn their language as quickly as she could.

"There is no time like the present." Cariña smiled at Máximo and he laughed in return as he realized what he had said. Those words had more meaning for them than for anyone else.

Leaving the Calusa braves to set up the tents they had brought with them, he loaded a casket of gold into the boat.

"I'm coming with you." Fighting off the waves of panic that seized her every time she even thought about getting into a boat, Cariña hitched up her skirts and waded out to the wooden rowing boat. She was fighting for their future and she couldn't let her phobia stand in the way.

Máximo helped her into the little craft and made sure she and Roberto were comfortable before he pushed it out into the waves and joined them. They accomplished the journey to Mound Key in silence, both of them wrapped in their own thoughts.

When they reached the new Calusa king's stronghold, Máximo hauled the boat ashore. Cariña waited on the familiar shell and bone bank as he lifted the casket from the little craft. Scooping a handful of gleaming coins from the chest, she made a pouch out of her long skirt, holding the hem up with her hand to secure them.

"While you go to the king, I will visit Sinapa."

"Is that wise?" Máximo's blue eyes were concerned as he scanned her face.

"Her problem is with me. Let me see if I can be the one to solve it."

He nodded. "Take care, my love."

"I intend to."

They reached the top of the first mound and went their separate ways. Máximo took the path toward the highest mound, while Cariña, still holding Roberto with one hand and securing the coins with the other, veered off toward the point where she knew Sinapa had her hut. The little building, built on stilts over the edge of the water, looked exactly as she remembered it. The old woman sat in the wooden doorway. *She has been expecting me.* The thought sent a shiver of fear thrilling through her. *I will only get one chance at this.*

Seating Roberto on the sand, where he immediately started grabbing at shells and pebbles, Cariña made sure he was safe, before going down on her knees before the wise woman, and pressing her head to the ground. When she rose, she held out her skirts, showing Sinapa the gold coins.

The old woman's eyes narrowed, traveling from her face to the coins and back again. She pointed to the scars on Cariña's neck and barked out a question. Cariña mimed falling into the Salto de Fe and was rewarded with a disbelieving snort of laughter in response. This was not going well.

Yargua's mother rose to her feet and came forward. She barely reached Cariña's shoulder. Her eyes fell to the gold coins and she gave an approving grunt. Reaching out a hand, she ran it down the sleeve of Cariña's gown, testing the fine material. Then she pointed to her own chest.

"This?" Cariña plucked at the garment. "You want my dress?"

Sinapa nodded, her eyes bright with the glee of avarice. Cariña hurried over to the hut and placed the pile of coins inside. Quickly unlacing her gown, she slid it down over her shoulders, stepping out of it and handing it over. Sinapa grabbed it from her with greedy hands, rubbing her face against the soft cloth. Eyeing Cariña thoughtfully, she pointed next to her embroidered slippers, then the jeweled combs she wore in her hair.

Sometime later, when Cariña rejoined Máximo at the boat, he raised his brows in surprise at her appearance. She wore only her shift, her hair hung loose down her back and her feet were bare. "I was starting to get worried."

She handed Roberto to him as she climbed into the boat. "It's a long story, but let's just say that the next group of Spaniards who land on these shores may be surprised to find the Calusa wise woman clad in the sort of elegant dress, slippers and jewels one of their own noblewomen might wear."

"And the curse?"

Her gaze was serene as he pushed the boat out into the open water. "She didn't mention it. I think she had other things on her mind."

Months passed with no further mention of the curse. The Calusa braves helped Máximo start to build a house and Cariña had very precise ideas for how it should look.

"You, my Cariña, are amazing," he told her one evening as they sat on the sand outside their tent, finishing their evening meal beside the fire.

"Be specific." She leaned her head against his shoulder with a contented sigh.

He waved a hand around the little camp. "You traveled back in time from a world where everything was easy, endured every hardship possible to find me. We had a pleasant home in Valladolid and I snatched it away from you to bring you back here to an island where we both know danger lurks. Yet you have faced every challenge with a smile. Now, we are living in a tent and you have made this into our home."

She laughed. Her Spanish had improved to the point where they could converse in that language now, even when they were alone together. "Máximo, you are forgetting what my life was like before I met you. I was running from a madman, dodging shadows, not knowing where my next meal was coming from. *You* are my home."

The kiss they shared was long and lingering. "There is no curse." His voice was filled with wonder.